A Spark
of Death

Books by Bernadette Pajer

A Spark of Death

A Spark of
Death

A Professor Bradshaw Mystery

Bernadette Pajer (signature)

Bernadette Pajer

Poisoned Pen Press

Poisoned Pen Press

Copyright © 2011 by Bernadette Pajer

First Edition 2011

10 9 8 7 6 5 4 3 2 1

Library of Congress Catalog Card Number: 2011920311

ISBN: 9781590589052   Hardcover
        9781590589076   Trade Paperback

The historical characters and events portrayed in this book are inventions of the author or used fictitiously.

Poisoned Pen Press
6962 E. First Ave., Ste. 103
Scottsdale, AZ 85251
www.poisonedpenpress.com
info@poisonedpenpress.com

Printed in the United States of America

To Bryan and Joey. You are my world.

Acknowledgments

I am indebted to Bill Beaty, an electrical engineer at the University of Washington, for reading my manuscript and advising on the electrical detail. His generosity in sharing his knowledge and ideas enhanced many aspects of this story. Any mistakes are mine alone.

The University of Washington Archives and Special Collections provide a rich resource I continue to gratefully explore, and the American Museum of Radio and Electricity in Bellingham, Washington, is a wonderland of invention, bringing the past alive. Professor Bradshaw and I would like to live there. We shall return.

I am also grateful to the many unseen people behind the sources, both printed and online, of historical and electrical detail so readily available for curious writers.

Jill Grosjean, my wonderful agent, will always have my deep and continued appreciation for her faith in me and this book. Annette Rogers, my brilliant editor, makes the exhausting editing process a joy.

Writing would be an impossibly lonely task were it not for the friendship and support of my circle of writing friends: Laron Glover, Barbara Long, Patricia Vincent, Joan Sells, Patricia Hall, Jeannie Dunlap, and Curt Colbert.

I am grateful for my friend and web designer Tracy Campbell, who listens patiently and encourages me to "think of this as an opportunity to…," and for Morgan, who gave me the priceless gift of time to write.

And finally, Becky, Bev, and Mom. My love and thanks for always believing. TNT.

Chapter One

A curtain of pale hair hid the young man's downturned face. His skinny fingers trembled as he toyed with the pencil. He'd been staring at his examination paper without making a single mark for ten minutes.

Test anxiety. Professor Benjamin Bradshaw knew it well. Bradshaw himself had never been good at written examinations. It was the blank page, the abstract theory that vexed him. Put him on a pole with a length of wire to string, give him the components of an electric motor to assemble, and his mind sang. This young man was much the same.

Professor Bradshaw spoke softly. "Mr. Daulton."

Oscar Daulton froze, gripping the pencil so tightly it snapped in two.

Bradshaw slid open his desk drawer and found a sharp lead pencil. As he stood, the squeal of his chair leg scraping the hardwood floor pierced the hollow silence. He crossed the empty classroom—the other students had long gone—and set the new pencil on the edge of Daulton's desk. The young man did not look up. He'd spread his hands protectively over his test, but Bradshaw could see some work had been done.

"Take your time." Bradshaw put a reassuring hand on the young man's shoulder. "I'm in no hurry."

He retreated to the window, his chest tight with the ghosts of his own youth. In his college years, he'd believed he would one day leave anxiety behind. Maturity and experience would sweep worry away. How wrong could he be? With age came new forms of anxiety. Apparently, thirty-five was the age of discovering oneself to be a plodding old fool, and the Kinetoscope, the modern-day mirror, reflecting what he'd been blissfully missing. Bradshaw squared his shoulders. Kinetoscopes be damned.

That blasted moving picture machine tick-tick-ticked in his mind. He saw himself once again—in black-and-white but unfortunately clear—trudge across the white plaster wall, the image growing larger, closer, until his own dour face stared out at him.

Professor Oglethorpe had laughed.

They'd all laughed at Bradshaw's ridiculous flickering image. To be fair, the students had laughed at everyone's image, their own included. But Oglethorpe's laugh had been loudest as Bradshaw lumbered about the moving picture, looking old, tired. Oglethorpe's laugh had been full of condescension and ridicule.

"Arrogant bastard," mumbled Bradshaw. He took a deep breath and thrust the flickering images, and Oglethorpe's laughter, from his mind.

The turret window of this second floor classroom projected forward, giving Bradshaw a view of the front of the building. He liked the way the sandstone and brick French Renaissance style building—complete with rounded turrets and conical candle-snuffer roofs—dwarfed the students climbing the steps to the portico entrance. The University of Washington, with its surrounding woodland and view of Mt. Rainier, inspired. He felt that was proper. Institutions of higher learning should humble those who enter them, encourage them to seek knowledge with a sense of awe.

Professor Oglethorpe was never awed. This morning, perfectly groomed and elegant in a navy suit, his wrists smugly buttoned with opal cufflinks, Oglethorpe had stood atop those impressive stairs as if he owned the building. His long frame limp with arrogance—he possessed odd, convex bones—he'd looked down his sharp nose with undisguised disgust as Bradshaw approached on his bicycle, sweating from his ride. With a sniff, he'd turned and entered the building, headed for that humiliating moving picture the entire engineering department was scheduled to view, leaving Bradshaw to park his bike and follow. A lamb to the slaughter.

Now the steps stood empty. Pink and white blossoms danced in the spring wind, drawing Bradshaw's gaze toward the expanse of green lawn and up to the shifting clouds.

Downstairs, the front doors banged shut, and a second later a student—Bradshaw recognized him as Artimus Lowe—hurried down the steps and onto the path only to disappear from view. The young man moved with a springing gait that Bradshaw envied. That's how I should move, he told himself. *That's how I will move!* He would stride as a professor ought to stride. He would not stew over his life like some addled old fool. He was far too young to be addled. A fool? Well, he could be that at any age.

He supposed he should be grateful he'd seen the truth of his appearance this morning, but he would much rather be ignorant. He hoped never again to see a recorded image of himself. He'd prefer not to see Professor Oglethorpe again either. If wishes were horses....

The Varsity Bell, in the belfry high atop the building, tolled. The pleasant note echoed until the wind erased the final resonance.

The classroom's electric lights blinked several times, mimicking the skittering clouds playing with the fading sunlight. "Name the causes of voltage fluctuations"—an exam question for another day.

"Sir?"

Professor Bradshaw turned. Unexpected surprise and pleasure temporarily lifted his melancholy. Oscar Daulton had completed his test quickly, once the pressure of time had been lifted. The young man, his fair hair now finger-combed out of his face, handed Bradshaw his paper with a blush of gratitude for the extra time he'd been given, then rushed out the door. Bradshaw wondered why the young were always in such a hurry. He then sighed. Better to be in a hurry than to plod.

He slid Daulton's exam into his leather satchel as stray rain-drops plinked against the window. He pulled on black rubber boots and a bright yellow slicker and descended the stairs to the main floor with a deliberate energetic bounce, but a steadying hand on the rail. In the main entryway, he thought of his son. He hoped the afternoon would clear long enough for a game of catch. Dour old men did not play catch with their sons. It stood to reason that he did not always appear as that film had captured him. Yes, a game of catch with Justin would lift his spirits tremendously if the weather would only cooperate. He'd reached the heavy oak doors, pushed one open, and a rush of damp wind whistled into his face and rustled his slicker. At the same moment, the building's lights flickered again, and the entry lamp in the ceiling directly above Bradshaw's head sizzled as the filament burned to a crisp. Bradshaw reluctantly hesitated, glancing about the entryway. The lamps in the wall sconces were dim as fireflies.

This was no simple fluctuation of the university's power plant, no fallen limb on a power line. Someone in the building was using a tremendous amount of power, and the only place tremen-dous amounts of power could be tapped was down in the electri-cal engineering lab. It was most likely Professor Oglethorpe down there causing trouble. Indeed, Bradshaw fumed, it was Professor Oglethorpe's interference, and not Edison's Kinetoscope, that was responsible for this entire, disastrous day.

Oglethorpe had provoked the students into building that modified Edison Kinetoscope by telling them they hadn't the skills to pull it off. Oglethorpe was responsible for Oscar Daulton's heightened test anxiety. Oglethorpe had all the electrical engineering students muddled and anxious with his indecipherable teaching method. And now, with the electrical students' big exhibition scheduled for tomorrow, Bradshaw suspected it could only be Oglethorpe down there in the lab, tampering with their Electric Machine in hopes of stealing all the glory for himself.

No, Bradshaw decided angrily. He wouldn't allow it. With a pang of regret, he abandoned thoughts of child and home and hurried instead to the stairwell, following the wide steps down to the basement. Before he reached the bottom step, he could hear the crackle of electric arcs. The pungent odor of ozone hovered outside the electrical engineering lab. Blue light danced erratically beneath the closed door. Bradshaw hesitated only a moment before putting his hand on the glass knob. He opened the door.

The laboratory lights were off, revealing the Electric Machine's full visual glory. Electric arcs erupted from the silver sphere atop the copper coil, and little needles of fiery purple arcs danced on the bars of the Faraday cage. Inside the cage, amidst the charged, poisonous, and deafening air, sat Professor Oglethorpe upon a three-legged stool, head propped against the metal bars, looking like a slumbering circus attraction: See Bird-Man in Giant Flaming Cage!

"Professor Oglethorpe!" Bradshaw buried his nose and mouth in the crook of his arm. What in God's name was Oglethorpe up to? Bradshaw flipped the switches that activated the lights and exhaust fans, and the roar of the blades joined the cacophony as they sucked the dangerous vapors from the building. "Oglethorpe!"

Professor Oglethorpe did not reply nor did he move. In the harsh glare of the overhead lights, Bradshaw couldn't see Oglethorpe's face, only the back of his dark, pomaded head. He was in shirtsleeves. His expensive navy cassimere vest and pants were not in their usual state of perfection, but askew. The vest rode high, revealing an expanse of white shirt. A pant leg bunched about the calf.

Bradshaw choked. A pompous black silk stocking adorned with white polka dots had broken free of its supporter. It had fallen into a puddle above Oglethorpe's polished leather shoe, exposing a pale ankle. The sight of it, above all else, sent a shiver of alarm through him.

He turned the safety key of the Electric Machine to the OFF position. Immediately, the arcing ceased. Only the ventilation fans now disturbed the air. He yanked the electric plug from the building supply socket as a final precaution. A burning acrid smell rose in a thin haze from the wires hanging from the ceiling that spelled "Welcome President McKinley" against hard, and now over-heated, black rubber plates.

A numb sort of unreality possessed him as he climbed the steps to the cage. Oglethorpe was so very still. Bradshaw avoided looking at the puddled polka dot sock, the exposed ankle. Slowly, he opened the cage door and stared in stunned silence at Oglethorpe's extended hand, at his slightly curved index finger protruding from the safety of the cage. The tip of the finger was blackish-red and swollen. A trickle of smoke rose from the charred flesh. The rest of the finger, the rest of the hand, was absent of color, bloodless.

He whispered, "Dear God," and staggered back away from the smell of cooked flesh.

And then Oglethorpe moved. Slowly at first, he began to tip sideways. His head lolled, his torso collapsed, his arms flopped uselessly. And then he dropped with a sickening thud to the wooden floor. His face was pasty white, his thin lips blue, his grey eyes clouded, staring vacantly directly at Bradshaw.

If wishes were horses—he hadn't meant it. He hadn't wished *this*.

Chapter Two

"Of course it killed him," barked Patrolman Mercer when the Electric Machine fell dark and silent after a brief demonstration. Mercer was a big man, jowly and fleshy and sloppily made. Even in a pressed blue uniform with brass buttons gleaming he looked rumpled. His dark eyes flashed, not with intelligence, but with the quick anger of a man more comfortable with brawn than brain. Oglethorpe's body had been removed to the morgue for autopsy after the coroner had done an initial examination, and it was Patrolman Mercer, without assistance, who had lifted the body from the cage. Now, glaring spitefully at the Electric Machine, he looked as if he wished he had some villain to tackle.

The patrolman narrowed his eyes at Bradshaw. "It's a wonder any of us in this room is still alive."

There were by that time only the two of them in the room. Bradshaw felt it prudent to retreat to the other side where he'd begun taking notes. "It may appear lethal," he said, picking up his pencil, "but I assure you, it's working as it was designed to work, and it's perfectly safe when scientific principles are carefully observed."

"Science!"

Bradshaw, ignoring Mercer's glare, perched himself upon a lab stool and continued making notes, his pencil moving with confident precision, listing every detail of the Electric Machine as it had been when he entered the room. He took care with the diagram showing the configuration of the Leyden Jars that provided the tremendous amount of required stored energy, and he described the ON position of the safety key, which now lay nestled in the safest place of all, the bottom of Patrolman Mercer's deep pocket.

"He was alone in that thing when you come in?" Patrolman Mercer's voice boomed so suddenly, Bradshaw jumped, toppling from his stool.

"Yes." Bradshaw regained his balance. "He was alone."

"So you think he turned on that contraption, crawled in that cage, and poked his finger through?"

"He couldn't have turned it on before he got in, it would be like walking through a lightning storm and grabbing hold of a lightning rod."

"Somebody else was here then?"

Bradshaw thought it probable, and said so, breathing more easily as the patrolman strolled away to cast his angry eye upon the Machine. Somebody else must have been here, but who? Had a student been assisting Oglethorpe, turned the key, then left Oglethorpe alone? No engineering student would do such a foolish thing. It was senseless, and more than anything Bradshaw abhorred senselessness. Especially in death. It unsettled him. It threw his own life into precarious balance, like watching that awful moving picture. What did it all mean? Why did any of them bother with life, with work, with caring, when it all came down to this? To sudden, irrational endings.

It was a scientific matter, he told himself, not a personal loss. *Not like before.*

Think of math, he told himself. Think of something safe. Algebra. Oglethorpe's sudden death was like an algebraic equation not yet deciphered. Yes. That was it.

He need only gather the pertinent information and solve for the unknown. Yes, the answer surely could be found in science. He jotted down the fundamental power equation, $P=EI$, and the orderliness of the algebra began to calm his mind. Mathematics had always appealed to him. There was nothing vague or cloudy in numbers. One did not have to second-guess the meaning of mathematical equations. They stood proudly and boldly, representing a universal truth. One plus one equaled two. Volts times amps equaled watts. In a world awash in confusion, algebra was a haven of clarity.

"What's that there mean? That zigzagging thing?"

Patrolman Mercer was once again breathing down his neck, but Bradshaw managed to stay seated. "It's the symbol for resistance." He launched into an explanation so full of scientific description it could have been one of Oglethorpe's own indecipherable lectures. It had the desired effect.

"Oh. Right." The patrolman was not quite able to mask his baffled expression with a frown. He strolled away to stand importantly in the doorway, rocking back and forth on his heels. Bradshaw, for the moment, could think in peace.

But the answer was going to be elusive. If something had gone wrong with the Machine, he couldn't see it. The students had done well. The Machine should have been completely safe when operated correctly. So what had Oglethorpe done wrong? Bradshaw saw no evidence that he had altered the Machine in any way. And Oglethorpe extending one of his curved fingers outside the cage was as foolish and unexpected an act as Patrolman Mercer tossing a loaded revolver into the air.

Why had he done it? Suicide? The loathsome word struck Bradshaw so powerfully, he snapped his pencil in two. He looked at the broken pieces in his hands and shook his head wryly. He had no more control over his anxiety than his student. The Patrolman lifted a suspicious eyebrow.

This was not suicide. He need not go there. Oglethorpe, the self-proclaimed genius of electrical engineering, would not have intentionally taken his own life. Behind the conceited confidence, Bradshaw hadn't detected an underlying insecurity. There'd been no hint of depression or desperation. The man had everything to live for and had bragged of it. A successful career, prominent friends, a new mansion paid for by shrewd investments.

Why, then, had Oglethorpe reached so foolishly outside of the cage?

And why, since the output of the Machine's secondary coil had a frequency and potential so very high and a current so very low, had the shock killed him rather than painfully jolted him? Bad luck? A weak heart? A stray current diverted from the relative safety of the outer surfaces of the body to the very core?

Lethal potential was there, of course, but if the safety rules were followed coils could be shown to the public. They were flashy and exciting, the science behind them loaded with possibilities for future invention. Why, next week…next week….

"You okay, Professor?"

Bradshaw realized he'd given a small gasp, but the thought that had provoked the gasp could not be spoken aloud, not to this oaf of a patrolman.

"You can't come in here, this is a crime scene."

Bradshaw turned to see the patrolman keeping Frank Graves from entering.

"It's all right, Officer. He's the University President."

Graves held out his hand, and the patrolman grudgingly shook it and allowed him entrance.

"I still can't believe it." Dr. Graves stared at the copper coils and metallic sphere of the Electric Machine, hands clasped behind his back.

Dr. Frank Pierrepont Graves, aged thirty-two, was three years younger than Bradshaw, but he'd amassed impressive credentials and a host of degrees. He was, in fact, the youngest university president in the country. Yet he exuded a polite, firm authority. Perhaps it was his prematurely receding and thinning hair, or the fuzzy sideburns that met a neatly trimmed mustache. Or the penetrating blue eyes that openly reflected his emotions as well as his intelligence. It certainly wasn't that dimple in his chin or those ears that stood out a bit further than was considered handsome. Those attributes caused certain females of the institution to call him "adorable," and he was wise enough to pretend not to notice.

Dr. Frank Graves was as lean and neat and organized in appearance as Patrolman Mercer was sloppy. Side-by-side they made a curious pair. Neither knew much about electrical energy; both knew enough to fear it.

Patrolman Mercer renewed his authority. "This room will have to be locked until Detective O'Brien gets here."

Dr. Graves said, "Yes, of course. And the Machine will be dismantled as soon as the police say." He shook his head and made a "tsk" sound of dismay. "It won't, of course, be shown to McKinley."

Bradshaw moaned silently.

"McKinley?" Patrolman Mercer's eyes shot wide.

Graves pointed up at the dark but readable welcome sign that had failed to light during the demonstration because of heat damage to the wire. "President McKinley was to see it next week when he toured Seattle."

Patrolman Mercer's jaw dropped. For several seconds he stared speechless and appalled, as if they'd intended exhibiting an assassination machine.

Bradshaw tried to catch Dr. Graves' eye, to beg him not to elaborate. But Graves paid him no attention. "McKinley was not to enter the cage, he was to be a spectator. He was to be given a specially made souvenir glass bulb that would light up in his hand when the Machine was running."

The patrolman's look of horror intensified.

Bradshaw wished Graves hadn't enlightened the rumpled patrolman, but it would have come out sooner or later. Eventually, the public would contemplate the what-ifs of next week's Presidential visit. What if the accident had happened when McKinley was here? What if McKinley had himself been injured, or killed?

Graves rubbed a sideburn thoughtfully, turning the full authority of his blue eyes upon Bradshaw. "Professor, I hate to ask you this, but Mrs. Oglethorpe, their two children...."

The polite but firm request in those sincere eyes couldn't be ignored. Bradshaw turned to his notes and underlined the word "potential" as he struggled with a way to decline. He said lamely,

"Sir, I hardly know her." He'd wished Oglethorpe gone even as the man was being electrocuted. He could not face the widow.

"We can't let her hear it from the police, and I won't be free to see her for several more hours." Graves laid a gentle hand on Bradshaw's shoulder.

Let her hear it from someone else then, Bradshaw thought. Not him. It would be better if some other teacher were to go, anybody but Bradshaw, not only because of his ill-timed wish, but also because it was well known, presumably also by Mrs. Oglethorpe, that Professor Oglethorpe despised Bradshaw and often called him a buffoon. And Bradshaw, in a frustrated moment that was unfortunately overheard, had once very recently called Oglethorpe an ass.

Graves squeezed Bradshaw's shoulder as if in direct answer to Bradshaw's thoughts. "I know you and Oglethorpe didn't get along, but that surely is unimportant under the circumstances. Mrs. Oglethorpe must be told immediately, with utmost care, and Bradshaw, I can't think of anyone who could handle it with more understanding and delicacy than you."

Bradshaw swallowed the bile rising in his throat. He did understand, far better than Graves realized. And who else was there, truly? Professor Hill was too young for such a task, and Professor Kelly, though kind at heart, had a tendency toward bluntness that wouldn't suit.

Bradshaw reluctantly agreed.

"It's imperative that I see to numerous details here immediately. Tomorrow's exhibition will, of course, be canceled."

"Yes, of course." His voice was a foreign, gravelly sound. He gathered his papers and hunted for courage. His head felt oddly light and fuzzy while his body dragged with the weight of lead. Somehow he moved across the lab, out the door. At the bottom of the staircase, he paused, looking up as if facing the icy crags of Mt. Rainier. How could he manage the task before him?

He took a deep breath that made his head all the lighter and his feet all the heavier.

He lifted his anvil foot and climbed.

Chapter Three

The Oglethorpes and the Bradshaws lived on the same street on Broadway Hill in Seattle. But 1204 Gallagher, the address of Bradshaw's modest two-story house was a world away from 1234 Gallagher, where Oglethorpe's spanking-new brick mansion reigned. Corinthian columns rose up from the porch through the second story balcony and brought the eye to a giant cameo-shaped window under the gable. The mansion took up the better part of two lots, but the yard and garden had not yet been planted. Planks had been laid across the mud as a temporary walk. Bradshaw propped his bicycle against a utility pole and followed the planks to the steps of the wide porch.

No sound came from within. All was eerily silent. Even the wind had momentarily hushed, the rain abated. Bradshaw took off his damp hat respectfully. A sick feeling, which hadn't left him since he'd seen Oglethorpe's dead body, rose in his throat as he rang the bell and heard the sound echo solemnly through the immense house.

He'd had to do this once before, eight years ago.

He'd stood before a door much like this one, preparing to tell his in-laws that his wife, their only daughter, was dead.

With a trembling hand, he rang the bell again.

When the door remained firmly shut, anger swept over him. If he must do this, he wanted it done now. He didn't want to have to return later, to have to spend the next hour, or hours, thinking about it. In a fit of anguish, he thought about leaving a note on the door. *So sorry*, he would write, *but Professor Wesley Oglethorpe, husband and father, has been unfortunately killed by the great Machine at the university. My deepest sympathy....*

Of course, he couldn't. He turned with a sigh and spotted a delivery wagon coming up the road, sprouting young slender trees, the limbs showing buds, the roots wrapped in burlap. There were young shrubs too, small green hydrangeas and budding rhododendrons. Amongst the limbs and leaves bobbed the plump faces of two eager children, a girl of about eight, and a boy of five. Both towheaded with noses upturned. Oglethorpe's children, Olive and Wesley, Jr.

Up front, next to the driver and a garden hand, sat Mrs. Marion Oglethorpe, as round-faced and towheaded as her children. Before the wagon had stopped, she was shouting good-natured instructions and soon all carried the greenery to the mud. Professor Bradshaw, on the porch, went unnoticed. He looked for an opportunity to make his presence known, but none came. They were all so exuberant about their task, so cheerfully argumentative about what was to go where, Bradshaw couldn't bring himself to interrupt. This might be the last carefree moment they had for a very long time. The girl Olive had distinct opinions as to the placement of the trees, and Bradshaw believed her calls to be good. The boy hadn't the same artistic eye as his sister and seemed merely concerned that he be noticed and get his own way. Very much like his father, in that respect. His father who, through some accident no doubt triggered by childish ego, now lay cold and dead in the morgue.

"Professor Bradshaw!" Mrs. Oglethorpe had spotted him.

Bradshaw's hand went numb. He dropped his hat, and it went tumbling down the steps to the mud. While he retrieved it, a girl on a bicycle rode up, apparently the maid, for she launched into explanations of tardiness. She was vaguely familiar to Bradshaw.

"Supper will be on the table well before Mr. Oglethorpe gets home from the university," the girl said to Mrs. Oglethorpe, then gave a quick nod and smile to Bradshaw. He took in her appearance as he returned her nod: frizzy brown hair, shiny face, intelligent blue eyes. Yes, he did know her. She'd aided Mrs. Prouty with deep spring cleaning several times over the past few years. She now hurried along the boards around toward the back of the house with her bicycle.

"It'll be cold if you put it out before he gets home, Sheila!" Mrs. Oglethorpe shook her head at the difficulties of maids, but she presented a beaming welcome to Professor Bradshaw.

"Come in, come in." She ushered him up the steps. "Olive, Wes! Come along, the men will finish up, time for homework. Not the front door," she added as the children clomped toward Bradshaw and the front porch. "You're not guests. Around back through the kitchen and leave your muddy shoes with Sheila."

She turned once again to the Professor. "Do come in, Professor Bradshaw, don't you worry about your overshoes, I see you've stayed to the boards and are clean. Let me take that hat and get the mud before it sets. Have a seat and I'll be right back."

Like a gust of stormy wind, Mrs. Oglethorpe swept him into the elegant polished hallway, removed his yellow slicker, and bade him pluck the rubbers from his shoes. She ushered Bradshaw into a front parlor that smelled as clean and new as the showroom floor of Frederick & Nelson, his housekeeper's favorite department store. He stood alone in the grand room with its maroon tassels and porcelain figures, listening to the bustling sounds of a happy, healthy family go about their routine. How on earth could he shatter their world? He forgot completely the words he had so carefully chosen on the way here.

Mrs. Oglethorpe returned with his now clean hat. "Good as new, Professor Bradshaw. Have a seat, please, and tell me what brings you here? Tomorrow's exhibition? Wesley is very excited about it."

He sat on the stiff settee, and she perched herself beside him, still talking. "I am so glad you came by, and I'm sorry we haven't been to see you since we moved in," she said quite earnestly, though Bradshaw knew her husband would never have made, nor allowed her to make, a social call to him down the street.

"…but as you can see things aren't quite settled yet. Besides the yard, we have entire rooms yet that are completely empty, and though we have Sheila, there's so much more to do in a house of this size, we'll have to hire another hand, temporarily of course, to get things in order. We certainly aren't the sort to have a house full of servants, we're down-to-earth simple folk, even though we've come into money and we're now in this grand house, but I do love maintaining house myself. Call me old-fashioned, but it gives me great pleasure to see to all the details. It's a sense of accomplishment, like what Wesley feels at the university, though he doesn't see it that way, and I'm sure what I do here isn't nearly as important, at least Wesley doesn't feel it's as important, but what would the world be if no one saw to home and hearth and made it a haven? Oh, but I do go on, and here you are so kind to pay a neighborly visit—why, Professor Bradshaw, you're white as a ghost, what is it? Has something happened?"

Bradshaw nodded, but he couldn't bring himself to say the words. He hoped wildly that she would continue talking in her tangential way and hit upon the horrible truth and then he wouldn't actually have to say it aloud.

But apparently, Marion Oglethorpe could be as silent and attentive as she could be talkative, and she took his hands and began patting them as if he were her child.

"I have very bad news, Mrs. Oglethorpe," he managed at last. "About your husband."

She raised eyebrows that were thick but so pale they could hardly be seen and gazed at him encouragingly, a kind smile still on her face. What on earth did she think he meant by "very bad news"? Why wasn't she bracing herself?

"There's been a terrible accident with the Machine."

Her face seemed to freeze. The smile was still there, but it was only skin deep and empty. A mask she was too fearful to remove.

"I'm so sorry. It was fatal." He wished he could assure her that her husband's death had been quick and painless, but death by electric shock could be both painful and prolonged. Oglethorpe could have been sitting in that chair for many agonizing minutes, his heart still beating but his lungs unable to draw a breath.

"Are you telling me my husband's dead?"

"Yes." It was he who now took her hands and patted them comfortingly.

"Dead?"

"I'm so sorry." This was not how it had gone with Rachel's parents those many years ago. The news of his wife's death had devastated them, yes, but not surprised them. They had not questioned his news. They hadn't had trouble taking it in at all. It was as if they had expected it.

"Dead? It can't be true. Sheila is preparing his dinner. He'll be home soon."

"No, Mrs. Oglethorpe. He won't be home."

She looked up at the ceiling, up, no doubt, toward her children's rooms, wondering how she could tell them their father was dead, how she could be strong for them, how they would all survive. She let go of Bradshaw to place one trembling palm over her mouth, the other over her belly. It was then that Bradshaw realized her roundness wasn't entirely due to a plump nature. Marion Oglethorpe was with child.

◇◇◇

A few minutes later, Professor Bradshaw pushed his bicycle along the cement sidewalk as he slowly walked home. His house was a humble little place, white and tidy, two stories high and simply dressed with white shutters and a leaded parlor window. A thin maple tree nearly as tall as the house stood in green relief against the white siding. And beneath the lace-curtained parlor window, in neglected flower beds, little white blooms of lily-of-the-valley bowed among the weeds in misty welcome.

Bradshaw had never been so affected by the sight. Standing outside the white picket gate, he felt strangely that his life had changed. That today, with all the traumatic events, he'd been turned slightly askew from the lonely road he'd been traveling. He'd seen himself in a new and disturbing light in that moving picture. Then death had arrived, shocking him yet again from the routine of his thoughts, his habits.

Change had come, and more change was to come.

He hated change.

Light glowed through the parlor curtains, but he couldn't bring himself to open the gate to enter the yard. He took a long deep breath of the cool damp air, and the front door flew open.

"Well, he's gone and good riddance, I say!" Mrs. Prouty's broad face was flushed, her sturdy frame braced with feet wide apart.

Bradshaw approached his housekeeper with a mixed feeling of admiration and shock. True Oglethorpe had been an egomaniac and generally annoying, but it was only common decency to express regret at a man's untimely death and forget his less likable attributes.

He said, before going around to the back of the house to put away his bicycle, "I understand your reaction, Mrs. Prouty, but I will hear no more ill spoken of the dead."

"Blimey, Professor, Henry Pratt ain't dead, he's gone to Alaska again in search of gold." She turned with a huff and closed the front door with a good deal more force than was necessary.

"Henry? Oh, oh. I see," he said to no one. It took his mind a moment to fully switch over from Wesley Oglethorpe to Henry Pratt, his longtime friend who boarded upstairs in the spare room. So, Henry had gone. Again. He'd known it was coming. Though unsuccessful in his first adventure in '98, gold fever had been growing in Henry for months. Boatloads of overnight millionaires no longer docked weekly in Seattle, but enough of them trickled in to keep the hope alive.

His bicycle stored, Bradshaw came in through the kitchen, then down the hall, and put his satchel beside his desk in the parlor. He thumbed through the mail, which Mrs. Prouty always left for him on the mantel, and found a letter for Henry addressed in a familiar hand. The letter-writer was Missouri Fremont, Henry's young niece who lived near Pittsburgh. For the briefest of moments, Bradshaw smiled, recalling the engaging stories Missouri had related over the years in that careful, flowing script.

It would be a week at least before he could forward the letter to Alaska. He propped the letter on the mantel as a reminder to send it on when he received word from Henry where he could be reached. Three years ago, that had been the general post office in the Klondike. Big syndicates now owned the most valuable claims in that region, and Henry would be wiser to try his luck in Nome, but he had some harebrained idea that a minuscule stream he'd filed a claim on was simply waiting for him to return to bestow its bountiful riches.

Bradshaw stared at the letter, but his mind was back at the university. He felt cold, and the house was suddenly too quiet. He called out to Mrs. Prouty, "Where's Justin?"

Her voice came in ever-increasing volume as she made her way down the hall. "Taking a bath. He must have jumped into every mud puddle on his way home from school." She was now standing before him, wiping her hands on her starched apron. "Now, what is it, Professor? You're white as sheet."

White as a sheet. White as a ghost. How many expressions were there for describing the pallor of a man who'd just delivered news of death?

"There's been a tragedy at the university. Professor Oglethorpe has been killed."

"No! Murdered, you mean? Who done it? A student or one of the staff?"

"No, not murdered." Good night, what a morbid mind she had, jumping to such a conclusion. "It was an accident with the Machine, Mrs. Prouty." Or was it? He was as bad as Mrs. Prouty, jumping to conclusions. He wanted it to have been an accident, but wanting did not make it so.

He climbed the stairs and found his son in the midst of a bubble bath war. Toy modern warships battled three-masted schooners. Pirates attacked navy sailors. Water sloshed triumphantly over the round edges of the enameled iron and was captured silently by thick white towels Mrs. Prouty had the foresight to spread across the wood floor. The boy, his fair hair still dry and messy, his pale skin gleaming with water and spotted with bubbles, declared a temporary truce when his father arrived.

"She made me take a bath even before dinner and now I'll have to get dressed in real clothes again and then have to get undressed and into pajamas!"

Bradshaw propped himself on the commode and hid a smile. The boy would run around filthy and naked, if he had his way. The chore of dressing was hated second only to bathing, although once in the tub, it was difficult getting him out.

"Did you know Henry went to Alaska?"

The boy sullenly sank the warship with a splash.

"He'll bring home exciting stories."

"So." The schooner followed the warship to the bottom of the tub, no doubt held submerged by the boy's toes. He could be as miserly in speech as his father, but that single word spoke volumes.

"Tell me what's wrong." Bradshaw's tone brooked no argument.

"He didn't even say good-bye."

"Oh, I see. And I agree. It was rude of him not to say good-bye. He was probably afraid I would try to talk him out of going."

"Would you have?"

"Yes. But he's gone now, and the best we can do is wish him safety and success."

Justin showed his disdain for this suggestion by sinking another ship. Bradshaw knew better than to try to force a change in attitude. The boy felt what he felt, but he listened to reason even if he didn't immediately embrace it. By the time Henry's first letter came, Justin would be eager to read it.

Bradshaw wished he could mimic his son's resilience. The heaviness of his chest was a constant physical reminder of today's events. He must be careful how he explained Oglethorpe's death. Too lightly, and the boy would treat the tragedy like some great adventure story; too heavily, and the boy would be frightened for his father's safety.

The sound of the doorbell diverted Bradshaw's attention and momentarily spared him the labor of finding the right words. He heard Mrs. Prouty at the door. A moment later, she shouted for him to come down.

He stood and stretched. "Behind the ears and between the toes," he commanded, leaving his son to the bubbles.

Bradshaw descended to the hall. Mrs. Prouty had returned to the kitchen, but she'd left the front door open. Two policemen stood on his porch. His heart gave a little leap—of what emotion, he couldn't say. Fear? Curiosity? Interest? Perhaps all three. He crossed to the threshold to greet Patrolman Mercer and another much smaller officer who identified himself as Sergeant Hoyle.

The small sergeant said, "You're wanted for questioning, Professor Bradshaw."

"Yes, certainly." He stood back to let them in. Curiosity and interest, most definitely.

"Not here. At headquarters."

"Shall I bring my notes?"

The policemen blinked blankly.

"Notes of the Machine? I took detailed notes of the lab and the Machine in case they were needed." He looked hopefully at Patrolman Mercer, who'd watched him taking those notes.

Patrolman Mercer said, with an exaggerated sarcasm Bradshaw found completely unwarranted, "Yes. Bring yer notes. By all means, bring yer notes."

Confused by their attitude, Bradshaw retrieved his engineering notebook from his parlor desk and returned to the open front door. Patrolman Mercer snatched the notebook from him, and Sergeant Hoyle unhooked a gleaming pair of handcuffs from his belt.

"Extend your wrists, Professor."

Bradshaw was too startled for words.

"I said extend your wrists."

"But—"

Hoyle placed a palm upon the hilt of his holstered revolver. "Don't make me say it a third time, Professor."

Bradshaw stared for a moment at the revolver. On his front porch. Threatening him.

Preposterous.

Impossible to ignore.

And so Professor Benjamin Bradshaw extended his wrists. He knew it was a moment he would never forget, even as sunlight winked off the steel and his mind went frightfully blank. The gusting wind brought him back to awareness, to the rattling of the back door with the change in air pressure. To Mrs. Prouty gasping as she emerged from the kitchen.

He heard a small intake of breath. He looked over his shoulder. Justin stood dripping bubbles, clutching a bath towel, at the top of the stairs.

Bradshaw's heart froze.

"Daddy?"

But before he could reply to his son, before he could assure him there was nothing to fear, Patrolman Mercer, whom Bradshaw now hated beyond reason, said, "Come now, Professor," and tugged on the cuffs, digging the metal into his wrists, ripping him from the threshold of his home.

Chapter Four

Professor Bradshaw was ushered into a tiny windowless office, given a chair, and told to sit. He sat.

The room had more in common with an over-sized closet than an office. A cheap wall-mounted electric fixture with a bare incandescent bulb filled the room with an unforgiving light. The detective wore a cheap brown suit of mixed cheviot and sat behind the desk that had been squeezed into the space. He did not extend his hand. Despite his lack of welcome, he had a friendly face, with smiling hazel eyes that were thick-lashed and thick-browed. His ears were large, sticking out from a close-cropped head. Freckles dotted his long, lean, angular face. His age was difficult to determine, nearing forty, perhaps, or a weathered thirty. He wore a cavalry style hat, a Roosevelt, with a high crown and flat brim. It looked like something a cowboy would wear, and Bradshaw wondered why the detective kept it on while indoors. He had the face of a stage actor—no, an Irish priest expecting a confession. Bradshaw certainly felt an unnatural compulsion to speak.

"You are Detective O'Brien?"

"Yes. I'm O'Brien." He sat back, hands entwined behind his neck, and smiled.

The smile did nothing to reassure Bradshaw. It was not that sort of smile.

"There's been a mistake." He lifted his wrists so that the metal cuffs jangled. His stomach twisted sickly again.

"There's been no mistake."

It would take time, that was all, thought Bradshaw. They needed factual detail of what had happened today at the university.

"I've brought my notes." Bradshaw opened his folder on the desktop. He sat forward and twisted sideways to better show the detective. It was not this detective's fault, he told himself, as the image of Justin clutching that bath towel flashed before him. This Detective O'Brien hadn't intended to traumatize a boy of eight.

For several minutes, Bradshaw pointed out the various features of the Electric Machine and the university's engineering lab, the handcuffs jangling with each page turn. Normally a quiet man, not given to casual discourse, he now fairly gushed with particulars of this deadly matter. This wasn't trite, manipulative, or wasteful conversation like most social interchange. It was conversation as useful and straightforward as an electric circuit. If all speech were such as this, Professor Bradshaw thought, his reputation wouldn't be taciturn but downright gabby.

Slowly, however, Bradshaw became aware that O'Brien's keen gaze was focused not on the notes, but on Bradshaw himself, and he appeared not to be listening.

"You must have taken your own notes of the scene, of course," said Bradshaw, "but I wanted to make sense of the tragedy, so I recorded all I felt might be significant. And I was able to record things exactly as they were when I arrived. This," he said, pointing at his precise drawing, trying to get O'Brien to pay attention, "is how the laboratory looked when I entered. I recorded even insignificant details, in case they might later lead us to a better understanding of the accident. Do you know anything about electricity, Detective?"

Detective O'Brien cocked his head sideways, still examining Bradshaw. He said, in a very deep and friendly voice, "Why didn't Professor Oglethorpe like you, Bradshaw? You appear a likeable enough fellow."

"Excuse me?"

"Not a single student or teacher I spoke with this afternoon failed to mention the animosity between the two of you."

Confused as to what this had to do with Professor Oglethorpe's death, Bradshaw shook his head. "It wasn't animosity, more like aversion. He's a physicist as well as engineer, a researcher and theorist. He believes—believed—all professors should be of the same nature."

"And you're not a professor of such nature?"

"I'm a practical man. My interest is in the mechanics and practical uses of electricity."

"I've read that Thomas Edison is such a man."

"Yes, he is." There was no warmth in Bradshaw's voice. He still hadn't forgiven Edison for devising the Kinetoscope. Had it really only been this morning that he'd witnessed that horrid moving picture?

The detective asked, "Did Oglethorpe admire Edison?"

"No. Oglethorpe acknowledged the cleverness of Edison's inventions, but overall, he considers—considered—Edison a lucky dabbler and talented salesman. And he thought Edison foolish for backing direct-current. Oglethorpe was a Tesla enthusiast. A Tesla rival would be more accurate. His research was in the same field of the wireless transmission of energy."

"Tesla? Is he the man who invented that contraption you had hooked up to that cage in your lab? The one Patrolman Mercer claimed produced lightning?"

"The oscillating coil, yes. That's Tesla's invention. But it's the university's lab, the engineering department's lab, not mine. And the Electric Machine was a student project overseen by the entire staff of electrical engineering, not just me."

"You're a very clever man, aren't you?"

Bradshaw didn't know how to reply to such a statement said in such an accusatory tone. A horse whinnied, the sound coming from beneath Bradshaw's feet. Apparently, this claustrophobic office was situated above the stables. Police headquarters, located within the City Hall building, had been recently extended as a result of Seattle's explosive population growth and corresponding crime rate.

Detective O'Brien's method of questioning was as incongruous as the building. "You've got a number of patents for electrical gadgets. Have they made you much money?"

Bradshaw stiffened. This turn in questioning hardly seemed conducive to the removal of the handcuffs. "I've invented a few gadgets, as you call them, and hold patents on improvements for certain electric motors. The income they provide make it possible for me to concentrate on teaching. Most of what comes in I save for my son's future." And it was his son's future that was most at stake here. Anger bubbled once more into Bradshaw's blood. He clenched his jaw in an attempt to control it.

O'Brien asked, "Why is it I've never heard of you before today?"

"Pardon me?" The words emerged hard and clipped.

"I've heard of Edison and Tesla. I've even heard of Professor W. T. Oglethorpe, the great university professor who solved, what was it, something or other about magnetism? But I've never heard of you, Professor Bradshaw, despite your patents."

"As I said, my patents are minor. The newspapers are more interested in the next great invention or theory."

"So you resented Oglethorpe for his more brilliant mind?"

Bradshaw nearly choked. "He understood theory better than I, yes. And if he'd used that understanding to enlighten his students and aid his fellow teachers, I might have admired him. But he didn't, and so I didn't. He used his talent as a magician uses tricks, to show off to his audience and keep them from understanding how his tricks are performed. If I resented anything, it was his high-and-mighty ineffective teaching method."

"You tutored many of Oglethorpe's students against his explicit request, I'm told."

"The man believed helping a student understand the material was some form of cheating."

"Did you help the students cheat?"

"I help the students understand the material so that they can pass their exams. It's called teaching, Detective. It's what I'm paid to do."

Bradshaw gripped his knees with his restricted palms and tried to regain his composure.

"I assumed that these," he said and again lifted his bound wrists, "were a mistake precipitated by my being first on the scene, but I fail to understand why you are mounting a personal attack."

"You don't deny you disliked Oglethorpe?"

What did his dislike of Oglethorpe have to do with his death? The detective was venturing into the sort of leading conversation Bradshaw so hated and that often kept him silent. He wanted no more of it. "Detective, wasn't I brought here to assist you in understanding Oglethorpe's death?"

The detective's eyes gleamed. "Yes."

"And despite my evidence, you believe I killed him."

O'Brien said nothing.

It was the first time in his life that Bradshaw truly understood that ignorance could be lethal. It was so ridiculous, if it weren't for the seriousness of the situation he would have laughed. They, O'Brien, Mercer, all of them, simply didn't understand the physical laws of electricity. Most people didn't. Knowing the names of prominent scientists like Edison and Tesla, which appeared almost daily in the newspapers, didn't make a man comprehend the complications of electric current. The deadliness of a single spark.

"If you would take a look at my notes. This diagram," he turned a drawing toward the detective, "shows precisely Oglethorpe's position. His index finger, here, is extended outside the Faraday cage. Not much, just a fraction of an inch, but that's all it takes to move from safety to danger. He foolishly, or carelessly, or for some reason I can't yet fathom, reached beyond the cage. The amount of current he was exposed to is not usually fatal at such high frequency, but the human body is not predictable when it comes to reacting to electricity. When the pathway of the discharge…" Bradshaw let his explanation hang in the air, unfinished.

Detective O'Brien was not looking at the diagram. His smile had taken on a new quality, that of a cat tired of playing with its prey and ready to put it out of its misery.

"Begin at the beginning, Bradshaw. Tell me when you decided to kill him, how you arranged it, and when you did it."

"I didn't do anything. You don't seem to understand. Professor Oglethorpe was killed by a tragic accident."

"You will be convicted. The only question is whether you get life or hanging. Your cooperation might make the difference."

"Would you stop accusing me!" The small airless room was suffocating him. "I didn't kill Oglethorpe."

"You'll have to be more convincing than that."

"I'm innocent. Why should I need to convince you of anything?"

"Would you like an attorney present, or will you give me your statement now?"

The detective's smiling eyes faded into cold stones. He stared long and hard, and Bradshaw returned the stare with what he hoped appeared equal nerve. He would not be drawn into some manipulative conversation by this professional interrogator. Any moment now, O'Brien would claim that one plus one equaled three. Bradshaw's unnatural desire to speak fled, and he clamped his jaw tight in silence.

"You're either innocent or the most cold-blooded killer I've yet encountered."

Let the detective say what he will, Bradshaw was through communicating.

The detective gave a huge sigh. "It's too easy, though. That's what I don't like. A man of your intelligence would surely go about murder with more caution. Or is that part of your scheme? Make yourself so obvious a suspect we don't suspect you at all?"

Bradshaw rose, clasping his notes firmly, knowing it a futile gesture made foolish by the jangle of the cuffs. He craved fresh air.

"What's your hurry, Professor? Your cell is being hosed down—the last occupant made a bit of a mess of it. But drunks will do that. We have time, anyway. Sit. Tell me about your day. Begin at the beginning. What did you have for breakfast?"

Chapter Five

O'Brien had told the truth—someone had been sick inside Bradshaw's dank stone cell. The lye soap and cold water splashed upon the mess had done nothing to dissipate the smell. For four hours, Bradshaw stood with his nose lifted to the tiny window high in the cell wall, breathing in wafts of hay and tar and dung. For another four, he lay stiffly upon the sagging cot, immune to all smells, but his hearing attuned to every drip, neigh, shout, and scuttle.

He'd refused to tell O'Brien about his breakfast—a mound of rashers and kippers Mrs. Prouty had served to him as she prattled on about how his mornings lacked protein. He refused to speak at all.

At six a.m., without explanation—innocent men did not summon attorneys, he believed—a key was slid into the lock of his door and he was set free. As he exited the jail, he was handed a thick document that turned out to be a summons to appear at Oglethorpe's inquest the following day.

He walked home through a thin drizzle that both restored his sense of smell and magnified the odor wafting from the wool of his suit. He skirted his house, entering the backyard gate from the alley. Standing before the charred remains of the burn pile beside Mrs. Prouty's compost bin, he stripped off his jacket and tie and shoes and socks and threw them onto the pile. For a moment, he stood in the drizzle, his face tilted up, letting the drops wash over him. Then he stepped gingerly across the wet lawn, up the steps and to the back door.

He found the kitchen deserted, the stove warm, water gently steaming from the kettle, the smell of something cooking—oats? Had Mrs. Prouty given up forcing kippers? The day was looking better. The hallway was deserted, as was the parlor where he placed the summons and his notes. But his luck ran out on the stairs.

Mrs. Prouty waited on the landing for him, her brows lifted at the sight of his bare toes. She leaned sideways to cast aspersions upon the damp footprints he'd left on the stairs.

"Good morning, Mrs. Prouty."

"You look a fright, Professor."

"How's Justin?"

"Won't come out from under the covers."

In his room, Bradshaw stripped off his shirt and trousers and tossed them out his window. The trousers hit the burn pile, but the shirt fluttered onto the compost. Only a deep-rooted sense of decency kept his underwear from a flight out the window. He took a scalding bath, using fully half a bar of Ivory soap, and emerged from the bathroom wrapped in an oversized white towel to find Justin, still in pajamas, sitting on the floor, Cloppy on his lap. Cloppy was a plump grey horse made from woolen socks and yarn. Mrs. Prouty had made it for Justin when he was a baby. Cloppy's appearance now indicated how troubled Justin was feeling. Bradshaw's heart tightened, but he forced his voice to be light.

"Well, well. We must stop meeting like this."

"Like what?"

"Never mind. Is your bed made? Had your breakfast yet?"

"Why did the police take you?"

"Because I was first on the scene. Did Mrs. Prouty explain to you about the accident and Professor Oglethorpe?"

"Did you kill him?"

Bradshaw looked gently into his son's eyes. "No, son. I did not kill Professor Oglethorpe."

"Then why did they put cuffs on you? Why did they take you away?"

"Electricity is a relatively new science, Justin. Most people don't understand it. I found poor Professor Oglethorpe dead from an accident with the Electric Machine. I understood that something must have gone wrong, but the police have never been educated on the subject. People are often afraid of things they don't understand."

"They're afraid of you?" Justin's eyes lit up, as if this were something wonderful.

"Well, I suppose they were a little bit last night. But I explained the circumstances, and now I'm home."

Bradshaw began down the hall to his room, and he heard Justin get up to follow.

"What was the jail like?"

"Cold and stinking."

"Stinking?"

"Yes, like vomit and horse manure."

Justin laughed. "Yuck!" And the tightness in Bradshaw's chest eased a bit.

Chapter Six

"Not an accident, Bradshaw?" President Graves pulled on Bradshaw's coat sleeve and drew him away from the open doors of Denny Hall. The murmur of students drifted out to them. "What are you saying?"

"I'm saying the police don't believe Oglethorpe's death to be an accident."

"You mean—murder?"

Before Bradshaw could reply, a cluster of hesitant parents in their Sunday best approached. One of the fathers spoke up. "Is this the Electric Show?"

Graves covered his anxiety with an official smile and an extended hand. "Yes, welcome. We decided to allow the students to briefly show their work to their families, but the exhibition has been canceled, so I must ask you to keep your visit short."

Many other parents were already in the hall, admiring their children's work as were curious members of the public who had ignored the cancellation signs posted on the doors, and newspaper reporters, who kept trying to sneak down to the basement labs and were blocked by a strategically positioned cadet officer in full uniform.

"This is getting out of hand," Graves said as they entered the hall behind the parents.

Bradshaw wasn't sure if he was referring to Oglethorpe's puzzling death or the growing crowd. Or both.

Graves had come to tell the students it was time to dismantle their projects, and Bradshaw had come to take the sting out of the request. Together, they moved from one table to the next. The students attempted to subdue their enthusiasm, but pride in a year's hard work was difficult to smother. Third year engineering student Glen Reeves failed entirely.

A square-jawed and popular fellow, Reeves had boundless energy, able to balance the demands of his studies with athletics, football and baseball, numerous debate clubs, and the social shenanigans of his fraternity. He manned a printing telegraph with a piano keyboard transmitter that sent messages to a receiver on the far side of the room. Each key corresponded with a letter of the alphabet. Reeves explained that he'd scrambled the letters and assigned them a musical note so that when a song was played, only a trained listener could decode the message.

"Nice work." Bradshaw shook Reeve's hand. It was a solid job of assembling components, but not the least bit innovative. Similar devices had been around for decades, although to be fair to Mr. Reeves, he had built a first-class modern version.

The miniature electric cars circling a miniature track had required more work and the application of both mechanical and electrical engineering lessons. The student trio responsible for it beamed at Bradshaw's praise.

The smell of bacon brought Bradshaw to an electric burner and Miss Sara Trout, a flirtatious junior with a fresh complexion, gleaming black hair, and mathematical mind.

She greeted President Graves politely, then turned to Bradshaw with a questioning expression that implied more than her teasing words. "Professor, I ask you, is it fair I'm forced to do the cooking because I'm a female?" The fact that she'd worn a frilled white apron and held a fork daintily over the sizzling pan countered her objection.

"Miss Trout, you chose the project yourself. How is the heat regulation?"

"Oh, it's troublesome, there is no middle heat where most cooking occurs. I triple-checked my calculations, and at the low and high current settings, the resistor coils are functioning correctly, giving me predicted temperatures, so the problem must lie in the current delivery."

"Don't discount the value of trial and error, Miss Trout. Continue your investigation and you might make an unexpected discovery."

She thanked him for his encouragement with a smile that lit her eyes. She attempted to hold his gaze longer than was necessary, or comfortable. He ushered Graves quickly to the final display.

Oscar Daulton stood alone at his table. He tucked his hair behind his ears at their approach, and with fumbling fingers, connected a bank of glass battery jars to screw terminals projecting from a handsome large wooden cigar box. A pair of short metal rods were attached to another set of terminals on the opposite end of the box. Daulton closed a switch, and a small flaming arc leaped between the two metal rods.

Bradshaw was intrigued. The flame was silent. Both the batteries and the absence of a noisy buzz told him the leaping flame was powered by direct current. But such a flame should not have been possible from the voltage provided by the batteries. "What have we here, Mr. Daulton?"

"My invention, sir. It steps up D.C. voltage." Daulton blushed nearly as much as Miss Trout.

Bradshaw was delightedly puzzled. "Impossible." He placed a hand over the cigar box, expecting heat. He felt none. Direct current couldn't be transformed like alternating current. Even if it could, surely the components necessary to do the job could not fit into such a small space. Yet there was that flame, defying reality.

"Is it a trick?"

Oscar shook his head. "No sir, it's my invention."

Bradshaw met the young man's eye and saw he was serious.

"Good heavens, Daulton. Have you gone and done something revolutionary?"

Daulton beamed.

"What about input, is polarity limited?"

"No, it will run from a standard A.C. outlet."

"Will you tell me what's in the box, or are you keeping it a secret until the patent's filed?"

Bradshaw had been half-teasing, but Daulton's shining eyes and tightly clamped mouth told him he wasn't far from the truth.

President Graves put a hand on Bradshaw's shoulder. "That's it then, time to go." He clearly did not understand that this humble electrical engineering student might have joined scientific history with his mysterious cigar box. Graves was still properly concerned with Oglethorpe's death. All else would have to wait.

Bradshaw shook Daulton's hand. "We'll talk later."

He followed Graves out the door, down the main stairwell, past the guarding cadet, and into the electrical engineering lab.

Bradshaw shut the door, closing them into an eerie silence. A faint residue of burnt rubber wafted from the charred welcome sign dangling from the ceiling. The Electric Machine, rendered harmless and impotent by the removal of the Leyden jars, had been dismantled. The individual components sat in a neat row along the back wall. Bradshaw crossed the room to examine them again.

"Murder," Graves whispered. His strength had vanished with the closing of the door. He ran a distracted hand through his thinning, frizzy hair, unwittingly mussing it. Odd strands fanned about his prominent ears, giving him a very youthful aspect. He was as yet, Bradshaw realized, untouched by deep tragedy in his life. This was his first encounter with senseless death.

"That's what the police suspect, sir."

The Faraday Cage was still intact. Bradshaw climbed the wooden steps and entered it, placing his index finger where the curved finger of Oglethorpe's right hand had been. With his finger still resting on the metal, he turned his face up to the roof of the cage, but found no dangling wires, no misplaced or broken bars, nothing that could have somehow come in contact with Oglethorpe. Nothing that could have brought dangerous current into the safety of the cage.

"I should have done something about him." Graves spoke quietly.

"Sir?"

"Oglethorpe, I mean." Graves shuddered. "Come out of there, will you, Bradshaw. I know it's unhooked, but you're giving me the willies, posing like that."

Bradshaw stepped out of the cage. "What should you have done about Oglethorpe?"

"I had a desk full of complaints about him from students, the faculty. And you, Bradshaw. I tried to steer Oglethorpe toward a more approachable teaching style, but he was not a man to accept direction. He was so brilliant."

"Brilliance is highly over-rated."

"Is it?" Graves wasn't really listening. "He studied abroad you know, after graduating from Columbia. In both England and Germany, with the most brilliant minds of the day. His research was so valuable to the university's reputation, I suppose I gave him too much latitude in his classes. I thought he'd eventually settle down to a more comprehensible teaching style."

"In the meantime, students were in danger of failing." Bradshaw thought for a moment that Graves would be offended, but he underestimated the man.

"Indeed, Professor Bradshaw," Graves said somberly. "Indeed."

Dr. Graves could not truly be faulted for his soft approach toward Oglethorpe. It was a difficult task, balancing the needs of the students with the requirements of the Board of Regents. His vision must be both immediate and long-sighted. It was thanks to Dr. Graves that the two new dormitories had been built and the faculty and enrollment of the university increased. Because of Dr. Graves, the ground would break for a new science hall in October and a new powerhouse would soon generate enough power to see the engineering department well into this new century. Inviting and keeping Oglethorpe, who'd been wooed by universities all across the country, was a clever chess move, designed for current prestige and future glory.

Dr. Graves sighed. "What happened, do you suppose? How did he get himself killed?"

Bradshaw strode along the line of disassembled components, eyeing them critically. "He could have come in contact with the primary coil, the Leyden jars, or the secondary coil. All are capable of discharging a fatal shock while the Machine is energized."

"Can any of those components be reached from inside the cage?"

Bradshaw paused before saying quietly, "No." He saw understanding in Graves' intense expression, in the way his mouth opened slightly. "Was it the students who took the Machine apart?"

"Yes, under Professor Kelly's supervision and with someone from the coroner's office and that hulking policeman watching."

Bradshaw hunkered down and studied the thick copper turns of the primary coil. He could think of no way for Oglethorpe to come in contact with lethal levels of current while inside the cage unless he'd made some ludicrous modification. Bradshaw didn't put it past him—Oglethorpe had actually once said he believed himself closer to God than the average man because he understood how God's greatest creations worked—but Bradshaw would have spotted any such modification when he studied the Machine yesterday and gave that brief demonstration of its power. Nothing had been altered, he was sure of it.

Graves' shoulders lifted as he shook a troubled head. "Someone must have been here when Oglethorpe died."

"I can think of no other explanation." And he would bet that Oglethorpe's body had been moved, but he didn't say so aloud. His speculations would not comfort Dr. Graves. Why move a body, unless to cover up a crime?

To cover up a fatal blunder? Was someone too afraid to come forward?

"I saw Mrs. Oglethorpe about an hour ago. She said you were very kind when delivering the news."

Bradshaw's throat tightened.

Graves said, "She's was bearing up quite well. Pale, but chin up. The children looked stunned. I'm not sure they understand, really, that their father won't be home."

Bradshaw tried not to imagine his own son in a similar circumstance.

They stood for a moment in silence, the weight of the situation a physical heaviness that made movement and thought as sluggish as running through mud. The scent of the burnt rubber sign made Bradshaw's nose itch. He rubbed it with the back of his hand and discovered an even more unpleasant scent on his skin. He'd touched so many electric components in the past half hour, the residue of chemicals must have unpleasantly combined. He washed his hands at the lab sink with pine tar soap.

Graves was silent until Bradshaw shut off the water and dried his hands on a clean lab towel. "I wired Dean Wilson about Oglethorpe's classes."

Wilson, the Dean of Engineering, was absent on leave with Northwest Engineering, a bridge-building company in Spokane. A sharp and very likable fellow. Bradshaw had missed his presence in the halls this past school year. He was one of the few people with whom Bradshaw enjoyed conversing.

"I thought it best to inform him at once. He sends his condolences, as well as his regards. He suggested you assume Oglethorpe's physics class until the end of term."

"Yes, of course."

"Professor Hill will take Electrical Design and Professor Griffin in Liberal Arts will take Industrial Problems."

So it was settled. Oglethorpe was gone, and already the flow of life was filling his space. How nature abhorred a vacuum.

A light knock sounded at the door, and a youthful voice spoke reverently. "Dr. Graves?"

Graves unlocked the door and Assistant Professor Tom Hill poked in his curly head. In his mid twenties, he still exuded the fun-loving demeanor of a student, though he did try to dampen his tone to fit the situation. "I beg pardon, sir, but the students are asking about Oglethorpe."

"Tell them I will speak to them soon. Have them gather in the small auditorium—no, make that Denny Hall once the exhibits are removed—and get word around the entire campus. I'll address all the colleges at once. Telephone the School of Law downtown. They can hop the streetcar."

"Yes, sir." Hill glanced at Bradshaw and pulled a face only a man still in his twenties would pull. "You found him? Tough luck." He looked to Dr. Graves. "Is it true McKinley's trip was canceled?"

"What?" Bradshaw was taken aback.

"Yes," Graves confirmed, "it was in the P. I. last night. Mrs. McKinley is ill. The President won't be coming to Seattle."

Bradshaw hadn't been given last night's edition while in that stinking jail cell, and this morning's paper sat unread at home on his kitchen table. He was relieved by the news. He wasn't exactly sure why, but he noted his reaction as something to examine later. Instinctive reactions, he'd painfully learned, should never be dismissed.

Tom made another face, this one of disappointment. "Tomorrow's engineering classes canceled, sir?"

"Yes."

Tom retreated and closed the door.

Graves took a deep breath. "Could the police be right? Could Oglethorpe's death have been intentional? He wasn't well-liked, but I don't believe he had actual enemies. Unless one of his failing students—but I can't see it. They come to you, don't they, Bradshaw, if they find themselves too awfully muddled?"

Graves already knew the answer. Bradshaw thought of the dozen students over the past year he'd tutored. It was impossible to believe any of them had plotted some sort of revenge, especially seeing that they'd all managed to pass their exams with decent scores.

"Do the police believe it was someone connected with the university?"

"It would have to be somebody knowledgeable about electricity."

"Aah, yes. True. That at least narrows the field."

And, he thought, someone who wouldn't realize that a coroner can often tell if a death has been staged, a body moved. He suddenly remembered Artimus Lowe, the student with the youthful gait he'd seen while he stood at the window yesterday afternoon waiting for Daulton to finish his exam. Last term, Lowe, a law student, had haunted the engineering laboratories for weeks, attempting to gain a rudimentary understanding of electrical hazards for a senior thesis entitled "Industrial Forensics." Bradshaw, despite his dislike of the arrogant Lowe, was intrigued by the topic. In this great age of industry, with machines continually finding their way into the everyday lives of everyday citizens, accidents were growing in number and the courts were increasingly in need of expert testimony and investigators able to understand the complex mechanisms.

Lowe was familiar with forensic medicine, and thanks to Bradshaw, he was familiar with the various dangers of electric current.

"You've thought of someone?" Graves asked.

"I—no, not likely." Lowe would have known moving the body wouldn't mask the truth.

"Whom do the police suspect? Did they say?"

Bradshaw felt his face grow hot and he knew it reddened for Graves' brow shot up inquisitively. "That would be me, sir."

"You?" To Bradshaw's relief, Graves laughed. "Why? Oh, because you discovered the body."

"Yes, and because the police learned that Oglethorpe and I weren't the best of friends."

"Mmm, yes." The laughter retreated from his eyes. "Even so, that's not much motive for murder."

"It was enough for the police. I spent last night in jail."

Graves' expression went blank. "Oh. But they let you go this morning."

"Here I am," he said, attempting to ease Graves' discomfiture with a lighthearted tone. He failed.

An uncomfortable silence hung between them. Graves broke it with a noncommittal, "Well then," before looking away, fixing his gaze in the direction of the Faraday cage.

"Do the police have any other suspects?"

"They didn't say. But I'm sure it hasn't escaped their attention that McKinley was to view the Electric Machine next week."

For the space of several heartbeats, Graves stared at Bradshaw. Staggered was the word that came to mind. Graves understood the enormity of the implication.

"Surely that has nothing to do with this."

"I'm an engineer, Dr. Graves. I never dismiss facts with assumptions."

Chapter Seven

"Have you ever testified at an inquest, Professor Bradshaw?"

He should not have paused, he knew, even though he was dreaming, even though he was aware he was dreaming. Yet the question came so unexpectedly, so out of his control, it stunned him.

The pause became a gaping silence. The Prosecuting Attorney, Harcourt, was the same attorney who'd questioned Bradshaw in Boston eight years ago at Rachel's inquest. He hadn't changed, not a lock of thin red hair, not a single piece of clothing. He wore that same hideous green tie, the color of steamed cabbage.

"Have you ever testified at an inquest, Professor Bradshaw?"

It was impossible to lie. "Yes."

"Tell us, please, the circumstances of that inquest."

Bradshaw could no longer see. He struggled to open his eyes.

"Tell us."

"My wife died."

"When did she die?"

"Eight years ago."

"And how did your wife die?"

Bradshaw turned his blind face in the direction of the judge on the bench. "He can't ask me about this. My wife's death has nothing to do with Professor Oglethorpe."

The judge's voice boomed like a command from God. "Answer the question."

She committed suicide. He merely thought the words, he didn't say them, but he heard the spectators in the courtroom gasp. Bradshaw fought violently now to wake up, to open his eyes. He needed to run home to his son, to somehow keep those words from echoing home to his son.

"By what method?"

Poison. Again, it had only been a thought. Again, a gasp told him they'd heard.

"And you say after your wife was poisoned, there was an inquest into her death? Why? If your wife's death was a suicide, then why was it investigated?"

He spoke this time, his words slurred. He was drunk with sleep. "The jury verdict was that of suicide."

"But why was the inquest called in the first place? Wasn't it because Mrs. Beatrice Bostwick, close friend and confidante of your late wife, feared foul play? Didn't she postulate that you had been involved in the poisoning and that you had carefully staged the event to make it appear to be suicide?"

No. No. It wasn't true. Mrs. Bostwick was very disturbed by his wife's death. She had been there when it happened. She later apologized for having made the accusation.

"You were angry at your wife on the day of her death?"

Yes, I was angry with her. Yes.

"You were angry at Professor Oglethorpe on the day of his death."

No. Yes.

"You were so angry with Professor Oglethorpe, you killed him. And you staged the event to look like suicide. You staged the event. You killed Oglethorpe."

No. No.

"You killed your wife."

"No!" Bradshaw's eyes finally opened, and he found himself staring at the ceiling, a strangled "no" in his throat.

Soft pre-dawn light filled his bedroom with a warm glow. Birds chirped happily. He stripped off his sweat-soaked pajamas and dried his cold damp skin with a cotton undershirt. He wrapped himself in his wool lounging robe and padded barefoot down the hall to his son's room.

The boy slept deeply in a tangle of bedclothes, his bare toes dangling off the bed. His blond hair stuck up in stiff spikes—he hadn't rinsed out the soap well enough. A look of complete peace sheltered the boy's face. He dreamed happy dreams. He didn't know about his mother. Bradshaw's own horrible dream had not slipped down the hall to snare his son, and the all-too-real nightmare of Bradshaw's arrest wasn't troubling the boy.

Quietly, he closed the door.

Chapter Eight

The fear that he'd publicly revealed the truth of his wife's death remained with Bradshaw all morning. It was there as he bathed and shaved and dressed. It was there as he ate his breakfast of oatmeal and sourdough bread. He was unable to meet Mrs. Prouty's eye as she lumbered about the kitchen, prattling about mundane things, the dampness of the weather, the cheekiness of the iceman, who'd made some comment last week about her ample bosom. She'd not yet forgiven him.

The feeling—a horrible, crushing sort of anguish—remained as he entered the heavy air of the windowless receiving parlor of Butterworth's Funeral Home. A policeman directed him through the crowd of spectators to the front row of folding chairs.

President Graves greeted Bradshaw with cool politeness. Tom Hill patted the empty seat beside him with boyish enthusiasm. "Here's your place, Bradshaw."

The strength gave out in Bradshaw's legs. He sank onto the chair.

Tom eagerly looked around. "I didn't expect such a big crowd for old Oglethorpe. Must be a couple hundred people here. Have you ever been to an inquest?"

Blood pounded in Bradshaw's ears as he stared blankly at Tom's eager freckled face.

"Egads." Tom lowered his voice. The crowd had suddenly hushed. "Here comes Oglethorpe."

Bradshaw forced himself to move, to turn his head, to breathe.

An examining table covered with a heavy white sheet mounded in the shape of a body emerged through a side door. The metal wheels squeak-squeaked until the uniformed bailiff parked the table before the makeshift judge's stand and a large portable blackboard.

The hushed voices dropped to whispers, then silence. Only Mrs. Oglethorpe's hiccupping sobs remained to greet Coroner Cline, Judge Philips, and the six gentlemen of the jury as they filed into the room and took their respective positions.

Coroner Cline was a short, stocky, middle-aged man with wiry hair. Though clean-shaven, his eyebrows were a grayish-black jungle beneath a grayish-black mop. He had intense black close-set eyes, and a disagreeable habit of breathing through his mouth, no doubt a consequence of working with disagreeably smelling corpses.

"Thank you all for coming." Coroner Cline's deep voice reached the back of the room and into the hall beyond. "I have called this inquest in order to discover what happened yesterday afternoon that may have caused the death of this man here." He pointed to the sheet-draped examining table. "For those of you who have never attended a coroner's inquest, I'd like to explain that this is not a criminal trial. We are here to gather facts so that this jury of six upstanding men," he made a sweeping gesture that took in the somber-faced jury, "can intelligently reach a verdict. We will establish three things today. The identity of the deceased, the circumstances surrounding his death, and the likely cause of his death. To do this, I will give the results of the autopsy that was performed yesterday afternoon. But first, several witnesses will be called to answer questions." He dropped his voice and turned to face Marion Oglethorpe. "If at any time this becomes too much for you, you may adjourn to the next room and Butterworth's staff will see to your needs."

Marion Oglethorpe lifted her chin stoically behind her black veil and gave one final hiccup.

Coroner Cline cleared his throat. "Professor Bradshaw, will you please come forward?"

As in his dream, Bradshaw sat stunned. He hadn't expected to be first. Prodding elbows from both Tom and Dr. Graves jolted him into action. He swore over a Bible to tell the truth then took the witness chair.

A sea of curious faced studied him. Detective O'Brien wore his perpetual smile. Patrolman Mercer scowled. The jurors were six men Bradshaw didn't know. Their ages ranged from perhaps thirty to sixty. Their expressions sober. Each wore a perfectly trimmed small dark mustache, curved and oiled and lifted at the ends in precise points.

Coroner Cline approached. For the time it took Bradshaw's heart to skip a beat, the Coroner studied him from beneath those wild brows. If Cline asked if he'd attended an inquest before, he thought he might be sick.

"Tell us your name, address, and occupation."

"I'm Professor Benjamin Bradshaw. I live at 1204 Gallagher, Seattle. I'm a professor of electrical engineering at the University of Washington." With those simple words spoken, Bradshaw's heart resumed beating, and his stomach ceased threatening upheaval. His home and profession were worlds away from that other inquest.

"Tell us, please, the events of yesterday afternoon. Begin at, let's say, one o'clock."

"One o'clock?" That was several hours before Oglethorpe died. He thought back. "At one I was in my office, at the university—"

"And where is your office?"

"On the third floor."

"For those unfamiliar with the university grounds, please tell us what building you are referring to."

"The Administration Building. It's the main building on campus and houses all the classrooms, faculty and staff offices. The library is in the attic and the laboratories are in the basement."

"Were you alone in your office?"

"Yes, I was preparing an answer-key for an exam on the theory of electromagnets I would be giving in an hour-and-a-half's time to my sophomore students."

"What is an answer-key, Professor?"

"A step-by-step explanation of how to solve examination questions. It takes some time to prepare because I use a mimeograph to provide duplicates for the students."

Cline lifted his tufted brows. "And after you made this exam-key?"

"At a quarter past two, I left my office and went down to the second floor classroom where I administered the examination."

"What is the title of this class?"

"Dynamo Electric Machinery and the Magnetic Circuit. There are four students enrolled, and all but one had completed his test and left the classroom when I first noticed the building lights falter."

"What are the names of the students who had left?"

"Jerry Carter, Melvin Sims, and Nat O'Neal."

"And the student who remained?"

"Oscar Daulton."

"And what time was it when the lights faltered?"

Bradshaw thought of the blustery afternoon. "Three-thirty."

"You're sure of the time?"

"Quite sure. The Varsity Bell had just tolled the half-hour."

"The lights had been working properly until half-past three? They didn't falter any other time that day?"

"I—well, I'm not sure. When I was in my office working, the room dimmed for a moment. I looked out the window and saw the weather was changing. At the time, I thought a moving cloud had caused the light fluctuation."

"And now?"

"It could have been the electric wall lamp that dimmed. I can't say for sure. I was concentrating on my work and didn't give it much thought beyond noticing the clouds. And I didn't check the time."

"And at 3:30, what did you think when the lights remained dim? Does this happen often?"

"I believed at first it might be the wind, a limb on a line, or there might be some problem with the university's power plant. But the lights had never faltered before, that I recall, except when we had the Electric Machine running."

"The Electric Machine is the student project in the engineering lab in the basement of the Administration building?"

"Yes."

"What happened next?"

"I went down to the lab to see if Oglethorpe had the Electric Machine going." He explained his discovery of Oglethorpe inside the Faraday cage with the Machine still running at full capacity.

"When you say Professor Oglethorpe, you are speaking of the deceased here." Cline pointed toward the examining table.

"Yes. Well, I assume yes. It was Oglethorpe in the lab. I haven't seen who's under that sheet."

A few laughs rippled through the spectators. Bradshaw hadn't meant to be funny. He glanced apologetically Mrs. Oglethorpe, but her head was down.

Cline strolled to the examination table and twitched back the sheet. Bradshaw rose halfway out of his seat to get a clear view. He recognized Oglethorpe's long face and sharp nose. He'd been embalmed. His pallor was an unearthly white. Small stitches along the hairline revealed the recent autopsy. In death, Oglethorpe looked innocuous, even kind.

"Yes, that's Professor Oglethorpe."

Cline replaced the sheet.

"Professor, would you mind drawing for us please, the Electric Machine you speak of." Cline handed Bradshaw a thick piece of white chalk and indicated the portable blackboard. "And then explain how it works. In simple terms, please."

Bradshaw took the chalk, and with a fairly steady hand, drew Tesla's oscillator and a Faraday cage. His drawing resembled a complicated street lamp, with all of its wiring showing, positioned beside a man-size birdcage. He cleared his throat before he addressed the mustached jury. He hadn't been warned he'd be giving a lecture.

"Do you know anything about electricity?"

The jurors blinked at him.

"You may answer his questions," instructed Coroner Cline.

The eldest-looking juror said, "I know I don't want it in my house. Don't know what was wrong with gas, we just had it installed ten year ago and now the wife says e-lec-tristy is what she wants. Cleaner, she says. Pooh, I say. What the heck is it? Can you see it? Can you smell it? Can you touch it without getting yourself killed?"

Professor Bradshaw took a deep breath. He would have to begin at the beginning.

Although it was inaccurate, he used the traditional water analogy, comparing electric current to the flow of water through a pipe. Alternating current didn't really flow, it simply vibrated in the wire, but he thought it best not to confuse them with such facts.

He explained amperage like water flow rate, potential like water pressure, and resistance like narrow or wide pipes. A half-hour later, the jury of six mustached men had grasped the fundamentals, though the elder fought it all the way.

Bradshaw now pointed to his diagram of Tesla's coil. "Here we have standard building current flowing into the Machine. The potential measures at this point 110 volts. If you have electricity in your house, it is the same strength as this. This very room is wired in this way." Bradshaw indicated the overhead electric lamps, and chins lifted to gaze thoughtfully.

"This electric strength is very practical. It operates a variety of motors and lighting fixtures. It is also very dangerous. While you are quite safe in turning on a lamp, you should never come in contact with the wires carrying the current. Like our water analogy. If you touch two conductors directly you are like a length of pipe that has been connected to the plumbing. Electricity will flow through you, like water flows through a pipe. And when electricity flows through your body, it can cause severe, even lethal damage."

Bradshaw examined the jurors' faces again and found he had not yet lost them, though a few other faces in the courtroom, including Patrolman Mercer's, looked puzzled. He was not concerned about them.

He turned again to his diagram. In simple terms as instructed, he explained how the electric current changed as it encountered various components of the Machine until it reached the Leyden jars.

"Electricity flows into these jars. Much like batteries, they hold electric potential until you are ready to use it."

Here, Bradshaw lost the jurors. Their eyes glazed as they tried to imagine stationary jars holding something as mobile as flowing electricity.

"Think of the jars as if they were a dam in a river, holding back the enormous weight of a manmade lake. Leyden jars, like a dam, hold in reserve powerful levels of potential energy." Thankfully, this explanation drew nods of understanding. "When the Leyden jars become full, they discharge, like a sluice gate opening, and the electricity flows into this coil of copper here of a few turns, and then into this coil of copper here of many hundreds of turns. By the very nature of the physical relationship of the materials," he said, knowing he had not attempted to explain induction or electro-magnetism, and that they would have to take it on pure faith what happened next "…the potential is increased while the current is decreased. This happens over and over again, the Leyden jars fill up, they overflow, they fill up, they overflow. This on-and-off activity is what we call frequency. By the time this oscillating energy reaches here," he pointed to the large sphere he'd drawn at the top of the Machine, "the potential has reached perhaps a million volts and the current is so low it is nearly safe to touch. The energy explodes from this component in electric arcs, like lightning bolts. These arcs, because they are at such a very high temperature, have the ability to cause severe pain and burns—an electric spark is much like a flame—but, in most

cases, won't cause death because the current is low and the frequency very high. High frequency energy is generally quite safe."

One of the jurors, the troublesome eldest, raised his hand as
if he were in class.

"Yes, sir?"

"Why the blazes would anyone want to make such a
contraption?"

There was a murmur of approval for the question.

"When electric current is transformed in such a way, amazing things happen. For instance, in the presence of an energized
coil, a man can stand several feet away holding phosphor-coated
gas-filled glass bulb, and the bulb will light up—without connecting wires. The energy travels through the air."

A few in the courtroom guffawed. Bradshaw didn't inform
his audience that President McKinley was to have had that
experience next week at the university before the same Electric
Machine they were all now dissecting because of Oglethorpe's
death. He glanced at O'Brien. The detective's poker face gave
nothing away.

A man in the back of the room suddenly stood. "It's true! I
saw it happen last summer at the world's fair!"

"That's right," said Bradshaw. "Demonstrations are often
given at fairs and exhibitions. Nikola Tesla, the man who
invented this machine, hopes to someday distribute electricity
around the world without a single wire. Houses will be lit, motors
run, vehicles moved, all by plucking high-frequency energy
from the air. The study of high frequency electricity has led to
inventions like Marconi's wireless telegraph. Messages have been
sent across the English Channel. Marconi is now working on a
project he hopes will send a wireless signal across the expanse
of the Atlantic Ocean."

The judge tapped his gavel lightly to silence the now babbling
courtroom. The wonders of science had threatened to divert
them from Oglethorpe's death.

Coroner Cline asked, "Professor Bradshaw, what is the purpose of that over-sized birdcage you have drawn?"

"It's a Faraday cage. A man can sit safely inside this cage while the Electric Machine is running and emitting arcs. Only the outer surfaces of the cage can become electrified. No charge enters the interior of the cage or even the inside surface of the bars."

"And you found Professor Oglethorpe dead inside that cage?"

"Yes, with the index finger of his right hand protruding through the bars." Bradshaw drew an "x" to mark where Oglethorpe's finger had been.

"That finger would have then been exposed to the high-potential arcs, is that right?"

"Yes."

"If you'd been in that cage when the Machine was operating, and you'd stuck your finger through the bars, what do you think would have happened to you?"

"I probably would have been struck by an electric arc. I would have felt pain at the point of contact. I would have pulled my hand away."

"Did Professor Oglethorpe pull away, do you suppose?"

"It doesn't look like he did. I found him with his finger still protruding and greatly burned."

"Thank you, Professor. That's all for now."

◇◇◇

The testimony began to paint a multi-dimensional view of Oglethorpe's final hours. Bradshaw hadn't realized how orderly and precisely the facts would be presented, like the elements in a complicated algebraic equation with dozens of possible variables. Would he have found Rachel's inquest as intriguing had he not been so emotionally involved?

He dug into his pockets and found his small leather diary but no pencil. He borrowed one from Dr. Graves. Immersed in the testimony, he filled his diary with meticulous notes.

An engineer from Seattle City Light testified that Bradshaw's explanations of electricity and the Electric Machine were simple but accurate. He agreed that a high-voltage, low-current shock would not likely have killed Oglethorpe but cause him to swiftly, reflexively, pull away.

"Can you think of any reason why a man would not react reflexively?"

"No man would leave his arm out there to be struck again, not unless he was dead."

Cline repeated the engineer's words, "Not unless he was dead."

Seven more witnesses followed. Each confirmed what others had already said, and three of them had noticed the Administration Building lights briefly dim at about a quarter to two. They all testified the building lights faltered greatly at half past three.

When the court took an hour break for lunch, the witnesses and jurors were asked not to speak to one another about the case. Professor Bradshaw walked down the street to the soda fountain on the corner. He sat alone, deep in thought, nursing a Coca-Cola and studying his notes.

The first witness to take the stand after court resumed was a student, the square-jawed Glen Reeves. He sat restlessly upon his chair, a bit flushed, hands restless. Having so recently departed from that chair, Bradshaw read no guilt into the behavior.

Cline asked Mr. Reeves to explain his whereabouts for the time in question.

"I was in Oglethorpe's class, Electrical Design, on the second floor of Admin, that's the Administration Building. The Professor had us all about ready to jump out the window—"

"Excuse me? Was this some sort of experiment?"

"Oh, no, what I meant was, we were that frustrated trying to understand what Oglethorpe was teaching. We had ten more minutes to go according to my pocket watch—"

"The specific time, Mr. Reeves?"

"Twenty minutes past one, sir."

"Go on."

"Well, that's when there was a knock at the door and a woman marched in and handed the Prof a piece of paper, sort of thrust it at him."

A woman marched into the classroom? Bradshaw sat forward. "Can you describe this woman?"

"She was older, my mother's age, I'd say. Near to fifty. And big, stout. She wore a blue suit of clothes and small blue hat. Her hair was fairish, I don't know if it were blond or gray. And she had a very stern face."

Good heavens, Bradshaw thought, sitting back. The boy could have been describing Mrs. Prouty.

"Did you know this woman? Had you seen her before?"

"No, sir. Never saw her before, and she didn't introduce herself. She gave Oglethorpe the paper, turned on her heel, and marched out. Oglethorpe read the note, said something rather nasty, then said class was adjourned."

"What was it he said that you considered 'rather nasty,' Mr. Reeves?"

"You want me to repeat it aloud?"

"Please."

Poor Mr. Reeves turned a deeper shade of red. He glanced at Professor Bradshaw sheepishly before casting his eyes down. "He said, 'Bradshaw, that stupid clod.'"

It was nothing Bradshaw hadn't heard before.

Cline moved on to another question, much to the relief of his witness. "Did Professor Oglethorpe leave the class immediately?"

"He was out the door right away. Prof Kelly took over the class."

"I thought you said you'd been dismissed."

"Yeah, well, we could've gone, but we've got an exam coming up and we needed Prof Kelly to make sense of the lecture for us. He'd been sitting in on the class."

Glen Reeves was dismissed. Bradshaw noticed he returned to a seat next to Miss Trout. The two didn't speak, yet by their high-coloring and fidgeting manner, Bradshaw knew they were keenly aware of each other. Miss Trout caught him studying them, and she gave him a shy smile from under her dark lashes.

He turned his focus back to the proceedings.

Detective O'Brien was called next, repeating and verifying details of Oglethorpe and the scene of his death.

"And the note Mr. Reeves tells us was handed to Professor Oglethorpe at twenty minutes past one yesterday afternoon—did you find it?"

"Yes. It was in Professor Oglethorpe's pocket." O'Brien produced the letter from his own pocket and handed it to the coroner.

Cline read it aloud. "*Oglethorpe. There is trouble with the Machine. I need you here at once. Bradshaw.*"

Bradshaw became uncomfortably aware of attention focused his way. Tom leaned over and whispered jokingly, "A note, Bradshaw? What were you thinking?"

Bradshaw couldn't reply. Cline had approached and now held the note under Bradshaw's nose.

It was typewritten, and Bradshaw noticed that "there" was spelled "thare."

"Did you type this note, Professor Bradshaw?"

"No."

Cline brought the note to the jury, and Tom leaned once more toward Bradshaw.

"Say, old man, you're in for it now."

"Be quiet," hissed Bradshaw.

"I'd like now to present to the jury our autopsy findings," Cline boomed, and Mrs. Oglethorpe rose, taking the arm of a gentleman her own age. He looked like a relation. His manner was brotherly and there was a familial similarity, same fair hair, same roundness of feature. When they'd left the parlor and the door closed with a click, Cline approached the examining table.

He folded back the sheet, revealing Oglethorpe's bleak head and upper torso. He bared Oglethorpe's long, uniquely curved legs, leaving only the private areas of his body covered.

"Now." Cline pointed to Oglethorpe's burnt fingertip, several burns to his right arm, and a slashing burn across his left palm. Necks craned and bottoms rose from seats as effort was made to see the damaged flesh. "The wounds we see here did not cause the death of the victim. The burn on the palm occurred before death, the others after. Professor Oglethorpe suffered immediate and irreversible heart failure such as can only be induced by contact with energy of a lethal current. Such a current, as testimony here today concluded, is not available inside the Faraday cage."

The room became silent. Bradshaw tried to breathe, but the thick air held too much perfume and sweat and exhaled breath.

"I arrived at the university approximately thirty minutes after receiving word of Professor Oglethorpe's death. I found the deceased still warm to the touch, which indicated he had been dead less than three hours, and yet rigor mortis, the stiffening of the muscles, had already begun in the jaw. Under normal conditions, rigor takes at least four hours to begin to be evident. In my experience, two factors can speed up the onset of rigor mortis. Violent action immediately before death, and electrocution. I conclude, therefore, in taking into account all the testimony here today, that Professor Wesley Thomas Oglethorpe met his demise between one-thirty and two o'clock yesterday afternoon when he was exposed to an as yet undetermined source of electric current."

The significance of Cline's words struck Bradshaw like a crackling arc from the Electric Machine. This was the reason Detective O'Brien had been so accusing. This was why Cline had asked him to explain his movements beginning two hours before he'd found Oglethorpe. It wasn't simply that Oglethorpe had died outside the cage, it was that Oglethorpe *hadn't* been killed while Bradshaw was administering the examination to his students. Oglethorpe died while Bradshaw had been in his office, writing up that exam key. Alone.

Chapter Nine

Bradshaw sank into his favorite easy chair with a mug of strong coffee and the morning newspaper. For a moment, he simply stared at the steam rising from his mug, aware of his home in every beloved detail, from the dusty attic above right down to the buttons in his chair's upholstery. He'd carefully built his life in this house, and yet until Oglethorpe's death he'd not realized how much it meant to him, or how easily he could lose it.

The sun angled into the parlor through the sheer lace curtains. Yesterday's clouds had departed, leaving a Saturday full of unexpected promise. Strange, he thought, how life could go on as usual while his life tilted and fractured. Mrs. Prouty stomped about upstairs cleaning Henry's room, and Justin played kick-the-can in the street with other neighborhood children. The sound of the boy's shouts and laughter came intermittently, reassuringly, to his ears. He didn't know what he'd do without Justin. And what would the boy do without him? His stomach tightened, and suddenly he didn't think he could drink his coffee. He set down the mug and lifted the paper.

The coroner's inquest over Oglethorpe's remains had made the front page. *INQUEST FINDS MURDER!* The article was neatly spaced between PHILIPPINE INSURGENTS ATTACK WITH KNIVES and the latest report on Mrs. McKinley, whose ill health in California had preempted the President's tour of the Northwest. Bradshaw skimmed the war news. The fighting in the Philippines had been far uglier than in Cuba. According to the papers, the insurgents were savages, oblivious to civilized rules of engagement, taken to hiding in villages behind their women. And American troops were in China, battling Boxers who wanted all foreign powers to leave. In Washington, D.C., the arguing continued between the expansionists and the anti-imperialists. Bradshaw thought it all a big moral mess. Stay or leave, as a new world power, the United States military brought salvation to some, death to others. There were no easy answers.

He turned to news of his own crisis. A sketch of his black-board drawing captioned "Bradshaw's Diagram of Electric Machine" was accurate, and a photograph of Oglethorpe taken last year, with a benevolent smile upon his face, not. Bradshaw was relieved to see no photograph of himself. In the article, the reporter had made a hero of Oglethorpe, praising his work at the university and his research efforts. Bradshaw, too, was praised, and then accused.

> *Professor Bradshaw so clearly explained the nature of electricity and its transforming power, even the least educated in the room could understand the basic principles of the Great Electric Machine and the Faraday cage in which Professor Oglethorpe's body was found. Exactly how Oglethorpe was killed, and who killed him, remains a mystery for the police to solve. The jury determined the cause of death to be murder by person or persons unknown.*
>
> *As helpful as Professor Bradshaw was, the overwhelming circumstantial evidence goes against him. He was arrested the night before the inquest and released the following morning with no charges....*

Justin came running into the front hall, the screen door slamming behind him as Mrs. Prouty descended the stairs. Bradshaw carefully folded the newspaper over the headlines.

"No running in the house," Bradshaw and Mrs. Prouty declared in unison. Mrs. Prouty disappeared down the hall, and Justin's steps slowed to a hurried walk as he approached his father in the parlor. Bradshaw didn't think he'd ever seen a sight as precious as his child, hair rumpled from play, knickers stained with grass, nose smudged with dirt.

"Dad, can I go to the zoo with Paul?"

"You and Paul are too young to be going to Woodland Park on your own, Justin." Paul's mother, Mrs. Dickerson, in the house across the street, had telephoned earlier to ask if she and her husband might bring Justin along. Either Mrs. Dickerson had not yet read the morning paper or she didn't believe it possible that Bradshaw was a murderer. Or maybe she did and inviting Justin was her way of rescuing the boy from his evil father for the afternoon.

Justin, oblivious to his father's thoughts, was nonetheless a clever boy for his age. He knew he was being teased. "I'm eight and one quarter, Dad. I know how to get to the zoo, and I'll be sure to keep Paul out of trouble."

"Very well then." He fished in his pocket for a dime and Justin took it eagerly. "Don't spend it all on sweets. And tell Mrs. Dickerson I said thank you for her generosity and that if you misbehave, she has my permission to feed you to the bears." And what would Mrs. Dickerson make of that comment, if the boy repeated it?

Justin giggled.

"Wash your face and change into your school suit."

"Aww, Dad."

"Or you can stay home."

"I'll change."

"Wear your winter knickers. You've nearly outgrown them and Mrs. Prouty won't complain if you get them dirty—and no," he said, in response to Justin's wicked pink-cheeked grin, "I am not giving you permission to get dirty."

Justin ran upstairs to change and was back in record time, looking decently enough put-together in woolen knickers, a slightly worn jacket and a soft cap. He'd washed enough to remove the dirt from his nose and his hair had been raked by wet fingers. He kissed his father good-bye, then was out the door, the screen door slapping noisily behind him.

A few minutes later, Mrs. Prouty passed down the hall with one of his suits draped over her arm, a pair of polished shoes in her hand. They looked suspiciously like those he'd deposited into the burn pile.

He called out to her, and she came to stand in the doorway, not meeting his gaze, her shoulders back defiantly.

He said, "I don't want those in this house."

She hesitated. "Waste is a sin, Professor."

"Then give them away."

She pursed her lips a moment, then her broad face relaxed. "Church bazaar?" She looked at him directly. "I'll be off in another quarter hour, Professor. That be alright?" She spent Saturday afternoons and evenings in the company of her cousin, who also had a live-in position. They did the town, first bargain shopping at The Great Western Company department store, then lunching at Frederick & Nelson's counter, followed by the new showing at the nickelodeon. A game of bridge amongst a troupe of housekeepers lasted well into the evening and so Mrs. Prouty stayed overnight with her cousin.

"Yes, of course."

"I'll be back at my usual time tomorrow morning. There's roast meat in the icebox and a pie cooling on the counter."

"Thank you, Mrs. Prouty. Enjoy yourself, and give your cousin my best regards."

"I could come home after the picture."

She made the same offer every Saturday, fussing and fretting as if she were to be gone a month rather than just one night. She'd been fussing longer than usual today. She'd read the newspaper article, too. And discovering his clothes in the burn pile yesterday had distressed her. He hadn't anticipated that.

"We'll be fine, Mrs. Prouty. See you in the morning."

After she'd finally closed the door behind her, Professor Bradshaw found himself alone and disliking it. With the street no longer carrying the sweet sound of children's voices, he felt restless. He checked his calendar, but the neatly printed entries in the precise white squares— "GRADE PAPERS" and "REBUILD MODEL GENERATOR"—didn't inspire. He went down to his basement shop and stared at the organized array of tools and gadgets, motors and copper coils along his workbench, then decided what he really wanted to do was to go to the university and look for what might have caused Oglethorpe's death. He couldn't just sit around while the police and the newspapers made him out to be a murderer. He had to clear his name soon, today if possible.

Like his son, he changed out of his casual clothes and into a proper suit. His thoughts were random, reviewing bits and pieces of yesterday's trial. Who had that woman been, the one who resembled Mrs. Prouty and had delivered that forged note? Did Detective O'Brien know?

That note. The very existence of that note pointed at murder with Oglethorpe as the intended victim. But what of President McKinley's visit? Bradshaw took the time now to ponder the instinctive feeling of relief he'd felt when Tom had said the visit was cancelled. That relief meant that Bradshaw's subconscious believed McKinley was somehow involved. Who would want to harm the President?

Anarchists. Not a day went by that the newspapers weren't reporting some anarchist somewhere in the country being arrested for plots to assassinate leading officials.

But an anarchist at the university? Had that woman who delivered the note to Oglethorpe been an anarchist? Had she followed Oglethorpe down to the lab? For what reason? McKinley hadn't been scheduled to see the Electric Machine for another week.

So what had been the purpose of the note? Why lure Oglethorpe down to the lab on that particular day?

Bradshaw left the house through the backdoor, eagerness energizing his step. He could not be accused of plodding today. Today he moved like a young man. He chastised himself as he rolled his bicycle to the sidewalk. He shouldn't be enthusiastic over this serious situation. Oglethorpe's death should sober him. A possible violent anarchist in their midst should anger him. Yet there it was. His step bounced. His mind hummed with ideas about whom he should see, what he should ask. God forgive him, he was enjoying himself.

At the street he paused. Northeast led to the university, southwest to downtown. He propped his bicycle inside his fence then headed south. If he were to cover so much ground today, he'd best save his legs and take the streetcar.

He walked roughly one mile southeastward to catch the Madison Line. Once he left the peace of his small section of Gallagher Street, he found himself constantly detoured by construction. Houses were springing up like out-of-control mushrooms, rising overnight from the cleared muddy soil. The last of the enormous stumps, which a decade ago had been towering giants of cedar and Douglas fir, were being ground and burned to make way for development. Pipes for new sewer and gas lines lay along the new cement sidewalks, bare power and telephone poles waited for linemen to string them. He could hear nothing but hammering and sawing, the rattle of wheels, the shouts of workers. The air was thick with noise and soot. It was a mad frenzy of human activity.

The commotion matched his mood. He found he couldn't sit still, so he rode the front platform of the streetcar with the motorman, the sun and breeze on his face. He disembarked on Fourth Avenue and soon came upon a crowd outside Butterworth's Funeral Home. The crowd was there, he understood from murmured conversations, to view the body.

Bradshaw didn't ask whose body. He heard his own name mentioned, and he was again grateful the newspaper had not printed his photograph. He tilted his hat low over his eyes, got in line, and slowly progressed into the funeral home. The crowd hushed, then silenced, as they moved down the dim paneled hall and into the parlor that yesterday had been a courtroom. Today, the room had been restored to a place of mourning. The overhead electric lights were off, and the gas wall sconces glowed softly.

The air was still and somber and slightly stale with the mingled smell of breath and wool and cloying perfumes emanating from the constant line of curious viewers filing by the open casket.

Bradshaw didn't linger when his turn came. Nor did he hesitate.

Oglethorpe's hands were crossed, palms down over his chest, hiding the burn marks. In one quick movement, Bradshaw reached into the casket, twisted Oglethorpe's cold left hand enough to see the burn, then returned the hand to its original position. The woman behind him gasped with horror, but then the same morbid curiosity that had compelled her to view the body of a complete stranger compelled her to imitate Bradshaw, to see what he'd had seen.

After she'd peered at Oglethorpe's palm, she whispered, "What do you make of it?"

Bradshaw shrugged. He began to move away then noticed a tiny speck of something reflective in Oglethorpe's hair. He reached into the casket again, pinched the sparkling black speck, capturing it between his thumb and index finger.

He went in search of an employee of the funeral home and found manning a desk a bored young clerk with a sour expression.

"Do you know where I might find Coroner Cline?" As County Coroner, Cline could be nearly anywhere in King County. He might be in his office up on "Profanity Hill" in the Courthouse, at any number of other funeral homes, or at some other death scene.

"He's indisposed." The clerk didn't bother to look up.

"Is he here?"

"He's indisposed."

"I need to speak with him."

"He's—"

Bradshaw leaned forward and the clerk not only looked up, he pulled back.

"I'm Professor Bradshaw. Maybe you read about me in the newspaper?"

The clerk's mouth dropped open. His eyes wide and staring, he sidled from behind the desk and down the hall. Bradshaw followed until they came to the back of the building, to an examination room brightly lit and smelling of something foul that a heavy dose of antiseptic hadn't masked.

The clerk appeared confused, as if he'd expected to find Cline in the room. "Wait here." He scurried out.

Bradshaw pulled a white handkerchief from his pocket and carefully deposited the shiny black speck onto the cloth. He folded the cloth and returned it to his pocket, trying hard not to breathe in too deeply. Across the room on a bier, a stark white sheet covered a mound far too large to be human. The foul odor was emanating from that general direction.

A few minutes passed. The silence was like a coldness. Or was it the room? He shivered. He'd never considered himself to be a morbidly curious man like that woman and the others out there gaping at Oglethorpe. Yet the shape beneath the sheet intrigued him.

He took a few steps toward the bier, and the smell increased exponentially. His shoes sounded gritty against the bare floor. He lifted the edge of the sheet half-expecting to see the hairy paw of a bear or the dorsal fin of a baby orca whale. But he found a human hand, an enormously fat hand, twice the size of his own, the skin hideously greenish-red.

He moved to the top of the bier and lifted the sheet slightly, revealing a head of thin brown hair, a greenish-red face, the nose and eyes and mouth too small for the mass of cheeks and jowls and quantities of chins. The smell was positively putrid.

"Recognize him?"

Bradshaw dropped the sheet and pressed his nose into the crook of his arm to breathe in the scent of clean wool. He shook his head at Coroner Cline and moved as far away from the corpse as he could get. "Should I?"

Cline stood beside the body, oblivious of the smell. "Only if you had need of a Pinkerton guard. He was found this morning in the bathtub of the Great Northern Hotel."

Surely, he hadn't drowned. It stretched the imagination to even picture him fitting into a hotel bath. "What killed him?"

"Overindulgence, most likely, although—well, never mind." Cline breathed for a moment through his mouth, the spittle gathering at the corners. He met Bradshaw's gaze as if measuring the wisdom of saying more. Factory managers who were worried about labor unions hired Pinkerton guards. And anarchists, as well as frustrated union organizers, attacked them. "What can I do for you this morning, Professor Bradshaw? I'm sure you didn't come to view my latest corpse."

Bradshaw lowered his arm and swallowed, then wished he hadn't. Now he could taste the putridness. "It's Oglethorpe. Did you find anything unusual on him? In his hair or on his clothing?"

Spittle bubbled at the corner of Coroner Cline's mouth as he breathed noisily, his bushy brows narrowed. "I removed a small quantity of black grit. Turned out to be dried India ink."

"Why wasn't this mentioned at the inquest?"

"Because none of the witnesses brought it up, and it's not my job to give away every piece of evidence at the inquest."

"Why are you telling me?"

Cline grinned. "Because you asked. And because I don't think you had anything to do with it."

It was the best news Bradshaw had heard in a long time. "Have you told Detective O'Brien your opinion?"

Cline shrugged. "I'm an expert at judging dead men, he's an expert at judging live ones. Is there anything else I can help you with? As you can see, I have an autopsy to perform."

"I do have a question. It's about the injuries to Oglethorpe's palm. Have you got a wire or rope or string handy?" He patted down his pockets in vain.

Cline opened a drawer and pulled out a length of suture.

"Something heavier."

Cline dug deeper into the drawer and found a ball of scratchy twine.

"Yes, that'll do. May I?" Bradshaw used his pocketknife to cut a five-foot length. "I've been puzzled about the mark on

Oglethorpe's left palm. He couldn't have sustained it while in the Faraday cage and being struck by arcs from the coil. I thought it might be connected to the fatal shock he received before being put in the cage. Now, if Oglethorpe had been holding a wire," he said, demonstrating how a man would typically hold a wire he was working with, "and if that wire became energized, say by the Leyden jars of the Electric Machine, the burn wound would be in this portion of the hand, running at about this angle." He indicated a line from the base of his index finger to the outside of his palm below the pinkie. "But the burn is lower, near the center of the palm and extending to the base of the thumb. As if he caught a wire falling from overhead." Bradshaw put up his hand, holding the twine as if keeping it from falling on him.

Cline watched Bradshaw's demonstration intently, not with O'Brien's accusatory grin, but with sincere skepticism. The doctor was not a clever manipulator, he was a scientist employed to seek out the truth. He wanted to know what had happened to Oglethorpe, but he was experienced enough not to trust everything he was told or shown.

"My assistant coroner observed the dismantling of the Electric Machine, Professor, and he examined the components as well as the room for any object that might have fallen onto the deceased. He found none."

"Under normal circumstances, that's what I would expect. I can't imagine a situation in which a non-insulated charged wire would be positioned above anyone, especially not in the lab."

"Circumstances appear to be far from normal, Professor."

"And the dried ink? Did you find it in the lab? I saw none when I was there."

"Maybe your esteemed colleague entered the lab having already encountered the ink elsewhere," Cline challenged.

Bradshaw shook his head. "He was meticulous about his appearance. The moment a speck of dried ink touched him, he would go shake out his clothes and hair if at all possible."

Cline's bushy brows lifted. Oglethorpe had not found it possible.

Chapter Ten

By the time Professor Bradshaw reached the university, he wished he'd taken his bicycle this morning after all. With its numerous stops and snarls with traffic the streetcar made for a slow and tedious journey.

He found the campus relaxed and basking in the rare spring sunshine. Co-eds with their parasols strolled arm-in-arm along the paths, making their way to the young uniformed men of the University of Washington Cadets. Bradshaw could hear them drilling on the grounds near the gymnasium.

The light sandstone towers of the Administration building glowed cheerfully, but inside echoed that empty feeling a school gets on Saturdays, when the school term is nearly over and minds have turned prematurely to summer folly. Bradshaw hurried down to the basement. He found the door unlocked, the Faraday cage still perched upon its insulating platform, and the disassembled components of Tesla's oscillator spread along the back wall.

"Come to decipher whodunit?"

Bradshaw jumped. Tom Hill stepped from behind the Faraday cage and laughed.

"Sorry, old man. I came down to have a look myself. It is a bit spooky in here, isn't it?"

Bradshaw doubted he'd ever be able to enter it again without seeing, for a split second, Oglethorpe's dead body topple over inside that cage. He said, "Since you're here, help me look." They approached the apparatus and began inspecting. The job would have been easier had the Machine been left intact. The guilty wire or component that actually caused Oglethorpe's death may have been inadvertently moved into some unsuspecting position.

They first examined the Leyden jars. Bradshaw even used a magnifying glass to peer at the connective metal knobs, but there was nothing whatsoever to indicate that the jars had discharged a fatal blow. Bradshaw and Tom moved slowly on to other components.

"What exactly is it that we're looking for, Bradshaw? A loose wire? A wire that doesn't belong?"

"Yes, anything that strikes you as being in any way out of place, but also look for dried ink."

"Ink?"

"India ink. It will look like black, sparkling dust or grit. There won't be much, the police have already looked." He explained to Tom what he'd learned this morning about the dried ink in Oglethorpe's hair and on his clothes.

"What does it mean?"

"I wish I knew. What other lethal sources of current are down here, Tom?"

They both scanned the room.

"We've got a couple induction coils, batteries, the generator, and of course big Stan." Tom was referring to the Stanley transformer on the wheeled dolly in the corner. Crucial to alternating current distribution, Big Stan was used to demonstrate step-down and step-up voltage, but it wasn't used indoors. Yes, it could conceivably deliver lethal current, but in what circumstances might Oglethorpe have been enticed to encounter such current? That was the unfathomable mystery of his death. He was far too knowledgeable to do anything stupid with any of the equipment in the room. And if Big Stan had been connected to the building's electric system, the lights would not have flashed and dimmed but tone out. The transformer would have blown the main building fuses. Bradshaw turned up his left palm, remembering the burn pattern on Oglethorpe's palm.

He left the lab in search of a ladder. He found one in the storage closet down the hall and set it up where the Electric Machine had stood when assembled. He put a hand on a rung and hesitated.

Fatherhood had brought him a host of unexpected emotions. Parental love, he'd learned, swelled with worry, anxiety, hope, frustration. And phobia. He knew the exact moment the phobia had come. He'd been carrying Justin down the stairs—a small babe in arms, the day after Rachel's death—when he stumbled and nearly fell. He'd recovered safely, no harm done to him or the child, physically. But the sudden attack of fear remained. It struck rarely, in situations where only balance kept him from falling, where there was nothing to grasp.

He looked up. The ladder shifted and swayed until he took a deep breath. The ladder stilled, but his stomach clenched. He climbed anyway. The ceiling was beyond his reach. He forced him himself to venture to the top step. The ladder—in fact, not mind—wobbled unsteadily.

"Uh, Tom. Would you mind?"

"Bradshaw!" Tom ran to put his weight onto the teetering legs of the ladder. "Are you hoping to find dried ink up there?"

"I won't know exactly what I hope to find until I've found it."

His heart pounding, his armpits stinging with sweat, he examined the conduit and the insulated wires that carried current to the connection at the wall tables. They moved the ladder several times, Bradshaw soldiering through each time, but nothing was amiss and the ceiling was clean. There wasn't even a cobweb.

Bradshaw put the ladder away, and when he returned, he resumed his examination of the Machine's components. Tom poked around the long lab tables, pulling open drawers, inspecting connection plugs and rolls of copper wire, switches and batteries, and a myriad of electrical components necessary to teach the fundamentals of electrical engineering.

"Say, Bradshaw, where's McKinley's bulb?"

The hair on the back of Bradshaw's neck prickled, a sensation he had in the past correlated with imminent discovery.

"Isn't it in the cabinet?"

Tom was now standing before the cabinet, the glass doors open. The ornate polished box, which usually held the specially blown glass of President McKinley's presentation bulb, was empty.

"It's nowhere else in the lab, I've been through everything."

"Then someone has taken it, or—" Bradshaw took a single step aside and looked at the chair sitting there so innocently. There were many chairs in the laboratory. Several high stools for the students to use at the tables, two swivel chairs, and three arm chairs near the bookshelves. This was the only chair with a high proud back, a padded leather seat, and ornate scrolled legs. This chair had been brought down from Graves' office for the sole use of President McKinley during his planned visit.

Bradshaw pulled the chair away from the wall, turned it around, and leaned in closely. There, clinging to a leg, was a flake of ink. Bradshaw picked up the chair and carried it to the center of the lab.

"Tom, help me find the mark."

Tom bent low and studied the floor. "Here it is." He pointed to the tiny red "x" that indicated where the front leg of the President's chair was to be positioned.

Bradshaw placed the chair precisely then sat. He held up his right hand as if gripping an incandescent bulb.

Tom quipped, "If you're trying to look like the Statue of Liberty, I believe you should be standing."

"I need a cloth, a colored cloth. Blue would be best."

Tom produced a yellow silk handkerchief.

Bradshaw snorted, got up, and began to root through the walk-in utility closet. "Cotton, Tom. And blue or green, ah, here!" He flourished a good thick pale blue cotton cleaning cloth. "Now, we get it damp." He took it to a lab sink and dipped it under the faucet where it darkened, then squeezed it nearly dry.

He returned to the chair, dropped carefully to his knees, and began to wipe the glossy surface of the fir floor. With each pass, he inspected the cloth. On the third pass, he beamed at Tom.

"I don't think I've ever seen you smile, Bradshaw. By golly, you're almost handsome."

"Be quiet, you dolt, and look at the cloth. What do you see?"

"It sparkles—black and white bits. India ink and—glass shards?"

"Not just any glass, phosphor-coated glass."

"McKinley's bulb? And ink? But what does it mean?"

Bradshaw felt his smile fade. "I don't know. Yet." He continued wiping in an ever-expanding circle until the cloth picked up no more glass. All the pieces together took up less space than a postage stamp.

"Where'd you learn that trick for picking up glass?"

"When my son began to crawl, I found I had to crawl, too. You've no idea how much filth and danger there is on the floor."

Bradshaw sat again on the chair.

Tom cocked his head with an amused smile. "I wish I knew what you were thinking," he began, and then his smile faded as the color drained from his face.

"Bradshaw, you don't think—"

"Yes, I do. President McKinley was supposed to sit here before the Machine, holding up his souvenir bulb."

"But not while the Machine was running. He was supposed to pose for a photograph, safe and sound and not in the least bit of danger."

The photograph was to be taken as Tom said, with the President in absolutely no danger. Then the photograph was to be double-exposed with the image of the Machine running in its full glory, arcs of lightning shooting from the sphere. Nikola Tesla had himself posed for similar photographs. Afterward, from a safer distance, the President was to have experienced the thrill of the bulb lighting in his hand.

"So what happened?" Tom asked. "Did Oglethorpe sit there, holding the bulb, while the Machine was actually running? By gum, he was a fool for a genius."

"The Machine couldn't have been running. Oglethorpe died no later than two o'clock. The Machine wasn't turned on until half past three."

Tom shook his head. "I don't see how it could have happened then, if he was sitting in that chair and the Machine was off. And where does the ink come into it?"

"I don't know. But somebody must. Oglethorpe couldn't have been alone. Somebody moved him. Somebody later turned on the Machine."

"Maybe it was that hefty woman, the one who delivered the note with your name on it."

"Maybe," Bradshaw said, but his thoughts had gone elsewhere. "Tom, you're scheduled to give tours up at the Snoqualmie power plant tomorrow, aren't you?" Before Tom could open his mouth to reply, he added, "Let me take your place."

Tom looked confused for a moment, then understanding lit his eyes. "You're thinking of McKinley's itinerary. Snoqualmie was one of his stops. But his trip to Seattle has been canceled."

"That didn't prevent a man from being killed here."

"What do you expect to find up there? Some lethal trap?"

He didn't know what he expected to find, he only knew he should go up and have a look round. "Can I take your place?"

"I don't mind. Actually, that works very well for me. The boys are having a tug-of-war rematch with the frats." Besides his teaching duties, Tom was steward of the men's dormitory, which currently housed several dozen boisterous young men. More a big brother than a father figure, he joined in their competitions and somehow, amidst the whoopla and backslapping, earned their respect as well as their obedience. Tom wiggled his brows. "You should see the mud hole they've dug."

"I hope you don't see it too closely yourself."

"Not this time. My boys have been exercising at the gymnasium. They're ready."

Chapter Eleven

At another university, tracking the whereabouts of students for any given time might prove difficult. It turned out to be a relatively easy task for Benjamin Bradshaw. The entire student body consisted of just under five hundred, of which only fifty belonged to the engineering department and twenty of those were in electrical engineering.

Because Oglethorpe also taught Industrial Problems, a political science course, another half-dozen students had been under his direct influence. By checking attendance records, Bradshaw was able to make an accurate list of students' whereabouts. Most were accounted for at the time the lights in the Administration Building faltered and for the two hours prior, when Oglethorpe had actually died. Most had been attending classes, which also put assistant professors Hill and Kelly clear of any possible involvement.

Four students remained unaccounted for. One was Artimus Lowe, the law student Bradshaw had seen rapidly departing the building at the time the lights faltered. The School of Law was downtown at the old university. Investigating Lowe's whereabouts would have to wait. The second student was Oscar Daulton, who'd been in Bradshaw's presence when the lights faltered, so he need only discover what the boy was doing for the two hours prior in order to clear him. The final two students were the very same who had witnessed that incriminating note being delivered to Oglethorpe. Glen Reeves, resident of Sigma Nu Fraternity, and Miss Sara C. Trout, whom Bradshaw hoped to find at home at the women's dorm.

◇◇◇

"Tea, Professor Bradshaw?"

Bradshaw accepted the proffered cup, declining milk, sugar, and lemon. He'd been lucky. He'd found not only Miss Trout at home and in the dormitory's visiting parlor but Glen Reeves with her, paying a call. Two in one blow, as they say.

The room was tidy, and the furniture comfortably worn. Bradshaw sat by the window in an upholstered easy chair trimmed with worsted fringe. Mr. Reeves and Miss Trout perched at opposite ends of a slippery, silk-covered armless sofa, looking as if they both might topple over with the slightest wrong move. Impossible, he imagined, to make love on that sofa, which was no doubt the very reason some parent had made the donation.

Like yesterday at the inquest, the pair were keenly aware of one another. Miss Trout fidgeted, her cheeks stained an unbecoming mottled red. Mr. Reeves fussed so much with the sofa's fringe, Bradshaw expected it to unravel any moment to his feet. No tingling sensation prickled the back of Bradshaw's neck, but still, there was something here to be discovered.

Were these two troubled souls, aching to unburden themselves? Had they been beguiled by the rhetoric of the anarchists? Misled by the passionate references to freedom? Thomas Jefferson and his call for revolution? The young could be so zealous about political injustice. But without life experience, they weren't able to properly evaluate dangerous stances like anarchism or socialism. Had these two foolishly made a pact to save the world from a capitalist leader and instead killed an engineering professor?

"You were both in Electrical Design when the note was delivered to Professor Oglethorpe?"

"Yes." Miss Trout looked at him through her eyelashes. "The woman came right in, without knocking."

"Did this woman say anything?"

"No." She flashed him one of her smiles, which he ignored. "She handed a note to Oglethorpe, looked him up and down like she thought he was beneath her contempt, then turned on her heel and walked out."

Mr. Reeves spoke up. "I thought he was being summoned by the law class. They've been doing that, holding mock trials and summoning people to appear. You don't have to go, not like a real summons. I was surprised when he mentioned your name and then stormed out."

"Thank goodness he did." Miss Trout didn't appear to realize how her words sounded considering Oglethorpe had left to attend his own death. "Professor Kelly came in and explained the lesson to us. He's kind like you, Professor Bradshaw."

Bradshaw ignored the compliment. "Can you describe the woman to me?"

"Of course. She was a big woman, strong-looking. Stout would be a good word to describe her. She wore a simple suit of blue wool, not the least fashionable. Something a charwoman or domestic might wear. She appeared to be near forty—"

Bradshaw interrupted. "Yesterday, Mr. Reeves testified she looked near fifty."

"Oh, what do boys know about age? To them a woman is either eligible to be courted or over-the-hill. No, she was near to forty, but I wouldn't say much over."

Mr. Reeves shrugged, taking the insult as his due.

"And you're sure you've never seen the woman before?" He looked from Miss Trout to Mr. Reeves. They both shook their heads emphatically.

"What time did you leave class?"

Reeves swallowed, his Adam's apple bobbing. Miss Trout looked at her hands, and her face, which had begun to fade to normal shades while speaking of the mystery woman, again began to mottle.

"Two," they said in unison again.

"But class was only scheduled until half past one."

"Yes," said Mr. Reeves, "but it took that long for Professor Kelly to go over next week's lessons. He looked ahead in Oglethorpe's lesson plan. He gave us a sort of head's up, so we'd be prepared. I was rather looking forward to that, showing old Oglethorpe that he didn't have us stumped."

The two o'clock time coincided perfectly with Professor Kelly's account, which meant so far as Bradshaw could tell, he was hearing the truth. Cline had given Oglethorpe's estimated time of death as approximately between half past one and two.

"And where did you go at two, after leaving Professor Kelly?"

Reeves got up and paced to the window. He stood with his hands shoved deep in his trouser pockets.

Bradshaw was encouraged. "You were both due in Oglethorpe's Industrial Problems class at three-thirty. Professor Kelly stepped in for that class also, when Oglethorpe didn't arrive. He marked the two of you tardy by approximately ten minutes. Where were you between two o'clock and twenty minutes to four?"

A door closed somewhere in the building. Light footsteps raced down wooden stairs, followed by giggling laughter. Outside, the faint echo of military drilling was drowned by the rumble and whistle of the Seattle and International Line that skirted Lake Washington on the edge of campus. It was a long train. No one spoke until the sound of drilling cadence could be heard again.

"You tell him, Sara." Reeves faced the window.

Miss Trout's eyes filled with apprehension as well as disappointment. She gazed at Glen Reeves' back with what could only be described as regret.

"We went for a walk."

"A walk? Where to?"

"You won't tell, will you, Professor? I'd be disowned. My mother would never forgive me."

"For taking a walk?"

All the mottled spaces of Miss Trout's face filled until she blushed pure scarlet.

Bradshaw said, "It was stormy that afternoon. Are you saying you were walking out in the wind and rain?"

She pressed her lips tight, then drew a tremulous breath with a small squeak of anguish. Her voice, when it emerged, was emotionally high-pitched. "There's a place in the woods, off the trail that leads to the lake. There's a hut there, an old woodshed, I think. It's sheltered—" she broke off, as if choking on the words. Reeves was absolutely no help at the window.

Miss Trout's hands fluttered protectively to her belly. A feminine gesture that could imply nothing, but it was exactly what Marion Oglethorpe had done when first hearing of her husband's death. And Mrs. Oglethorpe was with child.

"Did anyone see you while you were taking this walk?"

Miss Trout hid her shamed face in her hands. "Oscar did."

"Mr. Daulton?"

"H-he was studying in the hut. He left when we arrived."

Bradshaw sank wearily back into his chair. So Daulton had squirreled himself away rather than join a study group where he might possibly have bolstered his confidence. But his whereabouts had at least now been established. He'd left the hut after Oglethorpe had been killed. And these two young idiots were not anarchists, they were not assassins. They were foolish lovers who now found themselves in trouble, or at the very least in regret of their indiscretion. Well. He was now out of student suspects, other than Artimus Lowe.

"Both of you participate in the debate clubs here at the university?"

Reeves turned around. "Why do you want to know that?"

"Professor Oglethorpe led a number of debates. I thought you might recall a student who often took the side of labor, unions, or socialism."

"You mean someone who really believed in those things? Someone who would take a debate with Oglethorpe seriously?" Mr. Reeves asked.

"Yes."

"Professor, we all took debates with Oglethorpe seriously. It was impossible not to, the way he was so demeaning. He attacked his foe personally. Really, there was no sport in it, the way he cut you down."

"But was there someone who fought him more fiercely, with more skill, on the subject of labor rights or imperialist expansion?"

"Artimus Lowe," Miss Trout piped up, her eyes sparkling with an admiration that was absent when she looked upon Mr. Reeves. "A law student, Artimus Lowe," she said repeating the name as if the sound of it pleased her. "He was brilliant in debating Oglethorpe. Do you remember that debate last month, Glen? When the subject was 'Manifest Destiny and the War with Spain'? Oglethorpe led a team of pro-imperialist debaters, and Artimus Lowe led a team against them."

Mr. Reeves came away from the window to sit again, this time less precariously, on the center of the sofa. "Not much of a team on Lowe's side. Who'd he have? Trager, Lease, and Daulton? Trager and Lease weren't too bad, but Daulton, what a ninny." He shook his head and said under his breath, "Dormer."

Miss Trout gasped. "Dormer? Did you mean that as an insult? Have you forgotten I'm a dormer, Glen?"

A mischievous fire came into the fraternity lad's eyes and Bradshaw surmised he was imagining that tug-of-war rematch scheduled for tomorrow and seeing himself pull Assistant Professor Hill and all the dormers into the mud. But wisely he said, "I've got nothing against dormers in general, Sara, just Daulton. He got so tongue-tied, he nearly started crying. It was painful to watch."

"Poor Oscar." Miss Trout's face softened. "It was bad. I think he might have been convincing if he'd had a bit more composure. Oglethorpe attacked him with 'The White Man's Burden' and all Oscar could do was mutter 'but you weren't there, you didn't see the blood.'"

Bradshaw could very well imagine the scene, with Daulton's hair falling over his eyes as he crumbled before his opponent. If only his confidence matched his intelligence.

"He got sick, you know." Reeves gave a disdainful shake of his head. "In the Philippines. Dysentery. They sent him home."

Bradshaw let a silence hang in the air until Mr. Reeves swallowed nervously.

"I don't know the death toll so far in the Philippines, Mr. Reeves, but this morning's paper gave the total in Cuba. Nearly four hundred young men died in action. Over two *thousand* died of disease. Every one of them lost their lives serving his country. Each soldier that returns alive deserves respect."

"Yes, sir. I didn't mean—yes, sir."

"Yes, you did," said Miss Trout, with a you-don't-fool-me expression. She turned to Bradshaw. "After Oscar, Artimus Lowe got up and was brilliant. You should have heard the cheers when he tromped all of Oglethorpe's arguments into the dust. It was magnificent to see someone get the best of him."

"Does Mr. Lowe always take the side against imperialism?"

"Oh, no," said Reeves. "I've heard him argue for imperialism just as convincingly. I tell you, if I ever need a lawyer, I'll hire Lowe."

Artimus Lowe was a talented debater and had triumphed even against Oglethorpe. Oglethorpe must have been infuriated, but did Lowe have any reason to be angry with Oglethorpe?

"Well," said Bradshaw after a moment's silence during which the young couple on the slippery couch looked everywhere but at each other. There was no more to ask.

He left the women's dorm and followed the footpath to the edge of the playing field. The cadets marched smartly in their regulation gray, the sun on their young faces. The admiring co-eds with their parasols had spread out a blanket to watch while they picnicked. All first and second year male undergraduates were required to enroll in Military Science and Tactics training. Bradshaw spied Oscar Daulton among the troops, looking almost heroic with his chin up and shoulders back. What a difference that uniform made. Out there with his head held high, his appearance matched his keen intelligence. He was one of a handful of cadets who'd spent last year in Cuba or the Philippines as regular army volunteers. They'd all survived, thank heavens, to return to the idyll of campus life and hopeful futures.

For a moment, Bradshaw's thoughts turned inward, to a blurry future when his precious son was grown. Would Justin be called to war when he became a young man? Would he volunteer to wear a uniform and go forth in battle? Bradshaw closed his eyes briefly. He didn't think he could bear it. How did the parents of any of these young men bear it? He said a silent, desperate prayer for everlasting peace, then turned away from the field, toward home.

Chapter Twelve

Bradshaw needed to get organized. He rolled up his sleeves and sat at his drop-leaf desk in the parlor, his notes in a neat pile to his left, a blank sheet of drafting paper center, and a steaming mug of Postum, a drink he found uplifting without making him nervous, to his right. The mantel clock ticked steadily, and the fire shifted in the hearth taking the chill out of the evening air. Otherwise, all was quiet.

He glanced up at his daily calendar. He had scheduled himself nothing for this evening other than grading exams. How stale and pathetic the entry looked, as did all the entries in their neat white boxes. Study this text, write that exam, repair something about the house.

How had his life become so dull? It was no wonder he'd been enjoying another man's demise. Until now, he'd been sleep-walking. Oglethorpe's death had shaken him from this tightly structured existence that had been both his salvation and prison since his wife's death eight years ago. And yet, he still found the calendar, with his life tidily arranged in clean white boxes, comforting. Dull, but comforting.

He picked up a pencil and began. A half hour later, he had a graph of the day of Oglethorpe's death. As expected, the names of students, faculty, and staff and their corresponding activities for the crucial times checked off rapidly. When he finished, two names remained unchecked. One was his own because he still had no proof of his alibi for the approximate time of Oglethorpe's death, and if he had no proof, neither did the police. The other was Artimus Lowe. With his expensive clothes and lofty manner, Lowe hardly fit the anarchist profile, and he was far too familiar with the law and forensics to have moved Oglethorpe's body, but Bradshaw had seen Lowe leaving the building rather hurriedly immediately after the lights faltered. What had he been doing in the building? Where had he been two hours prior?

He studied Lowe's name and was unenthused. The back of his neck didn't tingle, nor did his arms feel the slightest bit goose bumpy. Maybe these weren't signs of imminent discovery after all, and this afternoon he'd merely been experiencing the excitement of the investigation. Maybe. But in the past, when tinkering in his basement he'd been on the verge of inventing a new type of motor gear, hadn't he felt that same prickling of anticipation? Hadn't it happened in other situations? Hadn't he felt it more powerfully than he ever hoped to again when Rachel had risen from the dinner table on the night of her death?

Sitting back with his Postum, Bradshaw scowled at the unchecked Artimus Lowe and felt not one iota of inspiration. Surely, when observing the name of a killer, he should feel some sort of emotion.

Bradshaw inhaled deeply and turned his mind to Oglethorpe himself. To that big new house and the two children who looked so much like their mother, to the other child on the way that would never know his father. Mrs. Oglethorpe's comments came back to him clearly. *I'm sure what I do here isn't nearly as important, at least Wesley doesn't feel it's as important.* Oglethorpe was belittling, even to his wife.

What if Oglethorpe *had* been the intended victim? Was Bradshaw missing something by attempting to link McKinley and the theory of an assassin?

Who else had Oglethorpe offended or angered? Did he have other family members in Seattle? Associates outside of the university? What of his clubs? Had he a jealous rival? Any member of the professional organization of electrical engineers would have the ability to stage Oglethorpe's death. Goodness,

Bradshaw couldn't go about nosing into the lives of Seattle's engineers. And as far as he knew, no engineer or inventor in Seattle rivaled Oglethorpe. Anyone even close to his caliber was back east, and they were the sort to make their attacks through strategic filings at the patent office.

Still, who else did Oglethorpe know who might have confronted him at the university? Who might have lured him to the lab with that note? Oglethorpe often bragged of his financial prowess. Had he angered an investment associate? It would have to be someone who also knew a goodly amount about electricity and the Machine. Bradshaw didn't know of any—wait a moment, yes, he did.

Good heavens, he did.

He knew Henry Pratt, friend, boarder, Alaska-bound gold-seeker. Henry! Bradshaw himself had shown Henry the Electric Machine. And Henry had picked up a basic understanding of electricity after so many years association with Bradshaw. And then there was the investment.

A year ago Henry had gotten himself unhappily involved in an investment scheme with Professor Wesley Oglethorpe. Henry, always between jobs, was one to dive in without thinking when a whiff of fast money was in the air. Bradshaw had brought home a printed flyer Oglethorpe had passed round to the faculty about some oil drilling company that was looking for investors. Bradshaw had tossed the flyer in the kindling pile near the fireplace. That's all he thought it was good for. But Henry had seen the words "Triple Your Investment—Guaranteed!" in bold black letters and rescued it from the fate of fire. He'd used the nest egg he'd been saving to go north again to buy into the scheme. Henry and Oglethorpe—Bradshaw still could not imagine the two men in the same room, let alone speaking. But a meeting had been arranged. Henry handed over his nest egg, and Oglethorpe promised big returns in three months.

But after a few weeks, Oglethorpe began to report setbacks. The drilling had run into trouble. Machinery broke, the ground was impenetrable. Six months passed without a penny payoff.

Henry had flown into a rage, wanting his investment back so he could try again up in the gold fields. Oglethorpe had guaranteed a profit! At Christmas time, Oglethorpe had bought out Henry's share of the investment, at half its original value, and Henry hadn't mentioned the deal again. But that returned half nest-egg wasn't near enough to finance a trip north, and Henry's wages weren't enough to make up for the deficit in a few months.

So where had Henry gotten the money to finance his Alaska expedition kit?

And why had Henry left on the very day Oglethorpe was killed?

Bradshaw had been so intensely pondering his old friend, he failed at first to realize he was vigorously rubbing his arms. He glanced down now to see goose bumps prickling his skin.

"Oh, God," he whispered. He rolled down his sleeves.

Had Henry typed that note? Henry's spelling was poor at best. He certainly was capable of writing "thare" instead of "there." Had he stormed up to the university and found some stern matron to deliver the note during Oglethorpe's Electrical Design class? For what purpose? He surely wasn't still angry over the lost investment. And what typewriter would Henry have used? Henry didn't possess one, neither did Bradshaw. He tried to imagine how such a scene would have unfolded. Had Henry, once he'd gotten Oglethorpe to the lab, forced him to sit in the chair before the Machine, holding McKinley's bulb aloft? And then what? Had Oglethorpe meekly sat there holding the bulb aloft while Henry concocted some method of electrocuting him?

Ridiculous.

Still, Bradshaw's skin tingled.

He got up from his desk and paced. Insane scenarios of Henry and Oglethorpe danced through his head. It couldn't be. It simply could not be.

Yet why had Henry gone so abruptly? Why on the day of Oglethorpe's death? And where had he gotten enough money to finance the trip?

"Henry, you fool!" Bradshaw growled, not because he believed the scenarios playing out in his mind but because Henry was not here to defend himself, to laugh at Bradshaw with that deep rolling laughter that could be heard at the end of the block. Well, he would prove his goose bumps wrong. He marched upstairs and into Henry's room. With dismay he took in the pristine space, the gleaming floor. The blue quilt on the bed and the white curtains on the window gave the room a clean, fresh fragrance. Every surface of the room gleamed. Mrs. Prouty had outdone herself.

The bedside table, the dresser drawers, even the large walk-in closet, held no clues to Henry's life other than the fact that he was not a man of material possessions. He lusted after fortune and fame, but what he would do if he ever attained them was unexplored territory. He'd taken all he owned with him. Bradshaw returned to the parlor.

So now what? Tell the police?

No. He couldn't. But if Henry were guilty, and the police didn't know to even suspect him—they would continue to focus their attention on Bradshaw. And he would be put on trial. He cast his gaze upwards toward his son's room.

A surge of love and of fear gripped his heart, pounding blood in his ears. If saving Henry meant condemning himself—did he truly have a choice? Standing trial, possibly hanging, for Henry's actions, for anybody's actions, would be suicidal. It would be like abandoning Justin the way his mother had.

Bradshaw sat again and with an unsteady hand entered Henry Pratt's name in the suspect column. He would prove Henry's innocence and then erase his friend's name from the chart.

"Daddy?"

Startled, Bradshaw jumped to his feet as Justin traipsed into the parlor, dressed as if from a discard table at a rummage sale in a striped nightshirt and a wool pullover sweater. His toes were bare, but his head was covered with a stocking cap.

Bradshaw moved away from his desk and stood by the hearth. Justin followed him. He was tall for his age and had pale blue eyes. Like Rachel's. Only Rachel's eyes had been shallow and cold. Like marbles. And the boy's were deep. The boy's eyes were full of love and trust, so full of belief in his father that it nearly broke his heart to look into them. He didn't fear seeing Rachel in his son, he feared the unknown, his son's future. He feared Justin ever finding out the truth of his mother's death.

"There's someone at the door," the boy said earnestly.

A steady knock verified this. Bradshaw raised an eyebrow. "Expecting company? Is that why you've put on your best attire?" How could he close up his desk without attracting his son's curiosity?

"No." The boy beamed up at him. So easily delighted

"Well, who could it be?"

The knock came again, and he had a dread feeling it was the police at the door come to arrest him again, or come to inquire about Henry Pratt.

Justin was giggling now. "Open the door and see, Daddy."

"Do you think we should?" He was hoping against hope that whoever was there would go away. He tried not to panic. If only Mrs. Prouty were home to take charge of Justin.

"Yes." Justin laughed. "Don't keep them waiting."

"Not polite, is it?"

"Daddy!"

"Oh, you want me to answer it. Where is that butler?" He looked about the room.

"We don't have a butler."

"The maid?"

"We just have Mrs. Prouty, and it's her night off."

"Oh, I see. Then who is to get the door?"

"You!"

Bradshaw allowed himself to be pushed, cussing the ineptitude of servants under his breath, drawing a string of wonderful childish giggles from Justin. With a flourish, he threw open the door, inwardly bracing to find the men in blue. How wrong could he be?

Chapter Thirteen

It had never occurred to Professor Bradshaw that he would find an apparition on his porch. But before him in a flat straw hat and thin summer suit stood a slender ghostly young woman, trembling as if the chilly spring evening were much too harsh for her.

The young woman spoke, and her words made no sense at all. "Mr. Bradshaw? It's me, Missouri Fremont."

Bradshaw opened his mouth to speak but merely managed to stammer incoherently. It wasn't possible that Henry's niece, the author of the letter on the mantelpiece, was standing before him, on his very own porch in Seattle.

At last he got out, "But you're in Pittsburgh."

"Oh dear, Uncle Henry didn't get my letter?"

"It—" He pointed over his shoulder, as well as over his son, in the general direction of the letter on the mantel, unable to explain that Henry had fled for Alaska, that the timing of his fleeing was unnerving because of the recent death of Wesley Oglethorpe.

He stared at her while his mind raced. She had been a child of three when the letters first began to arrive for her Uncle Henry back in their college years (mere scribbles addressed by her mother). That had been eighteen years ago. Somehow, despite the growing maturity of her letters, Bradshaw had never thought of Henry's niece as being grown up.

Underneath that straw sailor hat, Missouri Fremont's hair was cut short like Justin's, and it was straight and dark, the color of mahogany. She trembled. Her eyes were an unusual amber color, and they glistened with unshed tears. Why was she in tears? He scrutinized her other features more closely. The straight brows, the long nose, the narrow chin, the wide mouth and full lips. Not a pretty face. A plain unremarkable face beyond the distinctive long nose, were it not for color. The amber of her eyes, the mahogany of her hair, the paleness of her skin, these colors transformed her plainness into something, while not exactly beautiful, quite distinctive.

"You are Mr. Bradshaw?" Her voice was soft, throaty, almost husky. She looked at the boy, keeping a straight face as she took in his attire. "And Justin?"

"Yes, ma'am. Are you really her? Are you Missouri of the letters? Uncle Henry's Missouri?"

"Yes. I believe I am."

Her smile was wide and revealed lovely white teeth. Her shoulders drooped with relief that at last she'd been recognized. Bradshaw quit pointing foolishly over his shoulder and asked her in, taking her small traveling bag.

"Do you have more luggage? Shall I run down to the station?"

"No, thank you. It's to be delivered tomorrow."

"It's in your letter, I assume, that you were coming. But as you can see, we didn't open it." He pointed toward the letter on the mantel.

"Why hasn't my uncle read my letter?"

He hoped she couldn't read the apprehension in his face. "He left for Alaska before your letter arrived. I'm sorry."

She looked about to faint. He rushed to her side and helped her into the parlor, into his easy chair by the fire. He told Justin to hurry into the kitchen and make a strong pot of tea. The boy took off with speed.

"He makes tea? He's so young." Her voice had become vague.

"He's very careful with the kettle. His tea is usually quite good, but I don't recommend his sandwiches. He puts pickles on everything, even jam."

Bradshaw draped a russet afghan over the girl. She looked small and vulnerable beneath it. He stood with the breadth of the carved mantel between them, hands clasped firmly behind his back. His professorial pose, and he assumed it gratefully, like grabbing hold of a life jacket.

"Uncle Henry's in—Alaska?"

"On his way. I believe it takes about ten days in good weather for the boat to reach port. I was going to forward your letter as soon as he wrote me of an address."

She tried to smile, but the effort of staving off tears wouldn't permit it. She shook her head in apology and pointed to the mantelpiece.

"You want me to read it?"

"Please."

He took up the letter, opening it with his pocketknife, wondering if inside he would find Henry's reason for fleeing and her reason for arriving. Had Henry confided something to his niece that had compelled, perhaps frightened her into journeying clear across the country?

Justin came in with the tea, taking tiny steps to keep the good china from rattling. As he busied himself pouring out for their company, Bradshaw began to read. He got no further than 'Dear Uncle Henry' before he had to stop and readjust his mental image of the author from a little girl to the young woman now in the room.

"Dear Uncle Henry,

Oh, Uncle Henry. Mother, your dear sister, is gone. Influenza came to our valley. I nearly died myself, more so from a broken heart than from fever, and now I find myself alone and needing you...."
Bradshaw read the letter with some difficulty, feeling as if he were prying deeply where he should not.

Henry's niece wasn't here because of anything Henry had done. She was here because she had suffered a tragedy and was now alone in the world. He finished the letter, learning that Missouri's hair, that unusual glossy mahogany hair, had been sacrificed to a delirious fever. Missouri's life had been spared, but not that of her mother. Her father had died some years ago. And now she'd come to stay, believing she would find comfort and security with her Uncle Henry.

Bradshaw sensed his boy by his side and felt an overpowering pang of love. He placed a trembling hand on the blond head—the cap had apparently been shed in the kitchen—and felt the child's silky hair and warmth of life radiate to his palm.

"Is it bad news?" the boy asked in a whisper.

"I'm afraid so, son." But telling the boy would be a delicate task, and Bradshaw needed time to prepare. "It's time for you to get to bed."

"But, Dad—"

"We'll talk later. You can visit with Miss Fremont tomorrow. Now, go on."

The boy turned reluctantly. "It's very nice to meet you, Miss Fremont."

"I'd like it if both of you called me Missouri."

Justin smiled. "Good night, Missouri."

"Good night, Justin. I'm very pleased to meet you, too."

When Justin had gone, Bradshaw turned to Missouri. He wished he'd been better prepared to console her. He was ashamed to feel a flash of annoyance at having to deal with her now, with his life upside down. "You're not wearing black. People usually do."

"My mother wouldn't have wanted me to wear mourning clothes. She didn't believe in them. When my father died, we wore our brightest colors."

"Oh." He could think of nothing more to say to such a declaration.

The tea cupped in Missouri's delicate hands seeped warmth and apparently a bit of strength. Her voice was stronger, steadier. "Without death, life would have no boundaries and our days would not be so precious. My mother was a firm believer in the common sense of nature."

Again, he was stuck for a reply. "I'll go on up and prepare your room. You can stay in Henry's room." Thank heavens Mrs. Prouty had done such a thorough job of cleaning. "I'll come get you when it's ready. Unless—" He ran an eye over her slightly trembling frame. "Would you like a bath? We have a modern bath upstairs, and hot running water."

She sighed. "Back home, we dragged a tub into the kitchen and boiled water for an hour. I've never had a modern bath. Sounds like heaven, if it's not too much trouble."

"It's as easy as turning on the tap. I'll go up now and get things organized."

He hurried up the stairs, his mind finally working now that he had something to do. He pressed the chained plug into the bath and set the hot water flowing. He was searching the hall linen closet for the good towels when a faint voice rose up the stairs and made itself heard above the running water.

"Mr. Bradshaw?"

He crossed to the top of the stairs to find Missouri at the bottom, looking up at him.

"May I borrow your ink?"

"Ink?" His thoughts were on soap and wondering if Mrs. Prouty had anything more delicate than the Ivory bars she supplied for him and Justin.

"I want to write in my journal, and I've run out."

She looked so wan, he wondered she had the strength to even think of writing. "Oh, yes, certainly. You'll find a jar on the writing desk in the parlor."

She thanked him, and Bradshaw turned again to the linen closet, sniffing the shelves for the source of a slight whiff of lavender. He was rewarded with a paper-wrapped bar of fancy soap that Mrs. Prouty had wedged between a pile of sheets. But the moment he had the bar in hand, a dread came upon him. He had directed Missouri to his desk, where a murderous graph featuring himself and her uncle was spread. He spun on his heels, gripped the banister, and hurried carefully down the stairs. But he was too late.

Missouri stood at his desk, staring down at the graph of Oglethorpe's last day.

She looked up. "Who's Oglethorpe?"

Bradshaw explained, attempting to make the preposterous event, along with his murderous diagram, as mundane, as possible.

Missouri laughed, a delightful sound. A touch of color tinged her complexion. Bradshaw couldn't help but be glad that this awkward moment had taken her momentarily from her sorrow and weariness. "I'm sorry." She covered her smiling mouth with a slender hand. "A man's death isn't funny, but Uncle Henry would find it amusing to see his name on your list of suspects. Surely, you don't really believe he had anything to do with this Oglethorpe's death."

"In order to be completely fair and systematic, I have to include him because of as yet unexplained circumstances, until I'm able to exclude him."

"I see," she said, obviously fighting back more laughter. "Yes. Very fair of you not to take personal prejudice into consideration. Very commendable, Inspector Bradshaw. Is that why your own name is also listed? Do you consider yourself a suspect?"

"No, but the police do."

She stared at him, still smiling. "They do? Why?"

"Because I have no way to yet prove my innocence." As glad as he was of her calm, amused reaction, he was also concerned by it. Missouri had never met Bradshaw, she knew him solely through correspondence, and she hadn't seen her Uncle Henry since he last visited Pennsylvania, more than a decade ago. Her innocent faith in the both of them revealed a naiveté that was possibly dangerous for a young woman on her own. He wanted to tell her not to be so trusting, so imprudent. Instead, he crossed to the desk and handed her the bottle of ink. As she watched, he carefully folded his diagram and locked it within the desk.

"I don't want Justin to know of this diagram. He's very fond of your uncle, and he might not understand."

"Of course. It's our secret."

He couldn't meet her eye. She was too delicate, too trusting. Too feminine. "I'd better—" he said, pointing up where the rush of water could be heard filling the tub. He hurried up the stairs.

◇◇◇

The next morning, Missouri declined Professor Bradshaw's invitation to attend mass with him and Justin. She claimed she called no religion her own. The sky was her vaulted ceiling, she said with a completely straight-face, the trees her hallowed halls. "A hymn is sung in every bird song, a prayer whispers on the breeze."

Justin had looked at Bradshaw in puzzlement.

A bit later, while kneeling in a back pew beside Justin, Bradshaw wished he had chosen Missouri's cathedral rather than his own, for his own was full of people who turned to stare and whisper. They had read every word the newspapers had printed and listened to every bit of gossip concerning Oglethorpe's death. They didn't need a photograph to recognize him, they'd seen him in church every Sunday for the past eight years. And they judged him with an un-Christian like, even an un-American haste. Guilty until proven innocent, their glances said to him. He ignored their attention. He would not let them intimidate him into leaving his place of worship. Shame on them. A half hour later, he added a shame on Father Murphy for a sermon so blatantly about murder and confession. Did no one see Bradshaw's innocent son sitting beside him? For Justin's sake, Bradshaw kept his poise and dignity. For Justin's sake, Bradshaw went through the motions, kneeling at the appropriate times, reciting clearly the Latin responses, taking Holy Communion.

He felt eyes trail him even after they left the church. Twice Bradshaw turned around abruptly, positive he had seen someone following them. But no one had been there, and Justin had laughed at his father's strange behavior.

They arrived home to find Missouri kneeling in the flower-bed, digging away cheerfully. Justin hurried inside to change into play clothes, but Bradshaw lingered in the front yard, observing Henry's niece as she lovingly fluffed soil around a pink pansy she'd freed from the weeds. She looked as if she had no cares in the world. How did she do it? How, after all she'd been through, did she achieve such serenity so quickly? Literally overnight. He was jealous of her, he realized. Jealous that he still struggled to overcome his life's traumas while she, after one good night's sleep in a strange house, could so happily toil in a flowerbed as if it were her own. Jealous that she felt she didn't need traditions such as wearing mourning black or going to church and he so very much did.

She sat back, smiling radiantly up at him. "The lawn needs a cutting."

"That's Justin's chore. He'll be out after breakfast."

"Oh breakfast! I made biscuits and gravy, I hope you don't mind. I left a pan warming in the oven for you." She took in a great long breath. "I love digging in the dirt. I'm so glad you have flowers and a kitchen garden, Mr. Bradshaw. Children need to see things growing one season to the next. It helps them understand life, and death, the cycle of the human soul." She gestured with her trowel, a graceful, circular motion that somehow took in the universe.

"We like fresh vegetables."

She cocked her head, searching for deeper meaning where he meant none. He'd simply felt he ought to respond to at least one of her observations.

Her mention of cycles made him think of an empirical law of physics. Conservation of energy meant there was no waste, no loss of energy, no true end to anything, only transformations from one form to another. Bradshaw had never thought about life in terms of cycles, and he certainly had never lain awake thinking about the human soul in such terms. But he imagined Missouri Fremont did, and now he was afraid he would as well.

These thoughts were haunting him a moment later as he stood in the kitchen, licking clean a plate of the most delicious buttermilk biscuits and sausage gravy he'd ever tasted. He nearly leaped from his skin when the bass voice of Mrs. Prouty bellowed behind him.

"Professor Bradshaw! What's the meaning a this?"

He turned to his housekeeper as if every day she caught him licking his plate. "I believe it's called breakfast."

Mrs. Prouty wore a crisp white apron over her starched gray dress; sturdy shoes now braced in a wide stance supported her ample girth. She carried a tin bucket, bubbles still clinging to the wet insides, which meant she'd been home long enough this morning to have begun cleaning, and long enough to have met his house guest.

"Miss Fremont is what I mean, sir. Out there on her hands and knees, digging in the dirt. And her spending the night here, alone, with you!"

"Miss Fremont is Henry's niece, Mrs. Prouty. You've enjoyed her letters, as we have. She's practically family."

"Not your family, Professor. What'll people think, a professor spending the night alone with a young girl? It's bad enough the town's gone mad thinking you—"

Thinking he what? Killed Oglethorpe? He could see in Mrs. Prouty's flashing eyes that he'd guessed correctly what she was afraid to say aloud.

"Why didn't you come and get me?"

"There was no need, Mrs. Prouty."

"No need? No need?"

She shook as she bellowed, and her cockney accent grew thick as gravy. Her own cement-like gravy, not Missouri's light and flavorful gravy.

"What time did Henry leave on Thursday?"

"Now, listen 'ere, Professor Bradshaw—"

Bradshaw folded his arms, and raised a brow.

Mrs. Prouty grudgingly complied. "The last time Henry left the 'ouse Thursday, with a bag stuffed with all his clothes, it was just after lunch time. About noon."

"What do you mean, the last time?"

"He was in an out of here more than Justin on a snow day. In or out, I told him. Make up your mind."

"He didn't go to work?"

"He left like he was going, then I had to call him back because the telephone rang."

"Who was it that phoned him?"

"I haven't a clue. She didn't say. Henry left again, then came back an hour later, waving a rolled up newspaper like he was one a them orchestra conductors. He was gone again while I did the ironing, then back for half an hour. He didn't mention a word about leaving for good until he come down the stairs and said he was off to search for gold."

"Did he say anything about the university? Did you notice if he had black grit or specks on his clothes, they would have been shiny if you looked close, sparkling."

"Black grit? Sparkling? That man is always covered in filth. He brings home more of Denny Hill in his boots than he leaves behind."

"But was there anything on him Thursday? Any shiny black flakes in particular? In his room when you cleaned on Saturday?"

"A lot of gravel and grit, and more than one empty whiskey bottle, but not a speck of it sparkled that I recall. It was plain old dirt. What in the world do you want to know about sparkles for?"

"It's not important."

"Of course it's important. You wouldn't have asked—"

"Let it be, Mrs. Prouty."

She shrugged, indicating her willingness to let some subjects drop. "But as for Miss Fremont, now, it ain't my place to say—"

"Aah, at last we agree." He strode from the kitchen before she could get out another word. The telephone, of the candlestick variety, was located in the hall. He picked up the receiver, put it to his ear, and was greeted by a pleasant female voice asking, "What number please?"

He put his mouth to the transmitter. "No number, I was hoping you might answer a question for me. This is Professor Bradshaw. Last Thursday a call was placed here to my home. The call was for Mr. Henry Pratt. I don't suppose it was you who connected the call?"

"Last Thursday? No, sir. That would have been Melody."

"Could I speak with Melody?"

"She's not on duty. I could leave her a message, if you like. What is it you're wanting to know?"

"I'd like to know if she remembers who placed the call. Is that likely?"

"We place hundreds of calls each day, sir. But I'll pass the message on."

"Thank you." He dropped the receiver on the switch hook and checked his watch. Time to catch the train.

Chapter Fourteen

As part of their commitment to the community, faculty members of the University of Washington were expected to visit schools, attend benefits, and give lectures to women's and youth groups. Some projects Bradshaw avoided—anything with meals or music usually spelled the sort of mingling he detested. But educating the public on the wonders of science, the power of electricity, was something he thoroughly enjoyed. The tour at Snoqualmie Falls was his favorite.

Since he'd last journeyed to Snoqualmie two months ago, more logged land had been cleared of stumps, plowed, and planted with crops. At Bothell, Woodinville, and heading toward Redmond, second growth woods gasped for breath through the haze of burn piles scattered throughout the valley and into the foothills. Farmhouses had sprung up along with the new crops, and where the wind blew, clearing the haze, a picturesque homestead sparkled in the green and fertile land.

A half hour into the trip, Bradshaw yawned and stretched, and it was then he looked around and realized his fellow passengers had been observing him for some time. Hastily, heads turned away and voices lowered. But he felt their attention as intently as a man upon a stage feels the eyes of his audience. He hid behind the Sunday paper only to discover the reason for their recognition. His photograph. His official university photo, taking up nearly an eighth of the page.

He didn't intend to read the article. He didn't need reminding that the editorial staff had pinned the murder on him. Conjecturing was good for sales—no matter that it ruined an innocent man's life. But Henry's name leaped out at him.

Our sources tell us that Henry Pratt and Professor Benjamin Bradshaw have been friends since their college days. Until Professor Oglethorpe's electrocution at the university, Henry Pratt resided at 1204 Gallagher, Seattle, in the home of Benjamin Bradshaw. Is it a coincidence that on the very day murder was committed in this city Henry Pratt boarded a boat bound for Alaska? Is it a coincidence that the coroner's inquest verdict allowed for persons, in the plural, to have committed Oglethorpe's murder?

Detective O'Brien of the Seattle Police Department refused comment.

Dear God.

The excursion train picked up speed. Bradshaw hid in a cocoon of newspaper, staring unseeing at the passing scenery. Henry, what have you done to me?

His thoughts became a confused jumble in need of detangling. Those things he'd thought behind him, the future he avoided examining, the scope of his entire life niggled and nagged and wanted organization. He wanted to understand it all and devise a code to live by that would keep him in balance, keep him sane while he navigated this mess. But devising theorems, however much he found them useful, was never his strong point. He was a hands-on inventor. He needed to get hold of things, put them in terms of positive and negative, wires and switches, before he could understand them. And then he had to translate that understanding into words, find analogies to create visual images. His teaching method had grown from this need, from his own inability to easily grasp abstract ideas.

But his feelings would not be easily sorted.

He'd read somewhere that in every man's life there comes something that marks him. A secret that he cannot forget or bury but must carry with him, every moment of every day. His secret had nothing to do with Oglethorpe's death. His secret was Rachel.

"Professor?"

The deep voice was quite near. Bradshaw slowly lowered the newspaper and blinked. It took him a moment to recognize the face before him, so utterly had he been in his thoughts and so unexpected was the young man's appearance. Artimus Lowe. Bradshaw carefully folded the paper on his lap before saying, "Morning, Mr. Lowe."

"May I?" Lowe indicated the vacant seat opposite Bradshaw. He shrugged. Lowe sat.

A silent minute passed. Surely, Lowe had something to say or he wouldn't have joined him. Bradshaw waited. Lowe only smiled.

Bradshaw cleared his throat. "You're going up to Snoqualmie?"

"Yes, to take your tour."

"Why?"

"Why not?"

Bradshaw resisted rolling his eyes. Before him was a high society law student and proven debater. In other words, a master of circular conversation. Bradshaw didn't think he had the stomach for it. Ducking and weaving, tricks of language and subtle leading, all the arts of rhetoric would be necessary to get anything out of Lowe.

Lowe sat forward, brown eyes eager, black hair perfectly in place. He asked, "Professor Bradshaw, may I be honest with you?"

"Certainly," Bradshaw said. It couldn't be so easy as this. A confession from this cool and confidant young man?

"It's about the young woman staying with you. Miss Missouri Fremont?"

"How on earth do you know about her?"

Lowe sat back smugly. "I happened to be passing by your house this morning and I saw her, in your front garden. I was enchanted. I had to learn who she was and was pleased to find that she's the niece of one Henry Pratt, your friend and dormer now headed for Alaska, and that she's staying with you."

"How on earth," Bradshaw said again, unable to think of another expression of his astonishment, "did you discover that?"

"Basic investigative technique, Professor. A lawyer must know where to find information on the quick. The fastest way to find out what's going on in a man's home is to ask the help. I went around back and knocked."

Mrs. Prouty? He had managed to interview Mrs. Prouty?

"Why would this information about Henry's niece please you?"

"Because you can provide me with an introduction."

"Oh, is that a fact?"

The smugness drained from Artimus Lowe's handsome face. He sat forward again, pathetically earnest. "Professor, I apologize. I should not have assumed you would grant me an introduction. Forgive me. It is a great favor I ask, no, I beg of you."

Beg? Good grief, the passions of the young. "Mr. Lowe, I'm not in a position to grant your request."

"Who is?"

"She is."

"But, sir. I can't just walk up to her and introduce myself."

"Why not?"

"It's not done, that's why not."

"It's not done in society perhaps, but real people do it all the time."

"Is that meant as an insult, Professor?"

"Take it as you like. It is meant as a statement of fact."

"She would have nothing to do with me if I behaved so rudely."

"What is rude about saying hello?"

"But a lady is taught—"

"Miss Fremont is not a lady of society. She was raised on a farm. She knows very little of society's rules and that's what makes her so refreshing. There is nothing false about her."

"No, I could tell that by looking at her. She is the most intriguing girl I've ever seen."

A foolish dreaminess came into Lowe's eyes. Bradshaw felt a twinge in the pit of his stomach. He thought of Missouri, her too slender figure, her over-large nose, that cropped hair. All somehow appealing. He forgot for a moment to censor himself. "You think she's attractive?"

"Certainly. Not in the classic sense of course. She's no great beauty. But there's something about her that I find compelling."

"And?"

"And what, sir?"

"After you tell her you find her—compelling, then what?"

"I don't know. What happens, happens."

"Nothing happens, Mr. Lowe. You can forget it." Bradshaw's mind suddenly filled with the image of another young woman, the poor Miss Trout, her face scarlet, her hand resting protectively over her belly. And he recalled Missouri's innocent trust in him, a man she'd never met, and her Uncle Henry, whom she hadn't seen in years.

"Are you refusing me permission to speak with her?"

"Yes."

"But you just said—"

"That was before I realized the danger in doing so. It seems a young woman is not safe in this city without the protection of family, and since I am the closest thing she has, I will take on the role." *You arrogant young pup.*

The train slowed to a crawl as it rounded a steep bend at Gillman. Lush spring woods rolled by unseen as Bradshaw narrowed his gaze upon Lowe.

"Where were you between twenty after one and ten minutes to four on Thursday afternoon?"

"Me? A murder suspect. Certainly, you know I had nothing to do with it. I'm as innocent as you are."

Lowe's remark carried to the nearest passengers. No one turned to stare, but Bradshaw noticed a slight leaning of alertness.

Bradshaw lowered his voice. "Where were you?"

Lowe followed Bradshaw's lead, saying quietly, "I shall tell you what I told the police."

"I want the truth."

"Oh, well, the truth. Is there really such a thing? Don't we all create our own truths? My perception of events may totally differ from another man's perception of events, and yet we can both be telling the truth."

"Mr. Lowe, save your attempts at confusion for the jury. I have a simple one-track mind and am quite capable of ignoring anything you say that isn't a direct answer to my question. Now, where were you?"

Lowe gave Bradshaw a very odd, scrutinizing look.

"You didn't like Oglethorpe." Bradshaw tried Detective O'Brien's interrogation technique of tossing out remarks designed to probe.

"Nobody liked Oglethorpe." Artimus laughed, his wariness fading somewhat.

"But you had reason to dislike him more than most." The accusation had come of its own accord. As he watched Lowe's proud features drift into back into wariness, Bradshaw analyzed his suggestion. Did he really think there had been bad blood between Oglethorpe and this young Lowe? A heated debate over politics in a class designed for such debates need have no underlying vendetta. This was a long cast into a murky pond. But wasn't Lowe's reaction interesting?

"I don't know what you're intimating, Professor. I am not a man who seeks revenge through violence. If I had a quarrel with anyone, I would settle matters through the courts."

"The courts are now involved in Oglethorpe's death, Mr. Lowe. The matter will be settled in your favorite arena."

Bradshaw turned his gaze out the window to the passing scenery, letting the silence between them lengthen as he pondered what he knew about Lowe and Oglethorpe, and what possible connection, besides student-teacher, they could possibly have had.

Chapter Fifteen

The falls at Snoqualmie were more spectacular than Bradshaw had ever seen them. Spring runoff swelled the river, broadening the cascade from its usual slender form to churning white falls stretching the entire width of the brink. For two hundred and seventy feet, the raging water plunged before crashing into a thunderous cloud in the pool below.

Bradshaw, with Artimus Lowe in tow, climbed the narrow trail through the misty woods, inhaling the sweet fragrance that was a mixture of clean mountain water, evergreen trees, and spring blossoms. He paused often to simply stare, his gaze lifting to the very top of the falls. He stood solidly on the trail a fair distance from the steep slope, and felt not the slightest twinge of anxiety. There had once been a huge boulder in the very center of the brink known as the "Seattle Rock," but logs too often hung up causing dangerous jams and so last year it was blasted away. Now, only a few jagged black rocks pierced the deep flow. And there was something else.

Something that resembled a carriage wheel was impaled upon the tallest of the jutting rocks near the far bank above the churning water. The wheel, or whatever it was, and its curious predicament, as well as the sight of such a splendid force as the falls themselves, sent Bradshaw's calculative mind into happy overdrive.

How had that wheel gotten stuck above the water line? Why hadn't it been swept over the falls? What would be the speed of an object at the top of the falls, and what speed at the bottom? Bradshaw had in the past spent many happy hours studying the dynamic hydraulic forces of rivers. He remembered being fascinated by the unique forces that came into play immediately downstream of large rocks where eddies could form and cause the current to actually flow upstream.

Bradshaw breathed deeply and let problems of physics and motion come and go as they please. The falls sang a pleasant, powerful song, like the crash of the tide without the intermittent pause. It was no wonder the native Snoqualmie people worshipped here, the beauty and energy lifted one quite away from the petty concerns of man. Care had been taken in the modern invasion, and the forest surrounding the falls had barely been disturbed by the construction of the power plant. Except for the handsome brick powerhouse, only a few white cottages to the south of the railway station disturbed the natural scene. The dam behind the top of falls that regulated water flow was completely submerged and thus concealed from view. From below, the falls showed no obvious sign of this human tampering.

"Professor Bradshaw!" The superintendent of the plant, Mr. Dittmar, a big, balding man in a practical dark suit, came huffing down the path toward them, hand extended.

Bradshaw shook the superintendent's hand firmly then introduced Lowe.

Superintendent Dittmar's eyes shifted from Bradshaw, to Lowe, then back to Bradshaw. He said, "I didn't see you coming off the train. I couldn't believe it when I was told you were here, uh, I mean, I thought it was Professor Hill scheduled today. Honestly, I wasn't sure he would make it because of the whole Oglethorpe business, but I must say I certainly didn't expect, that is to say, I mean, Professor…" his words trailed off. Bradshaw pretended not to see the trepidation in his eyes.

"I've never seen the falls so full. Is there something trapped up at the brink? It looks like a wheel."

"A wheel?" Dittmar was slow to switch subjects. His gaze followed Bradshaw's to the brink of the falls. "Ah, yes. A wheel.

Trapped. Odd, the way it sits there, isn't it? We've tried to lasso it. The tourists are complaining it's ruining their photographs, but it won't budge. Maybe you could devise something for us, Professor."

"Certainly. After the tours, I'll take a look."

"But Professor, what I mean is—" said Dittmar, now dabbing his brow with a handkerchief. "I didn't expect anyone from the university to come. I made other tour arrangements."

"Oh?"

"Well, yes." His eyes shifted again to Lowe. He smiled a politician's sort of beaming grin that Lowe met with a single lifted eyebrow.

"You understand, of course," Dittmar said to Lowe.

"Me? Certainly not. Professor Bradshaw didn't kill Professor Oglethorpe. There's no reason he shouldn't give a public tour."

Dittmar babbled inarticulate apologies while Bradshaw bit back a smile. For a moment, he almost liked Lowe.

"That's not what I meant, not what I meant at all. It's just that I, that is we, the power company, it's been in the paper—I thought I'd give today's tour."

"There's no need for you to trouble yourself, since I'm here." Bradshaw turned and strode purposefully up the trail, Lowe on his heels. He heard the superintendent's footsteps clamor to catch up.

"Professor!" Dittmar chased breathlessly after them. They reached the top of the trail. "While I give the tours, you could assist Mr. Miller with the installation of the new meters, marvelous devices, really, newest on the market, I think you'll be most impressed by them, and we'd be most grateful for your assistance, I'm sure."

Bradshaw marched resolutely up the narrow path. The task was offered only because Dittmar hadn't the nerve to tell him to go home. He didn't slow his pace until they'd reached the dozen tourists who stood anxiously before the small wooden building that sheltered the power plant elevator. He'd had every intention of giving the tour as planned until he saw the change in the tourists' faces.

The women, stout matrons wearing "Improvement Society" sashes, inhaled audibly, and their husbands postured, squaring their shoulders and bracing their stances. Dittmar ushered them all into the elevator, talking over the few voices that attempted to complain.

The elevator attendant, a little man dressed in a cranberry uniform and box hat as dapper as any attendant in a fancy hotel, closed the grate. From very far below came the echo of a gong, and the elevator began to descend. Bradshaw experienced the very real sensation of his stomach dropping. Never in the past had the feeling triggered his vertigo.

Today it did, with a speed he found staggering. He gripped the brass hand rail and tried to breathe deeply without visibly gasping. He glanced at the tourists and found he wasn't alone in his panic. No one knew quite where to look or how to breathe. It wasn't fear of the plummeting elevator alone he saw on their faces. They pressed back as far as possible into the walls, into each other, so that even in the cramped space he stood alone.

If he didn't do something fast he would vomit. Speech was the only distraction within grasp. "Three years ago, engineers temporarily diverted the river from this area, exposing bedrock. Men with compressed air drills labored for a year, drilling straight down, two hundred and seventy feet through solid rock to form this tunnel, down which we are now descending. Beside us, parallel to this elevator, is a pipe called a penstock. A portion of the river above is dropping into the penstock, plunging much more swiftly than we are, heading toward the generating plant." These last words, Bradshaw shouted above the rising, constant thunder, and soon speech was impossible. Bradshaw gripped the rail and breathed.

Down the shaft they descended, while in the seven-and-a-half foot diameter pipe parallel to them, the river fell in roaring volumes. At one hundred feet down, the thunder of the water as it struck the revolving wheels of the generators bombarded their eardrums. By the time they reached the bottom, nearly three hundred feet below the surface of the river, they could barely hear their own thoughts.

Bradshaw was closest to the door when it opened. He hesitated a moment while equilibrium returned. The women were quite pale, the men's faces hostile. Lowe elbowed him, and Dittmar shouted, "Off we go now." Bradshaw stepped out. The tourists burst forth liked released prisoners.

The noise level was tolerable in the power chamber that had been carved out of the bedrock, and the air was cool and fresh. The women gasped and stretched their arms like birds testing their wings. The gentlemen strode to and fro, as if they'd been cramped for a week inside a steamer trunk. Artimus Lowe appeared unaffected by the claustrophobic descent, but his eyes gleamed and his mouth dropped open at the sight of four massive generators that stood in line down the tunnel-shaped space. Each generator was as large as a small house, making visitor's feel lost in a giant's world.

"Good golly, Professor," Lowe said. "This is—" Words failed him. He shook his head, laughing.

"I know." Lowe's reaction surprised Bradshaw. He hadn't expected the sophisticated young man to be impressed. It was impossible to believe that a man capable of such innocent delight could have recently committed murder. This, Bradshaw thought as he studied Lowe's astonishment, was how his mother probably saw him.

Bradshaw felt Dittmar's solid hand on his shoulder. "Thank you for that introductory lecture on the way down. Just what the tourists needed. That ride can be ghastly for first-timers. I'll take over from here while you assist Miller. I'm sure you'll find those new meters fascinating, really."

Bradshaw turned to look the superintendent squarely. "Are you sure you trust me with your equipment?"

Dittmar's fat cheeks reddened. "Professor," he said in a voice loud enough to only reach Bradshaw over the din of the machinery. "Of course I trust you, but as supervisor I must be sensitive to the public, to the tourists."

"In normal circumstances, I would accept your word. But a man's been killed and I've been made a suspect and so circumstances are far from normal. I can see that you don't fully trust me and yet to avoid a scene, you're not only allowing me to remain, but giving me a task vital to the running of this plant."

"I don't know what you mean, Professor. I'm not avoiding a scene."

"I don't care what you think of me, it's how you may have dealt with other visitors to this plant that concerns me. President McKinley was to visit here next week."

"Why, yes he was. But his trip has been cancelled." Dittmar's jaw suddenly dropped. "I—you—Professor, you don't think he would have been in danger. Do you?"

"Can you guarantee me that he would not have been?"

Dittmar's eyes darted about the cavernous room, over the massive generators, to the gaping door of the elevator, up to the rough ceiling that supported nearly three hundred feet of crushing rock. He swallowed hard.

"McKinley was to visit the university as well as this power plant." Bradshaw could see understanding dawn on Dittmar's stunned face. "While I'm here today, I'll be looking around. To be sure everything is exactly as it ought to be. I suggest you do the same."

"Yes. I will. Of course I will." The tourists approached them, questions raised above the din. Dittmar said hastily to Bradshaw, "You'll find Miller at the switchboard. He'll be very glad to see you."

"That'll be refreshing." Bradshaw squared his shoulders and accepted his banishment.

Chapter Sixteen

Three hours after descending into the cavernous depths, Bradshaw ascended to the surface and stepped into the fresh, relatively quiet air. By then, he was partially deaf and slightly hoarse from speaking over the constant thrum. Miller, a clever and boisterous young engineer with a full bushy beard, hadn't really needed Bradshaw's assistance but he'd more than welcomed the company. The meters had proved to be state-of-the-art and installing them therapeutic for Bradshaw. Afterward, he and Miller had gone on an inspection tour and found nothing out of place or tampered with, but that didn't give Bradshaw the sense of relief he'd hoped for. If he'd inspected the lab at the university before Oglethorpe's death, would he have found evidence that murder would soon take place?

Miller, however, had been relieved and satisfied with their findings as he'd walked Bradshaw to the elevator. He smiled and shook Bradshaw's hand. "Did Dittmar mention the wheel stuck at the top of the falls?"

"I saw it. Odd the way it's trapped above the waterline. It happened sometime last night?"

"Or maybe this morning. I saw a couple other wheels when I was fishing the lower river, no tires on any of them, about a quarter mile downstream. Looked as if they'd gone over the falls. Then at the top, there's that third one stuck like somebody chucked it, like a ring toss at the county fair. Funny thing is, not one wheel was the same."

"What? All different sizes?"

"Sizes and makes. Usually when a group of things come down the river, you can guess what happened. A logging wagon overturned, or a campsite washed away. But this morning, there were just those wheels."

Three unmatched wheels. How? Why? Bradshaw walked around the brick power house to the restricted personnel-only section of the river's edge. Here, the cement wall of the submerged dam formed a wide ledge a foot above the river's surface. Excellent for observation. Excellent for vertigo.

Mind—over—matter. He put one foot in front of the other and moved several yards along the ledge until he was as near the brink as he dared. He breathed through the threatening panic, diverting his thoughts to the safe elements of his surroundings. Many trees had been spared during the construction of the plant, and in three years' time the cleared places had filled with bushy undergrowth. With the late afternoon sun at a low angle, the bushes and trees formed a dark barrier beside Bradshaw. A pressing barrier. He turned to look directly at them, to tell himself there was nothing frightening about them. Shadows shifted and moved in the bushes, leaves fluttered then stilled. An animal, he told himself. A startled squirrel.

He turned to the river. The limitless blue sky, momentarily untouched by haze or clouds, offered nothing to grasp. Leaving a good foot of concrete between himself and the edge, he forced himself to study the river's surface, which was deceptively smooth where he stood, like a sheet of dark glass. Occasional miniature eddies, swirling deep into the darkness, revealed the true power and swiftness of the river as it neared the submerged dam and the hundred and fifty foot stretch of rough water before the brink.

He took a small step backward and realized part of his disorientation was due to deafness. He couldn't hear his own footsteps. His ears were in need of a good popping. The steady thunder of the falls, which from here sounded like a distant approaching train, was the only sound that could penetrate his muffled hearing. He yawned and swallowed and shook his head, but his ears remained stubbornly plugged.

He focused on the buggy wheel balanced at the precipice. It was much larger than he'd realized, over five feet in diameter. And it wasn't a buggy wheel at all but the front steel wheel of one of those ridiculously large three-wheeled velocipedes. Two of the thin strong spokes held it wedged on the exposed portion of granite near the brink. The steel rim caught the sunlight and winked. It did indeed look, as Miller had said, as if it had been purposefully thrown there, like a carnival game. Wheels of that size weighed twenty-five or thirty pounds, and the distance from shore was a good fifteen feet. Had it been tossed? Highly unlikely. It must have entered the river at some point upstream and when it arrived here, unlike its two mix-matched companions, somehow managed to become trapped horizontally above the waterline. Maybe it had a lucky bounce off a protruding rock.

The real question for Bradshaw was how it could be removed short of diverting all the water from the falls. Lassoing, Bradshaw could see, would be useless. From shore, a rope wouldn't be able to give the required leverage. The wheel would need to be lifted up with even pressure exerted on both sides. A pulley would have to be devised from some height.

Why not use the stuck wheel as a lesson for his students? He crouched down to look eye-level at the wheel, tilting his head to see if there were some protuberance on the rock formation holding it up. It appeared to be simply wedged between the spokes. He could devise a series of problems for the students, taking the wheel from the time it tumbled into the river, which would include the force of gravity, the weight of the object, resistance, and then the speed of its journey to the brink—his thoughts were suddenly interrupted. A sound filled his ears, coming from within his own head. It was like a cork being pulled slowly from a bottle. His ears went thwump, and all at once he could hear clearly the distant thunder of the falls, the wind in the trees. And footsteps.

The steps rasped against the cement ledge, rapid and light. Startled, Bradshaw shot to his feet, something solid hit his shoulder and pushed him forward. He teetered. The world began to spin. Instinctively, he flung his arm—not out for safety but inward, around Justin, around his infant son who was not there and yet who was always there. In this tight fetal position, he tumbled head-first into the ice-cold river.

Roaring bubbles engulfed him. The cold seized his stomach and lungs. He had an instant, terrifying sensation of being swallowed alive. He kicked, frantically reaching upward to break the surface, gasping and choking on white froth. He had enough clarity to understand what all the froth meant. He'd been swept over the submerged dam.

Nothing stood between him and the brink of the falls.

Nothing except a few jagged rocks and that blasted velocipede wheel.

The icy tentacles grasped his soaking clothes and limbs again and pulled him under, shooting him down the short stretch of rapids.

His head broke the surface again. He caught sight of a few feet of churning white water. Beyond there was nothing but empty sky. He knew he was going over. For a second that lasted an eternity he lived in pure, blind, screaming panic.

Then the river gripped him again, sucked him under, catapulted him forward, and splattered him against granite. His head and shoulders were above the icy jets pounding his spine, pinning him to the rock. Arms spread, fingertips splayed, he clung, unable to move, his cheek plastered against the cold wet rock.

He choked and coughed and finally breathed. His mouth open, he gulped damp air as he clung desperately and the river tried to pulverize him against the rock.

Breathe! Think! Hydraulic force. Current speed. If he could get on top of this rock, out of the water…the cacophony of churning water receded to the back of his mind as he pushed back the noise and panic. How long could a man last in such frigid water? Minutes? He needed to climb, but the force of the river pounding his spine and pinning his legs was too great. Not here. Not this side of the rock. The other side would—might—provide shelter. He needed an eddy. The rock he clung to now was wider than his stretched arms and he knew that big submerged rocks created hydraulic rotating forces and eddies that surged upriver.

He didn't give himself time to think. He closed his eyes, inched sideways, and felt the force of the water as he neared the edge of the rock, shifting and circular. He eased himself around, not looking, not thinking, feeling his way into the eddy.

Then it happened. The river grabbed him, pushed him down, and the astounding hydraulic force shot him around the rock, up into a calm pool of water no larger than his own body. He dug his fingers into slippery crags and said a fervent prayer of thanks.

He could feel the emptiness behind him. Absolutely nothing stood between him and the plummeting brink a few feet away. Just the miracle of hydraulic motion kept him bobbing in place. He could barely feel his legs and his feet were frozen inside his shoes, making climbing all the more difficult. But he climbed, lifting and shifting his numb feet, reaching hand-over-hand until he gripped the top of the rock and hauled himself up onto his stomach in a semi-sprawled position.

He hugged the rock, kissed the slick granite, then gave himself a quick inspection to be sure his limbs were all still attached. He was surprised to see that the current had sucked off his shoes and socks. It wasn't his shoes that had slipped on the granite, but his naked frozen toes. White with streaks of blood, they looked like they belonged to a corpse. But he was alive.

He said three Hail Marys and two Our Fathers while catching his breath. Then he carefully examined his position. To his left, the churning water stretched to a crumbling cliff face. To his right, between him and the shore lay fifteen feet of white water, the tips of a few jagged rocks—and a wheel. The velocipede wheel. Within reach. He laughed and coughed and spit up a lung full of water. When he'd recovered, he reached out and gripped the steel rim.

After testing its hold, he devised a plan. He would use the velocipede wheel as a bridge. He crawled across the wheel to the next rock, hefted the wheel overhead, and brought it clanking down on the rock beyond. Three times he used the wheel as a bridge between the jagged rocks to cross the raging river at the brink until at last the steel clanked down on the concrete dam ledge. He hauled himself and the blessed wheel to shore.

He found the full-bearded young engineer alone having a cigarette near the elevators. He gaped, taking in Bradshaw's dripping wet clothes and the velocipede wheel.

"How—"

"I swam."

Chapter Seventeen

"Those aren't your clothes, Professor!"

Bradshaw had hoped to be able to sneak into the house unnoticed, but as he slipped shivering into the kitchen through the back door, Mrs. Prouty entered through the dining room. She took in his ill-fitting borrowed suit first, his face second.

"Lord above us, you're white as a sheet again. Did somebody else get murdered?"

"Very nearly. Where's Justin?"

"Next door, I was about to holler for him to come home and wash for supper."

"Wait until I'm upstairs. And Missouri?"

"Miss Fremont," Mrs. Prouty said, her voice turning cold, "is having a lie down. I told her she was over-doing after such a long journey, but she wouldn't listen. Stubborn as her uncle, that one."

Bradshaw shuddered, and Mrs. Prouty took charge of him as if he were Justin, nagging him, in what was for her a gentle voice, up the stairs and into his room. She put a hand to his clammy forehead and scowled, wrapped him in a blanket then tucked him into his bed, his pillows propped behind him. She fetched him tea, thick with sugar and milk, and watched as he drank, prattling a steady stream of meaningless chatter about the house, her chores, her cousin, the latest show at the nickelodeon.

He began to feel human again.

She took his empty cup. "Well. What happened?"

It was difficult disobeying that stern motherly command. But Bradshaw thought of how easily Artimus Lowe had discovered Missouri's identity this morning from Mrs. Prouty, and he felt a hard, phantom pressure on his shoulder blade pushing him into the icy river. Except for Miller, who'd lent him dry clothes and promised his silence, no one knew of his tumble and near death. No one except whoever had made the sound of those footsteps that raced up behind him. Someone had wanted him to die while under the suspicion of Oglethorpe's death.

He'd spoken to no one on the train back to Seattle. He'd been in a state of shock and afraid that if he'd opened his mouth, his trauma would give way in a flood of gibberish. He'd had enough sense, however, to examine every single face aboard the train as he made his way down the aisle to the last seat. He recognized no one, though their sideways glances told him they recognized him. Artimus Lowe had not been aboard, and Bradshaw learned from the conductor upon debarking that Lowe had returned to Seattle three hours prior. He'd also learned that nearly two hundred people on a dozen scheduled runs had journeyed to the falls today. Who among them had tried to drown him? Or had another route been taken? A rough road up to the pass was under construction. And there was a bicycle trail used by local clubs, but it was many miles long, winding and steep, and not the fastest route to carry someone to and from a murder scene.

"Well?"

"Mrs. Prouty, if I were to tell you that I can't tell you, not yet, would you understand?"

She pursed her lips but didn't argue.

"And will you keep this to yourself, these clothes and my state when I got home?" Besides keeping it from Justin, he couldn't stomach the idea of the attention that would result. He doubted it would clear his name, and the sensationalism would make his attempt to find the truth impossible.

She set his tea cup on the tray then began tucking him in again, though he hadn't come loose. "Eight years I've been with you, Professor," she said meaningfully, then set her jaw. Her throat tightened as if she were swallowing back tears.

Bradshaw had hired her on the day he arrived in Seattle with his infant son. He had chosen her from an employment agency line-up downtown, in a stuffy office building. Justin had been fussy as Bradshaw held him and gazed over the line of house-keepers and nannies, all experienced and eager for employment. Mrs. Prouty had been new herself to Seattle, fresh off the boat from the poverty of London's East End. Middle-aged, childless, she'd recently lost Mr. Prouty to consumption and had come to America, to Seattle, in the wake of her younger cousin's immigration. She was as broad then as she was now, and as opinionated. And as protective.

While Bradshaw had tried to choose from the assortment of women, Justin had begun to cry. After five minutes of Justin's squalling, Mrs. Prouty had stepped forward from the line, taken the boy from his arms and said, "Sir, the lad needs his nappies changed. Are you deaf?" She had picked up the satchel that contained Justin's diapers. And without waiting for permission, she took charge of his boy, cooing without shame. Justin had stopped squalling. He'd gurgled delightedly. She made the diaper change in record time then squeezed back into the line-up. She'd been with them ever since, running their lives, keeping them clean and fed and out of trouble.

She now gave the blankets a final jab. He was wrapped so tightly he couldn't wiggle his toes. "I'd never do anything—"

"I know."

"If my keeping quiet will land you in more danger—"

"Keeping quiet might save me from danger."

She looked down at him, brow fierce, jaw slightly trembling.

"And I need you to be especially vigilant around the house. Let me know if anyone pays a call or if you see anyone come near, no matter how innocent they may seem."

She put roughened fingers to her lips, but a choked gasp escaped.

"I know about Mr. Lowe's visit this morning. What happened today had nothing to do with him, I don't think. But from now on, speak to no one until you've asked me first."

She nodded vigorously. "Mum's the word, I swear."

"I trust you."

She cleared her throat and gripped the tea tray. "Dinner's in an hour, Professor. You sleep until then, mind you."

◇◇◇

Bradshaw lifted a limp snow pea with his fork. They'd looked sweet and crisp when Mrs. Prouty brought them home from the farmer's market at the foot of Pike Street. He'd suggested that she lightly steam them, as did the Chinese in their small restaurant, but Mrs. Prouty did nothing lightly. She seemed to think all vegetables contained lethal toxins that required an hour's boiling to neutralize. The limp peas were accompanied by leathery roast beef, molasses-thick gravy, and watery mashed potatoes.

It wasn't Mrs. Prouty's heavy-handed cooking, however, that made each bite an effort. His digestion had long ago adjusted to her meals. It was her fierce protectiveness that manifested itself in bursts of rudeness. She now entered the dining room and slammed a basket of rolls onto the table with enough force to bounce the doughy things a good half-foot into the air.

Missouri caught one before it hit the table, which made Justin laugh. "Thank you, Mrs. Prouty." She received not so much as a grunt from the housekeeper.

This was the first time another female had entered Mrs. Prouty's territory. She'd been cool to Missouri all day, but now, charged with her promise to Bradshaw and troubled by fear, she was behaving like a mother hen with an invading bird in her nest.

"Pass the potatoes, please," said Justin with sing-song politeness.

Bradshaw passed the bowl of congealed starch to his son and his arm muscles sent him the first pangs of soreness. His mind flooded with the roar of Snoqualmie Falls, the icy froth, the weight of the velocipede wheel as he hefted it overhead. He felt not terror but exhilaration. It now took nearly as much strength to keep quiet about his amazing adventure. He did a rapid self-assessment and discovered what he felt was pride. He'd cheated death today. He'd faced a nightmare in that river and survived. He jabbed a hunk of beef and chewed happily.

Mrs. Prouty entered the dining room, muttering that she supposed her Saturday nights would be disrupted from now on until Miss Fremont moved out.

Bradshaw made a quick decision. "Missouri won't be moving out."

"She won't, Professor?"

"I won't?"

"She won't?" The delight in Justin's voice was a distinct contrast to the astonishment of the other two.

"No, she won't. Of course she won't. Henry would never forgive me if I let his niece live alone in some apartment."

"Mr. Bradshaw, I'm twenty-one."

"Age has nothing to do with it."

"I couldn't impose on you like that, Mr. Bradshaw. I'm most grateful for your hospitality, but I never meant for you to keep me for any length of time."

For the first time, Mrs. Prouty agreed with Missouri. "Many girls has their own places nowadays, Professor."

Bradshaw shot her a glance that not only silenced her but sent her waddling huffily back into the kitchen.

Missouri spread butter on her roll. "I'm not destitute you know, I have a small savings. Plenty to get by on, if I'm not excessive. Don't you think it would be best if I found an apartment?"

"No." He knew modern girls lived alone, and he knew Missouri in ordinary circumstances was capable of managing, but her uncle's name had been in today's paper, in connection with Bradshaw, in connection with murder.

She looked at him. "Do you really want me to stay?"

In the chandelier light, her brown eyes glowed like amber, and Bradshaw was struck anew at how her plain features were transformed by the radiance of her coloring. He could not send her out into the world alone. Not with her uncle a suspect, not with men like Artimus Lowe drawn to her "compelling" features like flies to honey. Not with a murderer still at large.

He now had two precious souls under his roof to protect. Three, if he counted Mrs. Prouty's ornery old soul. Four if he counted his own, which someone might again attempt to set free from his mortal being.

"Yes."

"Thank you," she said softly, and Justin shouted, "Hurrah!"

The bang of a pot hitting the floor echoed from the kitchen telling Bradshaw he had no need to pass on the decision.

◇◇◇

Later that evening, after discreetly going through the house and locking every door and window, Bradshaw lit a comfortable fire in the parlor. The front page of the newspaper gave flame to the kindling. His household would hear soon enough the city's speculation about Henry, he didn't need them to read of it tonight.

He sat in his favorite easy chair to at last grade those student papers. This afternoon's near-drowning drifted into a long-ago nightmare, yet he knew it was because of it he felt so alive, so keenly aware of the warmth and comfort of his home and small family.

Justin lay sprawled before the warm hearth with the children's page of the newspaper and a pair of scissors to cut out the "Puss'n Boots" puppet.

Missouri remained at the dining table, feet tucked beneath her, much as a child would sit, studying the help-wanted ads. She'd been in the city less than twenty-four hours, and already she showed more responsibility than her uncle. Thank heavens for that.

Bradshaw concentrated on the exams, losing himself in the logic of mathematical equations. He worked steadily for an hour. Oscar Daulton, he was glad to see, had done very well. He'd overcome his anxiety and his answers reflected how very hard he'd been studying. At the bottom of the test he'd written, as had all the students, *I have neither given nor received aid during the taking of this exam.* The words stood out boldly for he'd used Bradshaw's dark lead pencil to write them.

He thought of that oath. It represented honesty and fairness. Those were the virtues the university supported. Oglethorpe's death represented the very opposite. His death had been a sneak attack, his body moved. McKinley's bulb had been broken, the evidence all but erased. And today. Bradshaw had been pushed by an unseen hand. Someone had lain in wait for him. Someone wanted his death to look like an accident or suicide. Someone with a devious, murderous mind was still out there, still plotting.

"I could be a cook."

Bradshaw looked up. He blinked. It took considerable effort to return his mind to the young woman looking at him expectantly from his dining room.

"A cook?" His mouth watered at the thought of her biscuits and gravy, but he didn't like the idea of her in some seedy little kitchen in the back of one of Seattle's many restaurants.

"There are several listings for cooks." She leaned even further over the table, draped like some boneless creature, one long leg dangling to the floor. "But I do love cooking, and I'm so afraid that if it became my job, I'd hate it. Some things are like that, you know. You love to do them, say for your family, but it's tedious to do for pay. Still, it's something—"

"For crimeny sake, Missouri, you don't want to be a cook, go on to the other listings."

She looked at him, startled.

"I mean a cook would be a menial job, unsuited for a girl like, well, there must be something else."

"There must." She continued to look at him.

"You must reach up for your highest expectations." It sounded stuffy, even to his own ears, but it was the most profound thing he knew to say, and it was what he said to each new crop of students in the fall.

"That's my trouble, Mr. Bradshaw. I don't know what my highest expectations are. Everything has changed so immensely of late. I'm like, well, like a tadpole just changed into a frog and I don't know yet how I'm supposed to breathe."

Tadpole to frog? Good grief. She was dangerously close to talking about cycles again, and he surely didn't want to get onto the subject of life and death. Especially not death.

She continued gazing at him, her face expectant as if awaiting some great words of guidance. He set the exams aside and joined her at the dining table.

She glided back into a semi-seated position in her chair, her chin resting thoughtfully in a slim porcelain hand, her eyes focused steadily on him.

He cleared his throat. "What do you most enjoy doing?"

"Well, I love growing things, seeing a seed poke from the earth and grow toward the sun. I love swimming, you know, late on a hot summer afternoon. Slipping into the cool water when my skin is hot and dusty. I— "

"Missouri," he interrupted, still struggling with the image of her slim graceful figure slipping through the cool waters of a pond. "Do you have any skills that could translate into gainful employment here in the city? Can you use a typewriter, keep books? You'll have to stop in at the offices. Present yourself for hire, and see what you find."

For a few minutes, she was uncomfortably quiet. Bradshaw realized his casual proposition would not be so easy for her to undertake. She had no experience in navigating a city as large as Seattle. No experience in the business world. He wished he had not made the suggestion.

She bit her lip. "Would you come with me? Downtown?"

He looked away. He had classes tomorrow morning, and plans to investigate Artimus Lowe in the afternoon. He needed to sort out this horrid mess before anyone else was killed, himself included, or before the police came knocking again. He didn't have time to escort a country girl around the city.

"Please." Her husky voice pulled him back. Her eyes pleaded softly. Enticingly. Unexpected anger gripped him. How dare she show up here, now, needing him, confusing him, when his life was upside down?

"I'll be home at one." His words were hard and clipped, but she thanked him anyway and he felt like a beast. She was Henry's niece, he should be helping her, not fighting with himself because he found her inconvenient and—attractive. He was stunned by the thought. *She's as young as your students, Bradshaw! Give her advice not unwanted, inappropriate attention. She's too bright to spend her youth in some dingy office. Tell her that.* "You should find yourself a job for the summer. In the fall, you should attend the university."

Her eyes grew wide. "But I've never been to school. My mother taught me at home."

"According to your letters, your education was thorough. We have many home-schooled children attending. You can take an equivalency test."

"Do you think I could pass it? The test isn't too difficult?"

"I don't think so. With a little study, you could pass."

"Is it terribly expensive?"

"It's free, state funded. You need only buy your books."

"Oh!"

She threw her arms in the air as the idea coursed through her veins like a heady wine. Then she sank back into her chair, stretching her long legs beneath the table and her arms overhead, a song of laughter spilling from her.

The sight of her, as her eyes turned dark and dreamy with the possibility of a college degree, momentarily took Bradshaw's breath. His anger melted. He forgot everything. He had the feeling of time coming to a complete halt, of all existence hushing and slowing to gaze at the sight of this happy girl.

And then a giggle came from the other end of the table. Tearing his eyes from Missouri, he found the sound's origin in his son. Justin had approached silently, and he now too was mesmerized by Missouri. His eyes danced, his mouth hung open in awe as if observing some wonder of nature for the very first time. How long had it been since he'd seen his boy smile so?

Had he ever?

Chapter Eighteen

Black bunting drooped over the main entry of the Administration Building, and black armbands adorned many sleeves. It was a charade. The proper etiquette was being followed, but only on the surface. Beneath, a tense excitement vibrated. The students, even the staff, were unable to keep from gossiping, from wondering what had happened to Professor Oglethorpe. It was death without the usual sorrow, and for that Bradshaw felt an uncomfortable and quite unexpected pang of sympathy for Oglethorpe. No man's death should cause so many people so much entertainment. The poor dead bastard.

Outside Oglethorpe's office door, Bradshaw raised his hand to knock, then his palm fell silently to the glass knob. He entered hesitantly. The office was larger than Bradshaw's, with a window overlooking the oval. On a clear day, Mount Rainier would be framed in the glass, floating above the line of firs. Today, the view was blocked by a manmade haze of smoke and soot and dust rising from the never-ending construction. In another decade, Bradshaw wondered, would there be a native blade of grass or tree in the Northwest left standing?

And would there be any hills? He'd taken a long detour on his way to the university this morning, negotiating traffic and mud, construction and ditches, until he came at last to Henry's former place of employment, an enormous pile of dirt north of Pike Street. Denny Hill was being leveled in the name of progress, to make it easier for builders and horses and streetcars. Soon, other hills in the city would be taken down, one shovel-full at a time, until Seattle was as flat as Kansas. It was almost enough to tempt Bradshaw, who hated politics, into running for mayor to put a stop to the foolishness.

Henry hadn't reported to work last Thursday morning. The foreman said Henry had finally appeared on the job site at two-thirty only to say he'd quit and was heading north. Bradshaw had talked with the laborers, and they'd asked the same questions he'd intended to ask them. Since Henry was perpetually broke, where did he get the bankroll for the expedition kit? Why had he decided to go now, all-of-a-sudden? Why were the police asking questions about Henry? He saw in their eyes questions they withheld, questions about himself and the late Professor Oglethorpe.

Bradshaw kept telling himself that since Henry was on a boat, miserably and deservedly seasick, and had been since Thursday afternoon, he couldn't have had anything to do with yesterday's near fatal dunking. But the thought didn't provide the comfort it should. Henry had friends of questionable reputation. Friends with scars and a hundred violent stories who might have taken it upon themselves to push the blame to Bradshaw by pushing him over the falls.

"Professor?"

Bradshaw turned from the window to find a huddle of students in the open doorway. Among them were Oscar Daulton, Glen Reeves, and Sara Trout. They stared at him open-mouthed and aghast. He presumed they hadn't expected to see him at school, in Oglethorpe's office, after the newspaper's heavy hints of his guilt.

"The police took away some of his papers," said Mr. Reeves, glancing about the room.

The room did look as if it had been searched. The books on the shelf were askew, the cabinet drawers not fully closed. The desktop begged to be tidied, but Bradshaw fought his natural instinct to instill order.

Under the silent watchful eyes of the students, he continued with the task that had brought him here. He found in a cabinet drawer the syllabus, class notes, text book, and grade book for the class he was to assume for the final weeks of the term.

Under the students' still silent gaze, he began a slow and methodical search of Oglethorpe's things. It was such a violation, to poke about in a man's private desk, especially since that man couldn't possibly put a stop to it. In the back of the top desk drawer he found a small cardboard packet labeled *"Dr. Thompson's Kola Tablets for Improved Manhood."* He hastily shoved the packet back where he'd found it. Death, it occurred to him, was the end of a man's privacy, and he made a mental note to be watchful of leaving humiliating clues of his own private life. At the moment, he could think of nothing more embarrassing than castor oil in his medicine cabinet, but who knew what remedies he might someday need?

He continued his search, not knowing what he was looking for. He hoped something significant or meaningful would present itself. Of course, if there was some threatening letter from an anarchist, or from Henry, the police would have already confiscated it.

Though he tried to hide it, Bradshaw's entire body ached. His movements had no strength behind them. He felt bruised in places he didn't know he possessed. Even his hair hurt. The pain pressed an odd steadiness over Bradshaw's movements and, surprisingly, echoed pleasant memories of youth. He hadn't had sore muscles since his college days, and he wondered if he should start making use of the university's gymnasium.

"The police wanted to know if we'd ever heard you threaten Professor Oglethorpe," Reeves said at last. "We said you'd called him a pompous so-and-so under your breath, but you never mumbled anything about harming him." The students laughed nervously, but congenially.

"I must learn to mumble more quietly."

Reeves smiled, and Miss Trout said in surprise, "I think he's teasing us."

"Not Prof Bradshaw, he's always serious." This from Daulton, whose flushed face indicated he was pleased to be included in the small group.

"Maybe he's got more depth than we realized." Miss Trout's voice had turned dreamy. Bradshaw thought it wise to not look up. "They asked if you were a socialist or anarchist. And they wanted to know about your past, but we told them we didn't know anything about it except that you once lived in Boston and that you're a widower."

The words were like a vice on his heart. The police were asking questions about his past. He closed the final desk drawer then looked at the knot of students and found their curious faces surprisingly warm and kind.

"They wanted to know about your late wife's death, but we told them we didn't know and it was none of our business or theirs because you were a good and kind man and would never cause anyone a bit of harm." Miss Trout's expression turned protective as the others nodded emphatically.

Tears stung Bradshaw's eyes. He wanted to hug them all. "Thank you."

Reeves eyed the others, then said, "Besides, you couldn't have done it, we've figured it out."

He cleared his throat and got hold of his emotions. "Yes?"

"Well, it's what the inquest jury must have figured out, too. Since the power fluctuated while you were still giving an examination to Oscar here, then you couldn't have been down in the lab, moving the body and turning on the Machine. You're innocent."

Daulton pressed the hair from his eyes. "Good thing I'm lousy at exams. If I had finished sooner, you wouldn't have an alibi."

If you, Oscar Daulton, had finished your exam sooner, I would have been halfway home when the building lights sizzled, and it would have been some other poor soul who discovered Oglethorpe's body. But he didn't say so. Daulton had found a new confidence after his exam and the success of his exhibition project. That confidence was something fragile to nurture, not undermine.

Still, Bradshaw felt it prudent to explain the error of their logic. "You've missed one crucial point, Mr. Reeves. You're assuming I'm innocent because I have an alibi for the time the Machine was turned on. But I was alone in my office at the time the coroner says Oglethorpe actually died. I could have propped him in the cage, gone on to my class, then had an accomplice turn on the Machine while I was in another room with a witness."

The students stared at him in surprise. The idea of an accomplice was apparently new to them. They must not have read yesterday's article about Henry. They exchanged glances. What passed through their young minds, he could only guess. Poor Miss Trout turned a deathly pallor, white as a ghost or white as a sheet, either one would suffice.

Their voices rang as one. "But you didn't!"

Bradshaw's mouth twitched into a smile. "No, I didn't. But the police will be plotting out every possible scenario, and we must all strive to uncover the truth or someone innocent will hang. Possibly me."

Apparently, this was too much for Miss Trout.

"Catch her!" Reeves called, and she dropped in a dead faint into Daulton's arms.

Chapter Nineteen

"It'll take me ages to learn my way around Seattle, Mr. Bradshaw. Especially if the department stores dump me out in an entirely different place than I went in." They'd entered The Bon Marché through a main entrance on Second Avenue and emerged twenty minutes later from a small side exit onto a steep hill. He hadn't steered her this way to confuse her, but to avoid lingering too long on the street.

Accidents happened on the street. Lethal accidents. He'd beat the falls yesterday, but he didn't want to try his luck against a horse or a streetcar or a desk falling from a third floor window. He'd been trying to think deviously since last night and finding the world littered with potential death.

"Remember that if you're facing downhill and can see Elliott Bay, or at least ship masts, the avenue numbers get lower. Uphill, they get higher. And the streets follow a handy saying. There's an irreverent version, but the respectable version goes: Julius Caesar Made Seattle Under Protest."

"Julius Caesar? What are they teaching up at your university, Professor?"

"It's not meant to make sense, just be memorable. The first letter of each word matches the first letter of a street name, and the streets come by two's in the order of the saying. So Julius stands for Jefferson and James. Caesar for Cherry and Columbia, then Marion and Madison, Spring and Seneca, University and Union, Pike and Pine."

Missouri marched to the street corner and looked up at the sign mounted to the light pole, a slim hand on her straw hat to keep it from blowing away. "Pike, so Union or University is next, and behind us is Pine?"

She smiled, looking exactly what she was, a country girl straight off the train. And two blocks behind her, hat set at a jaunty angle, strode a city danger named Artimus Lowe.

"Go back inside."

"What?"

Bradshaw steered her back into The Bon, took out his wallet, and counted twenty dollars into the clean but worn palm of her gloved hand. "Buy yourself a complete suit of clothes." Twenty dollars ought to buy her a decent suit. He added another bill. "Shoes and gloves and a hat."

Her coppery eyes were huge as she stared at the bills. "Mr. Bradshaw, I can't take your money."

"Then consider it a long-term loan. You've seen how the city girls are dressed. You'll have to look like them to get a job. Go on now. I'd be no help, but there are plenty of shop girls who will help you make the right decisions. I've got some errands to run. I'll meet you back here in, say, one hour?"

He wouldn't let her argue. He saw her safely into the care of a well-dressed shop girl, and was on his way.

He hurried along Second Avenue, turned up University, and spied Lowe. Staying well back, he followed Lowe up to Fourth Avenue and the grounds of the old Territorial University. The main building with its four grand columns now housed the public library. North Hall, a boxy two-story building, temporarily housed the University of Washington's School of Law. Next year, the school was to be moved up to the new campus. Lowe vaulted up the short flight of steps and disappeared inside. A minute later, Bradshaw followed.

The narrow entry was empty and quiet but for the distant murmur of voices behind closed doors where classes were in session. Miss Peggy was on duty in the office. Bradshaw knew her. She'd worked for a short time on the main campus.

"Professor Bradshaw, how nice to see you." She had red curls and a round pretty face. He'd always wondered why she hadn't married. She must be near his own age.

"Nice to be seen, Miss Peggy."

She slid Lowe's academic file into his hand almost before he completed his request. She didn't question his motives, ask him about Oglethorpe, or give a hint of distrust. The world could use more Miss Peggy's.

Lowe's file proved interesting yet inconclusive. Lowe had classes here on Mondays and Wednesdays, and one class up on the main campus, Oglethorpe's Industrial Problems lecture, on Fridays. On Thursdays, the day Oglethorpe died, Lowe had no classes at all. So why had he been on the main campus? Why had Bradshaw seen him rush from the building?

Lowe's grades were impressive. He'd made the Dean's list every term for the past three years. Four letters of recommendation from his law professors were on file, praising his intelligence, his devotion, and his work ethic. Lowe had a bright future. Everything to hope for out of life—would he risk it all over an argument? A misguided ideal?

Bradshaw skimmed the application letter Lowe had submitted. He was from New York City, his father was an attorney by trade but supported by independent means. Old family money, he gathered. Lowe's current place of residence was the Cascade suite of the Lincoln, a nine-story first-class apartment hotel that catered to Seattle's elite.

"Can I do anything else for you, Professor?" Miss Peggy tilted her face up to his as he returned the file. For the first time in a very long time, Bradshaw actually paused to consider the personal implication of her question. He looked into her hazel eyes and saw interest. She really was very pretty. And unmarried. He could ask her to dinner. Not that he wanted to. But he could, and that's what he found unexpectedly interesting.

"No, but thank you."

He checked his pocket watch as he stepped out into the empty hall. He had forty-five minutes, if Lowe remained for the scheduled length of the lecture.

He left the law school and hurried over to Madison Avenue to the pristine white-bricked Lincoln Hotel. Inside the lobby, the polished floors gleamed and brass fixtures glowed. But he found no welcoming or policing presence, and no one in the office behind the front desk, which he entered as if he owned the place. He opened a few file drawers and quickly divined the numerical and alphabetical filing system. His pulse raced, but his mind was crystal clear and focused. Inside the Cascade suite file were a dozen bills for rent, receipts, and a few letters. He scanned them quickly, his eye catching such words as "late," "overdue," and "amount past limit." A carbon copy of a letter dated a few weeks past, addressed to a Mr. Lowe in New York and from the manager of the Lincoln, contained a summary of past and current debt. Bradshaw deftly folded the copy and slid into his suit pocket.

He was back out in the sunshine and noisy street before he had time to contemplate what he'd done. He quickly descended to Second Avenue, his limbs flooded with adrenaline.

As he neared The Bon, he felt a now familiar tingle at the back of his neck. His already heightened senses peaked. He slowed and turned, pretending to examine the display of shiny bicycles in a repair shop window as he studied the vague reflections of pedestrians passing behind him. Dark suits, light dresses, hats of all shapes floated by, but no figure moved to accost him.

He turned, hands in his pockets, and cast his gaze over the street as if considering which way to go. His examination touched on every face, the back of every head. He began walking again and had gone half a block when he felt a tug on his sleeve. In a split second, he calculated his safety—he was in public surrounded by a crowd of witnesses on foot and in buggies and taxis and the streetcar. He paused, took his hands from his pockets, and turned, ready to defend himself but not yet swinging.

"You walked right past me as if you didn't even know me!"

He blinked. He hadn't known her. In a slim, tailored blue walking suit and matching hat, Missouri Fremont was a new woman. A woman, not a girl. She laughed and turned around, holding her arms out to display her new attire. The new black button shoes upon her feet, he noted, had sensible heels and toes broad enough for a real foot to walk in comfort.

"Well?" She tilted her face up to his, like Miss Peggy had done. Only what he felt was so very different.

Missouri bubbled with joy and it was an effort to resist touching her glowing face, which began to fade with disappointment. She'd hoped, he realized, for something complimentary from him.

"I'd hire you myself, if I had a job to hire for."

Her glow returned. "Come with me." She took his arm and tugged, turning him completely round. "The girl who waited on me told me about a switchboard operator position at the Rainier Hotel where her sister works. It's on Sixth and Marion, so if I've got it straight, we must go uphill four blocks and over at least three until we reach the M's. You must tell me everything you know about telephones before we get there."

Even antisocial Bradshaw knew that the enormous Rainier Hotel-Apartment on the hill, with its ballrooms and restaurants and wide verandas, was all the rage for Seattle society. And it was but a short stroll from the Rainier to the Lincoln. Bradshaw didn't like the idea of Missouri working in a place so likely to be frequented by Lowe, but she looked so eager, and a job as a "hello girl" was a respectable position.

"Have you ever seen a switchboard?"

"Not up close. Back home, there was one in the post office, but the woman who ran it didn't like visitors. Sometimes, she'd leave the door open and you could see in. They're big and flat with lots of holes and wires and plugs."

"Hmm, yes. The big flat part is the upright panel, the holes have drop shutters connecting round apertures, and the plugged wires are jacks an operator inserts into apertures in order to connect a caller to a line." He spent the next several minutes as they marched, negotiating traffic and mud and paving projects, explaining the basic operation of a telephone switchboard. Missouri caught on quickly, grasping the concepts and terms with remarkable astuteness.

When they arrived, Bradshaw was encouraged by the sheer size of the hotel. The enormous handsome wooden structure had been erected in a record eighty days after the Great Fire of 1889. It took up an entire city block. There were so many people about, and so many entrances, it was possible that Missouri would find her way to and from work without meeting a love-smitten law student.

He saw her as far as the main entrance, then told her to go in alone. "I don't believe my presence or my reference would at the moment stand you in good stead."

She cocked her head considering this. "I suppose you're right. Will you wait for me?"

"Of course." She went in, and he found a comfortable chair on the wide covered verandah in sight of the main entrance. The city sprawled below him, Elliott Bay sparkled beyond, bustling with small steamers, large freighters, and sailing vessels. The grand Rainier radiated a holiday feel. Bradshaw didn't dare remove the letter from his pocket. He'd never stolen anything in his life. He felt giddy, ecstatic. Surprised.

Was this how Oglethorpe's killer felt? Was this what motivated his devious behavior, the secret thrill of deception? He analyzed the feeling. It was empowering. He had something he wasn't supposed to have because he'd been bold enough to simply take it. He hadn't followed the rules of polite society, he'd disregarded even the criminal code. He'd stolen, no one knew, and it was exciting.

But killing? What sort of person felt this thrill when killing? What sort of person felt no guilt or remorse? Or if the killer felt guilt but remained hidden, what did that tell him? That the killer felt justified. Someone believed his victim deserved to die. Why did this person feel Bradshaw deserved to die? Because he was a suspect? Because he was treading too near the truth? And what had he discovered so far? Nothing. Where had he been looking? At the university, in the lab, Snoqualmie Falls.

The minutes passed by slowly as Bradshaw pondered the psychology of Oglethorpe's murderer and reviewed the attempt on his own life where footsteps were his only clue.

He closed his eyes and began testing himself, listening to the footsteps of hotel visitors as they crossed the verandah. He found he could fairly easily discriminate between the steps of men and women, even young and old. Who had made those footsteps yesterday at Snoqualmie that had preceded his icy dunking? Light like a woman's, yet the sound had been solid somehow. Not the clunk of a wood heel but the tap of a leather sole on cement. A light running step. A young man's step.

Artimus Lowe was a young man with expensive leather-soled shoes. But he'd returned to Seattle hours before Bradshaw was pushed. Or had he? What was to stop him doubling back?

He now heard three distinctly different footsteps at once. A strong feminine tapping of what he guessed to be a heavyset woman, the scraping of sole grit of a somewhat lazy man, and the rapid patter of a child. He opened his eyes to verify his guesses and found he had two out of three correct. Coming toward him was Marion Oglethorpe on the arm of the gentleman relative who'd sat with her at the inquest.

Bradshaw stood as they approached, and then saw his error in the third set of footsteps. It wasn't a running child, it was Missouri, bounding from the hotel and past Mrs. Oglethorpe. "I got the position! I'm going to be a 'hello girl'!"

He put a steadying hand on her shoulder. "Miss Fremont, you can tell me all about it later." In appropriately subdued tones, he introduced her to Mrs. Oglethorpe, then Mrs. Oglethorpe introduced them to her escort, who turned out to be her physician Dr. Swenson.

"Dr. Swenson has so kindly helped me these past few days with all the arrangements. I don't know what I would have done without him."

The good doctor patted Mrs. Oglethorpe's hand where it lay tucked in his supporting arm.

"Everyone has been so kind and supportive. I haven't had to think of anything myself. Food keeps arriving at the door, and my dear friends, the Ladies of the Improvement Society, have organized a reception here, for tomorrow after the funeral."

Bradshaw nodded and murmured his agreement at the kindness being showed her, but he was remembering the three Improvement Society Ladies who'd looked at him with such fear and accusation yesterday up at Snoqualmie Falls. Those same women were caring for Mrs. Oglethorpe like devoted sisters. Had one of them made herself judge and jury and sentenced him over the raging falls? Could any of those stout women have produced the light tapping step he heard?

If one had, Mrs. Oglethorpe was oblivious to it. She stepped nearer to him. He could now see her eyes through her sheer black veil. "I don't believe a word those newspapers are saying about you, Professor. I know you didn't harm my husband. You will come to the funeral tomorrow?"

It was the last thing on earth he wanted to do. "If that's what you truly want, Mrs. Oglethorpe. I'll be there."

Chapter Twenty

"Dad!"

Bradshaw, in stockinged feet, the collars and cuffs of his best dress shirt not yet attached, ignored Justin's shout. He sat on the edge of his bed reading again through the letter he'd pilfered from Lowe's hotel file. The letter seemed to be about a different Artimus Lowe than the one on the Dean's list three years running. This Lowe was not winning the respect of anyone, least of all his landlord. The Lincoln Hotel-Apartments supplied its residents with not only luxurious rooms and suites, but all the other amenities of a fine hotel: maid service, fresh linens, restaurant or room service meals, and the services of a concierge. For the past year, Lowe had been late on rent nearly every month, and he'd charged a small fortune to his account. Intermittently, large checks had arrived from New York and been applied to the balance, but last month a letter from Lowe's father had arrived in lieu of a check, refusing to pay the bill recently submitted and any future bills.

"Dad!" It was Justin's sixth shout. Bradshaw tucked the letter away in his dresser and padded to the top of the stairs.

"Don't shout in the house, Justin. If you want me, come upstairs and find me."

Justin climbed the stairs until he stood directly below his father. "Hello," he said cheekily.

"Hello, young man. What may I do for you?"

"The telephone operator is on the line and says she remembers who called Uncle Henry last Thursday."

Bradshaw's stomach did a somersault, and his feet nearly followed as he slipped on the wooden stairs in his hurry to get down to the phone. He found the receiver dangling by its long braided cord.

"Hello? This is Professor Bradshaw."

"Good morning, Professor," said a very sweet voice, well articulated and slightly formal. "I was told you wanted to know about a call connected to your line last Thursday."

"Yes?"

"I was working last Thursday, and I placed two calls from the same party. One to a Henry Pratt, at your number, and immediately following, a call to a Mr. Lowe at the Lincoln Hotel."

"Mr. Artimus Lowe?"

"Yes, that was the name. I don't listen in to the conversations, Professor, it's a strict rule. But I do remember those calls, not because there was anything special about them at the time, but when it was reported that afternoon that Professor Oglethorpe had been killed, I remembered the name."

"You mean Oglethorpe? Professor Oglethorpe placed the calls? I understood it was a woman who called Henry Pratt."

"Oh, it was sir. It was Mrs. Oglethorpe."

"Mrs. O—I see. Thank you." Bradshaw replaced the receiver and realized Justin was staring up at him.

"Can I help you?"

"You didn't use the rail."

"I what?"

"The rail, coming down the stairs. You always use it, and you yell at me to use it, but just now you ran down the stairs and didn't use it and you almost fell."

Bradshaw looked at the stairs. He didn't even remember descending them. He climbed them now, as Justin watched. At the top, he turned around. Nothing. Not a twinge. He took a few steps, his hands by his sides, then tripped—in the light-footed sense of the word—down to the hall.

"Does that mean I don't have to hold on either?"

"No. Stairs are potentially dangerous, especially the way you throw yourself down them."

"Aah, shucks."

"Shucks are for corn, son." But he was smiling as he climbed up to finish dressing.

◇◇◇

Despite the tragedy, work in the Oglethorpe's yard had progressed over the past few days. The planks had been replaced with handsome stones that formed a walk to the front porch, then split off to encircle the house. The trees were now in the ground and grass seed sprinkled on the smoothed soil. But death marred the house. Black cloth draped the doorway, and the blinds were pulled against the sunshine. The maid Sheila opened the door to Professor Bradshaw and greeted him warmly. She told him that Mrs. Oglethorpe wouldn't be home until after the reception at the Rainier. A fact he already knew. He'd just come from the funeral, having endured not only the hateful stares of shocked mourners, but a eulogy so false it hurt to listen. Oglethorpe in death had metamorphosed into a saintly educator, a loving husband, and a generous father.

Sheila gave him a kind smile, revealing her unfortunately crooked teeth. He was invited in to wait. He followed her to the back of the house and the bright, modern kitchen. The coal stove and icebox were of the newest line, the linoleum a rich pattern of black and white squares. He glanced at the clock as she filled the kettle under the running tap. A half hour, and he'd be gone, long before Mrs. Oglethorpe returned.

"How's your young son, Professor?"

"Fine, thank you."

"I'm sorry I wasn't able to help your Mrs. Prouty this spring."

"Oh? Well, that's alright." He recalled Mrs. Prouty's recent bout of deep cleaning, blankets aired, drawers emptied, walls washed.

"Since I started working for the Oglethorpe's, I haven't had time to pick up the odd job. I miss the extra pocket money, but there's only so many hours in the day."

"Yes," he said. He wasn't used to small talk with maids. How would he even begin to question her?

She shut off the tap and sighed.

"I'm glad you've come today, Professor. Things have been so upsetting around here, I get gloomy when I'm alone too long, and to be totally honest, a little scared. Murder! Poor Mrs. Oglethorpe. Have a seat, Professor, and I'll get your tea. The police came yesterday, if you can imagine the gall. Come to ask me questions the day before Professor Oglethorpe is laid to rest."

Bradshaw sat at the rough oak table.

Sheila set the full kettle on the already hot stove. She removed the pressing iron from its nook in the stove, tapped a licked finger to the bottom, and at the sound of the sizzle, returned to her ironing board and began pressing a white apron. She said with an audible sigh, "I really shouldn't say on today of all days, Professor, but I won't miss the shouting."

Unsure of what she meant and hoping she would elaborate, Bradshaw ventured, "Arguing is never pleasant to overhear."

"No, it wasn't arguing, it was shouting, and all on Professor Oglethorpe's part. The Mrs. is such a strong woman when he isn't, or I should say wasn't around. I don't know why she took it. And treated him like a king, kept his house in perfect order, his meals always the way he liked them, and did all his typing to boot, not that he appreciated it. Seemed to think it was his due."

"She typed for him?" Oglethorpe had never mentioned that, taking full credit for the letter-perfect papers he was always submitting to scientific journals.

"Typing, filing, grading, you name it. She could have taught most of his classes herself, she knew his work so well."

"Helping and understanding are not exactly the same. Typing up notes and grading papers from an answer sheet—"

"Oh, no sir, Professor Bradshaw. Mrs. Oglethorpe often corrected the Professor's students' exams herself. Fifteen years they'd been married, and fifteen years she's been listening and learning. To tell the truth, she's handier around the house than he ever was. He might know about the things in books, but he wouldn't lift a finger to wire a lamp. It was Mrs. Oglethorpe who put in that fancy electric chandelier, 'electrolier' I think it's called, in the dining room."

Bradshaw imagined Marion Oglethorpe, that sturdily built woman, standing on a ladder, wiring the electric lamp. But then his mental image jumped to the engineering lab, and he saw as if watching a flickering moving picture, Mrs. Oglethorpe drag her husband into the Faraday cage and position him on the chair so that his arm reached outside the metal bars. He shook his head. "Sheila, did you tell this to the police?"

"They wanted to know did she know anything about electricity, and where was she when Mr. Oglethorpe was being killed. Can you imagine? They as good asked me if she did it? Well, I told them that Mrs. Oglethorpe knew as much as most people do about electricity, which wasn't a lie, she knows that and more, and that she loved her husband, which wasn't a lie either, though she had every reason to hate him."

"And did you tell them where she was?"

"I didn't know where she was."

"The children were in school?"

"Olive and Wes were in school, I was here, and Mrs. Oglethorpe was out, she didn't tell me where, and before you ask like the police did, yes, she often went out without telling me where she was going. I didn't tell the police exactly when she left, I was vague about that and did it drive them mad! I knew exactly what time it was, one o'clock on the very nose because she slammed the door as the hall clock struck and I thought to myself now I could put my feet up for a spell and read a bit of my new novel. It's all about a poor girl in England who meets a prince, only she doesn't know he's a prince."

Sheila could be as talkative as her mistress, once she got started. Professor Bradshaw feared the conversation was about to become mired in her dime novel, and he carefully steered it back to Marion Oglethorpe.

"Isn't it unusual for a mistress not to tell her maid where she's going or when she'd return? Did she have an appointment?"

"I worked for another woman who did the same thing, though for different reasons. She was just mean. Didn't trust anybody and was always thinking the worst of people. Mrs. Oglethorpe, I think she went out to feel a bit of independence, if you know what I mean. It was bad enough she had to answer to him all the time, she didn't need to answer to me."

Artimus Lowe had been so right. How easy it was to get information from a household employee. And how alarming. A maid or a housekeeper was privy to all the private and intimate aspects of one's life, seeing and hearing as much, perhaps even more, than a spouse. Yet a servant hadn't the same loyalty as a spouse. A servant hadn't the same fierce protective instincts born of love to stifle the desire to gossip. Sheila barely knew him, had simply worked in his home a few times with his housekeeper, and here she was, talking to him like an old friend.

He tried to think what sort of things Mrs. Prouty knew about him, his eating habits, the nightmares that woke him in a drenching sweat. But he couldn't imagine Mrs. Prouty sitting in his kitchen and revealing such intimacies to a guest. Telling Artimus Lowe about Missouri Fremont was one thing—Bradshaw's soaked sheets were quite another.

"She's a good woman, and I wouldn't like to see her come to harm. It sounds real mean of me, but I'm glad he's gone. He was so awful about the baby on the way."

He felt a twinge of dread. "Professor Oglethorpe wasn't—pleased?"

Sheila shook her head, her mouth firmly closed. She seemed to suddenly realize she had been imparting extremely personal information about her employer. Her face infused with color. A tickle of awareness crept up Bradshaw's neck. He turned to find Marion Oglethorpe standing in the doorway, in black cape and veiled hat. She came forward swiftly, lifting her veil to reveal a face as pale as her maid's was red. Bradshaw stood with a greeting that was ignored.

"No, Professor Bradshaw, my husband was not pleased about having another child." She reprimanded the maid with a silent glare, then her brave manner crumbled. He hastily pulled out a chair and she sank into it while Sheila busied herself pouring a cup of tea.

"To be carrying a child," Marion said in a voice near a whisper, "and to be told it's not wanted...."

Bradshaw covered Marion's cold hands with his own. "I'm so sorry. I do understand, more than you know. My wife," he began, then tried to censor himself, but it was too late. There in her eyes he saw the need to hear, to share and be truly understood. "The entire time my wife carried my son, she didn't want him. I did, desperately. I felt so helpless. If I could have carried the child for her, I would have."

Tears filled Marion's eyes and a smile trembled at her lips. "You, Professor? With child? Wouldn't you be a sight?"

"Not a pretty one," he agreed, also smiling, and they both took much needed sips of their tea.

"You're widowed, too, aren't you?"

"Yes."

Her eyes still pleaded for help.

"It really will get better." He didn't say how long it would take. He didn't explain that he had only started getting better when her husband died, that his death had brought him new life. "Mrs. Oglethorpe, if ever you want to talk—"

She wiped the dampness from her eyes with a handkerchief procured from her sleeve. "Oh, dear Professor Bradshaw. You think I did it? Well, you can rest easy. I was at the doctor's most of the afternoon, and the police have already confirmed my alibi. Is it called an alibi when it's the truth? It doesn't matter. There were times I wished Wesley were dead, but I could never kill him. You might find this hard to believe, but I loved him. Oh, I know, my Wesley seemed so unlovable, but that was the face he showed the world. He was terrified of failure. The higher his chin went, the more arrogant his boasting, the more afraid he was. Only rarely, once in fact, did he tell me how he truly felt. But he didn't have to tell me. I knew. From the moment I met him, I knew. Sometimes he nearly broke my heart because I couldn't help him, he wouldn't let me help him. He could get so very mean in his proud ways. I admit there were times I was sorry I married him. There were times I wanted to beat some sense into him. But I never could hit him. I certainly couldn't kill him. It would be like killing a defenseless child."

This should not have been a revelation to Bradshaw. As a man often judged by his own misunderstood behavior, he should have stopped to consider what drove Oglethorpe to be so domineering. But he hadn't. Like everyone else, he'd assumed Professor Wesley T. Oglethorpe was a selfish bastard and looked no further.

"Do you know of anyone who would kill him? Or anyone who might be so angry with him that an argument might get out of hand? Someone who might think killing him would help you?"

"Why would anyone think murdering my husband would help me? Oh, there are hundreds who had reason to argue with him, but I can't think of anyone who would actually want to kill him. I would think you'd have to hate someone passionately to do something so violent, and he never let anyone get close enough to truly know him, except me."

Another thing he never knew he had in common with Oglethorpe. Only Bradshaw didn't even have a wife to confide in. "Did your husband know anyone who might be an anarchist?"

"You're thinking of McKinley's visit. I wish I knew of such a person. That would give Wesley's death more of a noble meaning. He would have liked that. He wouldn't like to know that someone killed him because he was so nasty."

Bradshaw had a final question he hated to ask.

"On the day your husband died, why did you telephone Henry Pratt and Artimus Lowe?"

She exhaled wearily. "Because I learned from the morning paper—you know about the oil investment? How Wesley found others to buy the shares? The stock was all in Wesley's name, but that didn't make it right."

"Didn't make what right?"

"How he cheated them. He gave both men, technically, what the stock was worth when they demanded it back, even though he knew the price was about shoot up. What Wesley did was legal. But it wasn't moral. I thought they had a right to know."

Chapter Twenty-one

Bradshaw stood before his house, hesitating as he had five nights ago with a sense of comfort that this humble dwelling was home. Change had entered his life, and he sensed much more change was yet to come. Yet there was a relief to it, in a way. He had never shared with another soul Rachel's hatred of her pregnancy. Sharing that hadn't hurt as he'd expected it too, but it had comforted Mrs. Oglethorpe to know she was not alone. What sort of a life had she been living under her domineering husband? What sort of emotional sacrifices had she endured for the sake of the children? For the sake of the man she loved despite his unwillingness to be helped?

Bradshaw's gaze drifted up to the second floor of his house, to Henry Pratt's room now occupied by Henry's innocent and disturbingly compelling niece. He turned his thoughts from Missouri to Henry, as Mrs. Prouty had described him behaving the morning he left, waving the newspaper about like a man conducting an orchestra. A joyful action, conducting. An action suggesting excitement, eagerness. Good fortune.

"Is this a new habit of yours, Professor!" Mrs. Prouty shouted from the front door, pulling him from his deep reverie. "Standing out there, staring at your own house?"

Bradshaw opened the gate and strode up the path to the porch. "Do we still have last Thursday morning's newspaper, Mrs. Prouty?"

"It's in the compost heap, if that's what you mean."

Bradshaw retreated down the porch steps and headed around to the back of the house. He heard Mrs. Prouty's heavy steps behind him.

She had a system for composting. The refuse was divided into three chicken-wire bins, all in different stages of decay. The first held a ripe mixture of kitchen scraps and old torn-up newspapers, the second a more decayed and steaming pile, the third a nearly black and earthy mixture she shoveled lavishly each spring and fall onto the vegetable garden along the back fence. Thursday's paper would be, of course, in the first and foulest bin.

Mrs. Prouty behaved as if Bradshaw had gone mad as he poked through the mess with a stick and pulled out ragged, limp bits of newspaper. When he continued his search, despite her protests, she at last offered helpful advice.

"Look for paper rolled up tight. I didn't have the patience to unroll it after Henry'd been using it like, what's it called, a baton."

He found it then, covered in coffee grounds and sodden with rain and heaven knows what else. Carefully, he unrolled the pages, spreading them out over the grass. He peeled one page from the next until he found the headline he sought.

```
Cascade Oil Strikes Black Gold – Again.

    Last December holders of Cascade Oil Stock
found the value of their shares increase
tenfold when drilling struck rich supplies
far sooner than expected. Last week, in order
to allow more investors an opportunity to
participate, the stock split three-for-one.
Within hours the value of the new shares
had risen to exceed the old, making lucky
shareholders thousands of dollars.
```

No wonder Henry had been waving the paper about with such glee. He thought he'd struck it rich.

Bradshaw tore the article from the page and tossed the rest of the paper back in the compost heap. He followed Mrs. Prouty into the kitchen where, after flattening the article on a dish towel to dry, he washed the grime and grounds from his hands.

"Mrs. Prouty, on Sunday, when Artimus Lowe dropped by, what exactly did he say, do you remember?"

Mrs. Prouty actually blushed. "Oh, he's a handsome young man, that one. And quite the talker. I don't know what he sees in Henry's niece, but he seemed quite taken with her."

"But did Mr. Lowe ask about Missouri when he first arrived? Or did he ask to see Henry?"

"Now you mention it, he did ask first for Henry Pratt. I was a bit surprised, a dandified young man like that wanting to see Henry. Most of Henry's friends I wouldn't let onto the front porch. Mr. Lowe said it was on some matter of urgent business. When I told him Henry had up and gone to Alaska, he smiled, and what a nice smile that lad has. He said maybe I could tell him about the young woman in the front yard, and it was then I realized he'd seen Henry's niece and had taken a fancy to her."

"Hmm. Indeed he has, but trust your initial impression of Artimus Lowe, Mrs. Prouty. If he comes around again, shoo him off the porch with your broom like you would any other of Henry's visitors."

Mrs. Prouty gleamed happily. "I've got a new broom, Professor. The bristles are sharp enough to sting."

◇◇◇

Midnight found Bradshaw wandering the streets of Seattle in search of anarchists. He'd spent the first part of the evening arranging and rearranging facts and getting nowhere. Never before had he been faced with so much discordant information, positive it fit together in some logical way but unable to believe any scenario he could piece together. The dry facts fit—Marion, Henry, and Artimus Lowe all had motive. Henry and Lowe had opportunity. They all could have had help. But in order to believe any or all of them had killed Oglethorpe and attempted to kill Bradshaw, he'd have to dismiss his assessment of their natures. And he couldn't. He refused to believe he'd learned nothing over these past eight years. He might have lived in isolation, but he hadn't been blind. He'd watched. He'd practiced reading people, their voices and expressions and gestures. To ensure he never again made the mistake he'd made with Rachel, he'd learned to be observant and trust his instincts. To do otherwise courted disaster.

His instincts told him he was missing something vital. McKinley's visit remained a nagging fact with no leads. His visit was like an odd electrical component with no visible purpose. What was he missing? Where should he even begin?

With anarchists. A single phone call to the UW's Professor of Political and Social Science told him where to look.

And so midnight found him in the yellow glow of street lamps, hat low over his eyes, hands deep in his pockets as he mimicked other lone men. He passed by bars where music and laughter flooded into the streets, he heard the scuff of his own footsteps as he passed laundries and druggists and shoe shops all locked up tight. The air was damp and carried various scents to him, metallic oils, sweet perfumes, the fishiness of the nearby tide flats, even the warm yeastiness of a bread company baking loaves for early morning delivery.

On Third Avenue, between the darkened windows of Mme. Melbourne, Clairvoyant and Queen City Leather Goods, he spotted the sign. FREEDOM. Black block letters against a red background, the simple word was the only thing visible behind the glass in the dark curtained window. Chinks of light escaped the edge. There was no welcome sign on the door.

Now what? Did he march inside and start making accusations? Demand answers?

"Out late for a school night, aren't you Professor?"

The voice had come from the shadows of the recessed doorway of the clairvoyant. It caused him dismay but not alarm. He stepped closer to better see Detective O'Brien.

"Good evening, Bradshaw."

"Have you found a connection? Between Oglethorpe's death and McKinley's visit?"

"I've been watching the anarchists for years. A hobby of mine. It's ironic, don't you think, that the very freedom they say doesn't exist in this country allows them to meet in secret and plot the overthrow of the government?'

"Is there a connection? Has McKinley been warned?"

"It's hard to protect a man who refuses to be adequately guarded, but yes, a message has been sent. You've got your own troubles. It wouldn't be smart for you to be seen here. I wouldn't go inside."

"Like you said, it's a free country."

"It's not me who would make something of it. It's the citizens of this fair city. They want this crime solved, they want to feel safe again—well, safe as long as they don't venture into the Tenderloin district. They've marked you as their man and they'd love to have some sinister motive to add to their belief in your guilt. They've already decided your friend Pratt was your accomplice."

"Yes, I've seen the papers."

"There's more than what's in the papers. They've formed a committee and they want an arrest."

"They? Who are they?"

"Upstanding citizens. You know the type. You've been doing your own investigating, Professor. What have you learned?"

Bradshaw looked out at the empty street. What had he learned? What could he say definitively? How could he point at Henry, at Marion when he didn't believe them capable of murder? Even Lowe, whom he disliked, who was clever and opportunistic and in debt, whose tread was light and swift—even he seemed incapable of murder. To save himself, to save his son, was he willing to sacrifice a potentially innocent person? Point a finger without absolute proof?

"Haven't *you* got any other suspects?"

O'Brien laughed. "You're as good at redirection as me, Professor. I will say that I've interviewed a few of the same people you have."

"Then why ask me for my opinion?"

"They might have been more forthcoming with you. Most people don't like to open up to a police detective."

"I can't imagine why."

O'Brien suddenly grabbed his arm and pulled him deeper into the dark recess. Bradshaw saw the familiar figure on the sidewalk, hat lower over the eyes than usual. The sound of his light footsteps, the expensive leather upon the gritty pavement, sent a chill up Bradshaw's spine.

At the freedom sign, Artimus Lowe rapped three times on the door, paused, then gave another single knock. When the door swung in, he disappeared inside.

Bradshaw searched O'Brien's gaze. The guarded eyes told him nothing.

"Go home, Professor. If you think of anything you'd like to share, come see me."

Chapter Twenty-two

Before breakfast the next morning, Bradshaw went down to police headquarters, but not to share any information with O'Brien. He'd been summoned by a messenger boy.

In the cellar of the old City Hall, smelling of damp and mold and unwashed bodies, Bradshaw found Artimus Lowe behind the iron bars of the same jail cell he had occupied himself a few nights ago. Lowe looked none the worse for his experience. His blue cashmere suit and tan vest were of the latest fashion and untouched by jail grime, and his handsome young face unlined by the trauma.

"Thank God, you've come!" Lowe approached the bars but didn't grasp them.

"Good morning, Mr. Lowe."

"Please, Professor. You must help me. Tell them I'm innocent and get me out of here."

Bradshaw waited until the jailor retreated to a chair near the cellar door and snapped open the morning paper. "Mr. Lowe, I don't understand why you've asked for my help. Surely, you realize what you need is a lawyer."

"I don't need representation, I need someone to tell them I'm innocent."

"I don't know that you're innocent."

Lowe gripped the bars, so upset he forgot to avoid the filth. "Help me, Professor."

"Did you push me in the river?"

"What?"

"You were seen returning to the falls," Bradshaw lied, watching Lowe carefully.

"What are you talking about? The falls? I was arrested last night for Oglethorpe's murder."

Was he a good actor or was his puzzlement genuine? "You must have given them good reason to arrest you."

"I didn't do it, you know I didn't. Oglethorpe was dead when I got there, I swear to God."

"You were there?"

"You know I was. And I would have told the police about Henry Pratt by now if it weren't for his niece."

Bradshaw's legs suddenly grew weak, but the only chair in sight was beneath the jailor. He joined Lowe, gripping the filthy cold bars for support.

"Mr. Lowe, I think you'd better start at the beginning."

"Can't we do this later, when I'm out of here?"

"Are you an anarchist?"

"No! I attended a few meetings to learn how they think, but I'm no anarchist, you must believe me."

"What, another thesis paper?"

"The law school is holding a mock trial of the Haymarket anarchists next week. It counts as half our final grade. I'm defending August Spies, the leader who was convicted and sentenced to hang, so of course I needed to learn all I could about anarchy. But the police say I used that as an excuse to attend the meetings. They think I was plotting to kill the President, for God's sake!"

"You left the Administration Building at half past three. I saw you. And you admitted to me a moment ago that you'd seen Oglethorpe."

"But he was dead when I got there. In that birdcage. Just sitting there. It was horrible. I panicked and left. I didn't see any reason why I should get involved. I have enough on my plate with school and my parents refusing me money—I didn't need the complication."

"Why were you visiting Oglethorpe? Was it you who sent that woman with the note summoning him to the lab?"

"You mean you really don't know?"

"Tell me."

"Your friend Henry Pratt sent that note. He had some cousin of your housekeeper's deliver it. You didn't seem to know last Sunday on the train, but I felt sure Henry would have sent you word by now or your housekeeper would have learned from her cousin. You really don't know?"

Bradshaw dropped his head. A tremendous weight pushed on his shoulders. His bones had turned to lead. Henry Pratt. Mrs. Prouty's cousin.

"I can't believe it," he said hoarsely. "Henry—"

"No, Professor. Henry Pratt didn't kill Oglethorpe. At least, I don't think he did. Listen, I'd better start at the beginning. Last year, Pratt and I both invested in Oglethorpe's oil stock."

"Yes, I know about that, and that you learned from Mrs. Oglethorpe that you'd been cheated."

"I was in a bind, Professor—my father—well, that's a whole other story. My parents are annoyed enough that I chose to go to school in a frontier town, they'd never forgive me for losing so much on a bad investment. My father's never lost a cent. Now I'm up to my neck in debt. I thought I could convince Oglethorpe to pay up, to do the right thing. He was damned conniving about the whole deal."

"So what did you do when Mrs. Oglethorpe telephoned?"

"I was in a lecture when she telephoned and didn't get the message until after noon. I wanted to confront Oglethorpe, but I figured there was strength in numbers, so I went to find Pratt to go up to the university with me."

"What time was it, when you went in search of Henry?"

"A little after two."

"And did you find him?"

"He was at the bar across from Cooper and Levy Outfitters, whistling Dixie, and buying drinks on the house. He took me aside and told me how he'd gotten his fair share. He knew

Oglethorpe would never leave class at his summons, so he typed up a note using your name and the Electric Machine as the bait. Once he'd gotten Oglethorpe alone in the lab, he threatened him, said he'd to go to the police with how Oglethorpe had cheated us, he'd tell the newspapers, anyone who would listen, and of course the scandal would have ruined the Professor, so he paid up. It wasn't for the full amount Henry would have made, but it was enough to satisfy him. Enough to buy a full Klondike outfit."

"And Oglethorpe was alive when Henry left?"

"I assume so. Henry told me to get up the university and get my share, too. I went, but I didn't get my money because Oglethorpe was dead, as I told you, in that cage. Oglethorpe lied to me, yes. He stole from me, yes again. And I was bitterly angry—but I didn't kill him."

Bradshaw rubbed his temples. "You said you knew on Thursday that Henry was going to Alaska."

"Yes."

"Then why did you come to my house on Sunday and tell my housekeeper you wanted to speak to him?"

Lowe actually looked sheepish. "Because I knew he wasn't there. I came by to talk to you about the whole mess. You were at the end of your street when I got there, with your son, and I was going to run to catch up, but then I saw in your front garden the most intriguing girl—"

"Yes, yes," Bradshaw interrupted, not wanting to hear again the young man turn into a lovesick fool. "I take it your infatuation made you question the correct course of action."

"I was dying to know who she was. I went round back to talk to your housekeeper. Once I learned Henry was her uncle, I didn't dare risk getting him involved. How could I do something so horrible to such an exquisite—"

"The truth, Mr. Lowe, is always the best course of action. Your delay has only made things worse."

"But you'll get me out of here."

"I have no proof of your innocence, only your word. I do believe you, but do you really want me to go upstairs and tell them that they have the wrong man? That they should be sending men to Alaska to search for Henry Pratt? They certainly won't set you free simply because I tell them you're innocent."

"We don't know it was Henry. I don't think he would have sent me up to the university to see Oglethorpe if he had just killed him."

"Frankly, Mr. Lowe, I don't know what to think. But I won't betray my friend unless I know for certain he has done wrong."

"But that means I must stay here."

"That's up to you."

"But Professor, if I tell them about Henry, and he is innocent, even if he's guilty, then his niece will hate me forever."

"So you asked me here to tell the police for you? So that Missouri would hate me instead of you?"

"It's different for you. You're her uncle's friend, you're her self-appointed guardian. She would understand if you—"

"She would not understand, and she would not forgive."

Lowe looked as if he wanted to argue further, to say that it couldn't possibly matter what a lovely young creature like Missouri thought of a dour old man like Professor Bradshaw. The words weren't spoken, but Bradshaw understood what he saw in the young man's eyes.

Anger, or perhaps jealousy, gave him the energy to stand tall, shoulders back.

"I can't help you, Mr. Lowe. Not now. If I learn more, I will let you know. In the meantime, tell the police whatever you like. If I were you, I'd get a good lawyer."

◇◇◇

When the back door of the mansion opened, Bradshaw didn't know what to say. He'd known from Mrs. Prouty's prattling that her cousin worked for the Peterson family on First Hill, but in all these years Mrs. Prouty had never mentioned, that he recalled, her cousin's name. The Japanese boy who answered the door stared at him silently.

"If it's the ice man, tell him to leave an extra block," came a replica of Mrs. Prouty's voice from the depths of the kitchen.

"Not ice, Mrs. Gertie. A stranger."

"I'm Professor Bradshaw, young man. Would you ask Mrs. Gertie if I might have a word?"

Mrs. Gertie appeared behind the boy, younger than Mrs. Prouty by a few years, not quite as stout, but equally stern. She positively glowered at Bradshaw.

"Yes, what is it?"

"I'm Professor Bradshaw."

"I know it."

"Could I speak to you for a few minutes?"

"Haven't got the time, I've a house to run." She began to shut the door.

"It's about Henry…" the door continued to swing, "but if you're busy, I'll just ask the police."

The door reversed direction, and a moment later, Bradshaw found himself seated in a tiny servants' parlor, a cup of strong tea balanced on his knee. He'd been given tea by Miss Trout, tea by the Oglethorpe's maid, and now tea by Mrs. Prouty's cousin. Was it this way for Detective O'Brien, he wondered? Tea with each interview? A man would have to possess healthy kidneys and a strong bladder to get through a full day of questioning suspects.

"You didn't say nothing to Gladys, did you, Professor?"

"Gladys? Oh, Mrs. Prouty. No, no. Your cousin has no idea that you are involved with Henry."

"We're not *involved*, Professor," she said with a contradictory blush. "I've merely stepped out a few times with him, gone to the moving pictures like, had lunch at the park. He's a nice fellow. He makes me laugh," and as she spoke, she miraculously looked younger, prettier, and quite capable of laughing. Henry, he thought, you old dog. "Gladys would never understand. She's that set against him."

"Tell me about last Thursday."

"I didn't do nothing wrong, mind you. And neither did Henry. It's not our fault some murderer chose that very afternoon to kill Professor Oglethorpe. I couldn't see no sense in going to the police when we had nothing to do with it."

"But you're afraid that the police might learn that you delivered the note."

"Of course I'm afraid. It doesn't look good, now, does it? Innocent people have hung before, Professor."

"You might not be able to keep it from the police for long, Mrs. Gertie. Artimus Lowe is in jail, and he knows about you and Henry. He's not said anything yet, but he still might if he finds it's the only way to prove his own innocence. Why don't you tell me what happened, and I'll see what I can do to help you if the need arises."

The story unraveled with much elaboration and a prodigious use of adjectives, but Bradshaw listened attentively and weeded through to the facts. Henry had enticed Mrs. Gertie Nolan—the "Mrs." was strictly an honorary title, she'd never been married—to type a note for him on her employer's typewriting machine. He then convinced her to go up with him to the university and present the note to Professor Oglethorpe.

"I could see his side a things, couldn't I? He's been wanting to go back up to Alaska for the longest time, and he could've done if he'd gotten his fair gains from that investment."

Henry Pratt and Gertie Nolan had taken the streetcar to the university and parted company outside Oglethorpe's classroom door. She went in with the note, and Henry took off down the stairs to await Oglethorpe in the lab. Gertie wasn't sure about the time, some minutes after one o'clock she guessed. After delivering the note, she left the Administration Building, followed the path toward 14th Avenue, and waited as planned on the corner.

"Henry came a running about ten minutes later, flapping a bit of paper in the air like a flag. He was happy, he was. It was a letter he had, telling that Professor's bank to pay Henry a tidy sum. Said he was going back to mine his claim on the Klondike and make a million dollars. We rode back to town as far as 7th and Pike, then he got off and I came back here."

"Could you have mistaken happiness for anxiety? Did he seem flustered, upset?"

She got to her feet. "Shame on you, Professor. He's your friend more than mine. How dare you think he would harm a hair on Professor Oglethorpe's head, no matter how much he despised the man. I should've trusted my instincts and not let you in the door, but you threatened me with the police, and—"

"Did Henry mention if he'd seen anyone else in the lab? Or nearby?"

"No." She turned her back on him and led him through the kitchen and to the door.

"Yes."

Bradshaw, already on the porch, turned. "Yes?"

"I forgot until you asked. Henry did say he almost knocked down some poor kid as he ran out the door."

"A child? Running?"

"No, no, Henry was the one running, happy with his money. He meant a student, of course."

"Did he describe this student?"

"No." She slammed the door.

Ten minutes later, Bradshaw entered the telegraph office and dictated a message to be sent twice. Once, in care of the general post office in Skagway, where Henry's ship would dock, and again in care of the general post office in the Klondike, in case the fool didn't check for messages before heading to his claim.

To Henry Pratt: Wire Home At Once. Explain Your Departure. Wire for Return Fare if Needed. Missouri Is Here. B. Bradshaw.

Chapter Twenty-three

Professor Bradshaw drew upon the blackboard a rectangular box representing a piece of electrical equipment. He indicated the external power supply to be a standard electric wall outlet and damaged insulation causing an unwanted connection to the housing of the equipment.

"Mr. Myers, please come to the board and draw for me as best you can, a graduate of this college who has been called to fix that piece of equipment."

Mr. Meyers, a thin, pimple-faced youth, came forward and drew a stick figure fellow with a cocked hat and big shoes, but no other clothing. Chuckles resounded from the other five students. There should have been six, but Graves had informed Bradshaw this morning that a parent had pulled his son out of school and threatened action if Bradshaw remained on staff. Graves had defended Bradshaw and refused to be pressured. He'd ensured Bradshaw that his job was safe, but how long would it be if other students were forced to leave?

"Sir?"

Bradshaw brought his thoughts back to Mr. Meyers. No part of the stick man touched the drawing of the electrical equipment.

"Tell us, please. What is this fine graduate doing?"

"He is examining the situation from a distance to be sure no hazard exists."

"Very good. A graduate who values his life and digits."

"Oh, yes, sir." Mr. Meyers wriggled his fingers to the delight of his classmates.

"And does a hazard exist?"

"Uh—" Mr. Meyers examined the diagram. "I don't believe it would be safe to touch the equipment or housing."

"Why not?"

"Because then I, or I mean he," he pointed to his stick man, "might become part of the circuit."

"You can tell that by the diagram because I've shown damaged insulation. In the real world, Mr. Meyers, would you be able to see a hazard as you approached?"

"No, sir. Being a well-trained engineer in the electrical field I always assume a faulty piece of equipment poses a hazard until I safely prove otherwise."

"Exactly so. Very good. What, then, would be your first move?"

"I'd find a way to safely disconnect the power supply."

Mr. Meyers stood waiting for further instruction. But Bradshaw's mind had diverted from imaginary dilemmas to a very real one, and the diagram before him on the blackboard teased him with a promise of solution.

If Oglethorpe were represented by that stick figure, and the rest of the circuit showed the path and faults necessary for him to be electrocuted, then who and what caused that fault?

Bradshaw had gone over the details of the Electric Machine a hundred times. He'd mentally assembled dozens of devices to produce a lethal shock using components in the engineering lab, but none of them fit the known facts. The solution, the electrical solution, eluded him.

But what if he considered the human solution? The human path of connections? The energy of anger or passion or hatred that led to Oglethorpe's death? Maybe the answer could be found not in how it was done, but who did it and why.

Bradshaw examined the drawing on the board. Who was represented by the power supply? Who in the human equation provided the most substantial and constant motive? Henry? No,

Henry wasn't a man with constant, streaming anger. Henry didn't let his emotions fester, he let them out whenever he felt like it. He was impulsive and explosive, but then instantly forgiving. Henry was like a capacitor.

"Mr. Meyers, please add a capacitor to the circuit, in parallel with the power supply, before the fault."

Mr. Meyers drew in the requested component, and Bradshaw examined the diagram once more. He pressed aside his instinct to see the diagram as an electric circuit and focused instead on human energy.

Anger over being swindled about the oil stock would have infuriated Henry. Bradshaw knew for a fact he'd confronted Oglethorpe, had extracted money from him. Had he also, in a surge of released anger, killed Oglethorpe? But the set-up had been elaborate and time-consuming. It had been planned by somebody very carefully, not hastily improvised in a matter of minutes. Had Henry then been unwittingly used? Had his explosive anger somehow instigated or triggered the real killer's plan?

And where did Lowe fit in? Artimus Lowe was neither a man of impulse nor revenge, although he could be passionate. His actions were always self-serving. What was the electrical equivalent of a leech?

Mr. Myers scratched his head. "Professor, what are we making?"

Bradshaw didn't reply. He was devising a human circuit, not an electrical one. Was anarchy involved here? Had McKinley been the intended victim? Had the lethal current been diverted from its intended path to Oglethorpe by accident? Was the anarchist the power source, the source of lethal anger? But what was the connection between Henry Pratt and Artimus Lowe and some unknown anarchist? Or was Lowe the anarchist? Had he tricked Henry into to typing and delivering that note? And what would be the point? It kept coming back to that note! Why involve Oglethorpe at all if McKinley were the target? And why the attempt on Bradshaw's life?

He got up and paced to the blackboard, rubbing his chin thoughtfully. Why did both Henry and young Lowe pay a visit to Oglethorpe on Thursday? Because they learned they'd been cheated. Because of the article in the newspaper. Because Marion Oglethorpe had telephoned to tell them to read the article in the newspaper.

Bradshaw stood very still, barely breathing.

Mrs. Marion Oglethorpe had lived with and loved Wesley Oglethorpe for fifteen years. She spent those years devotedly caring for him, bearing his children, aiding him with his career, providing a comfortable home for him—all the while he belittled and berated her. Did it anger him that she understood electrical theory? Did he both use and resent her intelligence? When he learned of her recent pregnancy, he cruelly told her the child was not wanted. After a lifetime of build-up, his rejection of her child must have been too much. She had the electrical know-how. She saw a way out and she took it, cleverly adding unnecessary elements to the circuit to confuse and distract the police. McKinley's future visit was a false path already in place. A telephone call to Henry sent him racing off to the university with a misleading note. Another call sent Artimus Lowe, who by mere chance had been studying anarchists, also to call on Oglethorpe.

Bradshaw turned slowly. His young students eyed him curiously.

"We've done enough for today," he said to their amazement. "Class dismissed."

◇◇◇

Bradshaw sat in the plush waiting parlor on a wide velvet chair designed for the proportions of expectant mothers. The seat was rather high, and it struck his backside more quickly than expected on the way down, but made it all the more easy to rise when the nurse, a saintly-looking girl in starched gray, told him Doctor Swenson was now available.

He was led through a polished door to a book-lined office where Marion Oglethorpe's doctor rose from behind a mahogany desk. Bradshaw again noticed the familial similarity between

Swenson and Mrs. Oglethorpe, the big-boned frame, the fair hair, the plump face.

"Professor Bradshaw, how may I help you?"

"Doctor Swenson," Bradshaw said, shaking the offered hand. "I'm not sure. Are you a relation of Mrs. Oglethorpe's? An uncle or brother?"

The doctor indicated a chair, and Bradshaw sat, hat in hand. Doctor Swenson eased into the plush chair behind his desk. The springs gave a small protesting squeak.

"No, no. I'm no relation. I'm merely attending Mrs. Oglethorpe more closely than usual because of her delicate condition. I want to be sure she doesn't become too upset."

"Yes, I see. You must admit there's a similarity between you. You could pass for a relative."

"We're both Swedish, Professor. Our families have been friends for many years. They immigrated to this country together forty years ago. I've known Marion since she was a child. I assure you, we are not related. Was that what you came to ask me?"

"I came to ask you what the police already have. Did Marion Oglethorpe visit your office last Thursday, and if so, what time was she here?"

"She was here for several hours of observation. She'd had some pain and I wanted to be sure labor wasn't coming on prematurely."

"Wouldn't it be more usual for you to go to her home, especially under such circumstances?"

"She was downtown when the pain came on. It was closer for her to come here. But if you'll pardon my rudeness, I don't see how this is any business of yours, Professor."

"Professor Oglethorpe's death has touched many lives, Doctor. A young man is in jail because last Thursday he received a telephone call from Mrs. Oglethorpe. I am simply trying to understand the connection. Was Mrs. Oglethorpe upset? Nervous? Did she seem anxious?"

"She was deeply concerned about the fate of her child. She was anxious and distraught until the pain matured into a simple case of indigestion."

"Nothing else seemed to be distracting her?"

Doctor Swenson smiled politely, shaking his head. He was not about to volunteer anything about his patient, and if he were lying about Marion Oglethorpe's whereabouts last Thursday, he certainly wasn't going to admit it to Bradshaw.

"I'm sorry I troubled you." As Bradshaw rose to leave, his gaze skimmed the bookshelves with their many medical tomes. Amidst the books nearest the doctor's desk, skewed away from visitors, were two small picture frames. An impulse made Bradshaw cock his head and lean forward to catch a glimpse of the photographs behind the glass. Towheaded children—a boy and a girl—smiled out at him. Bradshaw, dropped his hat on the desk, boldly strode to the photographs and took them up, one in each hand. There was no mistaking them. The girl was Olive Oglethorpe, the boy, Wesley Jr. The photos were recent.

Bradshaw quickly surveyed the rest of the shelves.

"I delivered those two," the doctor said hastily. "I like to keep photographs of the children I brought into the world."

"But you have no others, Doctor. Only the Oglethorpe children. And these aren't birth photographs. These were taken recently."

"Marion gave them to me," he said defensively, then seemed to be searching for more of an explanation. But he wasn't very good at impromptu excuses. He wiped his mouth with his hand.

Bradshaw examined the photographs closely. The children resembled their mother. Neither had their father's concave bones, sharp features, or dark coloring. They had wide-set eyes and fair brows and noses like....

Bradshaw's gaze went from the children's slightly upturned noses to the doctor's upturned nose, and then his fearful eyes.

"You've been having a love affair with Marion Oglethorpe for many years. Olive is eight years old."

"No, it wasn't that way."

"Then how was it?"

Bradshaw, still clutching the framed children, returned to his chair, sinking upon it automatically, his mind and body heavy with his discovery.

Dr. Swenson tried to explain. "Professor Oglethorpe was unable to father children. Marion wanted them. Desperately. She came to me several years after her marriage and I gave her a thorough examination. After finding nothing wrong with her, I suggested she tell her husband he should be examined, but he refused. He was very angry that she even suggested the problem could possibly be him."

Bradshaw recalled the packet he'd found in Oglethorpe's desk, the pills that promised to restore a man's lost virility. He could easily imagine Oglethorpe, so proud, so vain, exploding at the suggestion that his manhood was flawed but secretly seeking a solution. And since deep beneath that vanity insecurity festered, as Marion had revealed to Bradshaw, confronting him must have been one of the most difficult things she'd ever done.

"I failed to understand why," Doctor Swenson went on, "but Marion loved her husband. She wanted to find a way to have children without letting her husband know he'd failed her. I was appalled when she asked me if I would provide what her husband could not. But I was really her only option. As you noticed, we look enough alike that a child born to her would not be questioned. It would be thought simply that her children favored her and not their father, which they do. For a year, I refused. Marion grew depressed. Despondent. With each child I delivered to my other patients, the more I ached for poor Marion. The joy I saw, the pure love on the faces of the new mothers, that was something I knew, that without my help, Marion would never have." Swenson glanced briefly at Bradshaw. "She told her husband that it was the new tonic I had given her that had enabled her to get pregnant. He believed her."

A tonic, indeed. Bradshaw took a deep breath and let it out slowly. He could understand Swenson's kind-hearted desire to give to Marion the children she so desperately wanted. But the actual carrying out of the deception? There would have been clandestine meetings, and the intimacy of procreation, the progression of the pregnancy knowing the child was his, and the delivery—how had this man delivered his own precious children into the world? Heard those first cries, felt the fragile warm weight in his arms, and then handed them over to another man? A man he neither liked nor respected. Not once, but twice. And a third on the way.

"Professor Oglethorpe found out after they moved into the new house that she was pregnant again, and this time he knew it couldn't be his. He hadn't slept in her bed in months. She hadn't told me. I never would have agreed to try for another child if I'd known."

Bradshaw shook his head, stunned and appalled. No wonder life in the new mansion had been so full of shouting. "Did she tell him the truth? That he hadn't fathered any of their children?"

"No. Even in the face of his brutal anger she wanted to protect him. She tried to convince him he'd merely forgotten a night of intimacy. She'd plied him with drink a few times, trying to lure him to her bed in order to validate her pregnancy. It hadn't worked. That's what saddens her the most. He died believing she'd been unfaithful."

"She had been unfaithful."

"She didn't see it that way. Her heart never strayed."

Swenson clasped his pale hands tightly together. Bradshaw had never seen anyone actually wring his hands before. Swenson's eyes were alive with troubled emotion.

Bradshaw said, "You must have hated him."

"Hate is a very strong word. I certainly hated that Marion loved a man who didn't deserve her."

Bradshaw set the photographs of Olive and Wes on the desk, facing the doctor. "What about the children. Do you love them?"

Unshed tears filled the doctor's eyes as he looked at his two children.

"Do you love them so much you found a way to be a part of their lives? Were you afraid your new child would grow up unloved in Oglethorpe's house?"

Dr. Swenson touched the photographs tenderly with his fingertips. "The funny thing is, I thought about his death. I'd imagine some accident, a runaway horse, double pneumonia. Some sudden and rapid fatality, always brought on by his own stupid arrogance. I imagined myself comforting Marion, and her turning to me, realizing it was me she loved all along. But now that it's happened—well, it's not like the fantasy. Marion's mourning, the children's sorrow, and my guilt. Oh, I didn't do it, Professor. I had nothing to do with Oglethorpe's death in that electric contraption, but I as good as wished it upon him. Marion is turning to me, but as a friend only. She's changed toward me. I think maybe she'd had thoughts, too, about what life would be like without her troublesome husband. Now his death has killed any chance of a future for us. I think she means to honor her late husband by denying me the chance to be a father to my own children."

◇◇◇

Bradshaw stood on the steps of Doctor Swenson's office building unsure what to do next. Traffic was heavy, and the policeman at the intersection was busy keeping the vehicles untangled. A shiny new motorcar was causing a stir with its sputtering progress, spooking horses and drawing pedestrians dangerously into the street for a closer view.

The bustling activity only made Bradshaw more unsure of what to believe. Marion Oglethorpe had borne children of her doctor, and Oglethorpe had recently learned that the child she now carried wasn't his own. Had maternal protective instinct driven her to kill her own husband? Had she arranged it all, persuading Henry to lure Oglethorpe to the lab where she hid, waiting to end her misery with a shocking jolt?

Or was it Dr. Swenson, who had foolishly given Marion Oglethorpe the children she so wanted, that had waited in the lab and done the deed once Henry had gone? Did Swenson kill Oglethorpe at Marion's request, or of his own accord so that he could become father to his own children and husband to Marion? Had Swenson been up at Snoqualmie and pushed Bradshaw into the river?

And what of Artimus Lowe? Who so neatly tied all elements together, from anarchy to revenge, and even the lightness of his footstep?

And then there was Henry. Henry, by all accounts, was responsible for that note that summoned Oglethorpe down to the lab and hence his death. Henry had been in the lab near the time of Oglethorpe's death, for he'd extracted that payment from Oglethorpe sometime after the note was delivered. And Henry had fled on the first boat out of Seattle to Alaska.

Who was the guilty party? They all had motive, all had opportunity, and all had ability. The possible circuit paths to Oglethorpe's death formed and reformed in Bradshaw's mind, components rearranging themselves, wires crossing and short-ing at so fast a rate for a moment Bradshaw thought he could hear the crackle of the circuit, smell the sharp odor of burning wire and metal.

Not until the policeman directing traffic shouted "Fire!" did Bradshaw understand that what he heard and smelled was real.

Traffic became a snarled mess as the policeman abandoned his intersection. Drivers jumped from their vehicles and the motorman and passengers leaped from the streetcar to join the pedestrians running down the hill in the direction of the black smoke. Bradshaw was among them. He'd not been living in Seattle in '89 when the Great Fire consumed thirty blocks of the city's very heart, but many of those around him had, and he saw the panic on their faces.

Seattle had been rebuilt upon more solid foundations above the burned-out rubble, and the buildings now were mostly of stone and brick. But there was enough fuel even in the newer, safer construction to fan flames of fear.

Fire alarms rang and shouts for help were heeded.

Unfortunately, it was the Seattle Tent Factory that burned, a three-story wooden building, formerly a hotel, built hastily after the Great Fire to be a temporary structure and never replaced.

Huge flames leaped from broken windows, and choking black smoke billowed into the sky. The fire department had not yet arrived, but the creamery across the street had thrown open its doors and tossed out every vessel and container available. A bucket brigade had been formed, and Bradshaw joined in, passing the sloshing tin pails and rope-handled tubs along the line.

"Is everybody out?" Bradshaw shouted above the din to the denim-clad man beside him.

"Everybody but the boss. Started in his office."

The buckets were passed so rapidly, talking became impossible. The heat of the fire added to the heat of hard work. Bradshaw soon soaked through his shirt and was glad for the cooling water that sloshed upon his hands and feet.

The fire wagon arrived with bells clanging, and within seconds their blasting hoses attacked the flames. The makeshift buckets were set down with relief.

Bradshaw stood back with the others to rest and watch and hope. The denim-clad worker was still beside him.

"Did you say you worked there?"

"On the production line, folding and packaging."

"Any idea what started it? You said it began in the manager's office?"

"It was probably an accident, but we'll get the blame."

"You mean the employees?"

"We've been trying to bring in the union and get fair wages. The boss said he'd fire every one of us. They'll blame it on the organizers, you wait and see. Organizers or some dang fool anarchist."

◇◇◇

The setting sun illuminated the charred and dripping remains with an amber glow. The firemen had gone, as had the helpful crowd, but Bradshaw, wet and soot-covered, sat wearily upon the hydrant, wondering what the world was coming to. Unhappy marriages, underpaid workers, zealous anarchists. Behind every face lurked secrets, even behind his own. He didn't know whom to trust or where to turn. Only in his son's precious face did he believe pure goodness and innocence existed—and he felt unworthy, just now, to behold it. So he sat.

Detective O'Brien, looking impossibly clean in his brown suit and Roosevelt hat, emerged from the black depths of the destroyed building, mildly surprised to see Bradshaw.

"You knew Gordon Purdy?"

"Who? Oh, you must mean the manager. No, I didn't know him. He had family, I suppose?"

"Wife, three grown children, one grandchild."

What a night this would be for them. "I hope it was an accident."

"Why?"

"Intentional death is so much harder to live with. The anger and bitterness never go away."

"You're speaking from personal experience."

Bradshaw looked O'Brien square in the eye. "You know I am."

O'Brien shrugged. "We had to investigate every possibility." He extended a hand. Bradshaw accepted it. It wasn't an apology O'Brien was offering, but a truce of sorts. An acknowledgment of Bradshaw's having withstood both the inquest and the uncovering of his personal past with dignity.

"Artimus Lowe is only part of the puzzle, you know, Bradshaw. That committee I told you about wanted an arrest. I gave them one. We're still investigating Oglethorpe's death. We may have to question you about Henry Pratt."

Bradshaw nodded, waiting for questions to follow. But O'Brien was content for now with giving him the warning. He had another, more immediate concern.

"There's something I want you to see."

Together, they walked through the gutted first floor of the tent factory. The smell was sharp, like having one's head stuck up a chimney. In what must have been the manager's office, O'Brien crouched before the charred remains of an inner wall. He pointed to a blackened bell that had been part of a signal system. The connecting wires were completely melted.

"I don't know why, but when I first saw that, the hair on the back of my neck stood up. The fire chief believes that's where the fire started."

Bradshaw stared at O'Brien for a moment. He wondered if everyone went about this world, getting insight and clues to important events in the form of tingles and goose bumps.

O'Brien pointed again at the wires. "What do you think?"

Bradshaw hunkered down and examined the burnt wires. "There was a short in the wiring. You see this here? It takes much higher temperature than normal fire to melt copper this way. There must have been an electrical arc, but the battery power needed for a bell system shouldn't have caused all this, not unless there was something highly combustible nearby. Did anyone mention if the lights went off before the fire?"

"Yes, as a matter-of-fact. The conveyor system, too."

"That would explain it then, there must be a transformer for the bells wired into building's electrical system. Plenty of power there for a short to cause damage."

O'Brien rubbed his neck. "The production foreman said the bell hadn't been working properly since yesterday. Would you be able to tell if something was deliberately tampered with?"

"Not now. All the evidence will have been destroyed by the flames," he said, but the hair on the back of his neck was now standing up, too.

"This is the second death in Seattle this week connected to union organizers."

"Second?"

"Charles Jackson was the first. He was found dead in his hotel bath of apparent heart failure. The coroner suspects electrical shock may have been involved, but he can't prove it. There's no evidence on the body, but an electrician was summoned the evening before Jackson's body was found because of trouble with the lights."

"Was this Jackson a very large individual?"

"Professor, you continue to amaze me. Yes, an extremely large individual. You didn't know him, by chance?"

"No. I saw the body at the funeral home."

"He'd been traveling under a false name, but a man of that size doesn't easily blend into a crowd. He worked for the Pinkerton Detective Agency and was here to dredge up business. A half-dozen factory owners whose employees have been trying to unionize had already signed on when Jackson was found, dead in the tub. It took six men to haul him out."

"The workers here, in this factory, were talking to the union, I was told. Are the deaths connected, Jackson's and Purdy's?"

"I believe so, but I have no proof. All I have are questions."

Bradshaw stood, his muscles and joints complaining all the way. He followed O'Brien out of the damaged building to the evening air.

"I'd like to use you as an expert witness, Bradshaw. For this case, and for Jackson's, if Cline can come up with enough evidence. Would you be interested?"

Bradshaw took a deep breath, but he still smelled and tasted soot. "Is this typical in police work, Detective? Unending questions, unearthing people's personal traumas, and deaths with no solutions?"

O'Brien pushed up the brim of his hat and chuckled. "That's only on the bad days. On the good days what gets me out of bed in the morning are the unending questions, unearthing people's traumas, and the challenge of investigating deaths with no obvious solutions."

Bradshaw shook his head. "I believe I know what you mean. Call on me, Detective. If you feel I can be of service. I'm going home now. Before I fall down."

Chapter Twenty-four

"Mr. Bradshaw?"

"Hmm?" Bradshaw sat heavy in his easy chair staring into the hearth fire, too tired to drag himself upstairs to bed. Too tired to think. He'd bathed and changed, but the scent of soot had seeped into his pores.

Missouri sat opposite him, studying a book about the operation of the telephone and switchboard at her new place of employment. He expected a question about crossed lines or faulty switches.

"The police questioned me today."

He took a weary breath. She was going to ask about Henry, and Gertie, and that note.

"They came to the hotel and Mr. Padelford had to relieve me at my post. They asked about Uncle Henry and you and Artimus Lowe. They even asked about anarchy."

"What did you tell them?"

"That I don't know anything. What could I know? I only arrived in Seattle on Saturday. And all I know about anarchy I read in the newspapers."

She gripped her book so tightly her knuckles shone white.

"You were correct to tell the police whatever they asked."

"It's not what I told them that concerns me, it's what they told me. And it has nothing to do with Professor Oglethorpe or any sort of assassination plot."

"They told you about that possibility?"

"I figured it out for myself from the sort of questions they were asking."

"So what is concerning you?" He looked into her amber eyes, made deep and simmering by the firelight.

She chewed her lip. "They said that your wife committed suicide."

He tore his gaze away.

"I think they were trying to unnerve me. They seemed to believe I knew much more about you than I was telling. I told them that although I'd been corresponding to my uncle for years, and that I knew my uncle shared my letters with you, I truly knew very little about you. I certainly know nothing of your politics, or my uncle's, nor especially Artimus Lowe's. I think they're trying to put together some conspiracy that involves all of you but can't make it fit together."

He got to his feet, eyes on the hall, the stairs, escape from this conversation. "I don't know what happened to Professor Oglethorpe, Missouri. I can't promise you that your uncle isn't involved. I'm fairly sure Mr. Lowe will eventually be released from jail. I only know for certain that I am not guilty of murder or anarchy. You are safe here in my home."

He took a few steps.

"But is it true? About your wife?"

He stopped, his back toward her. "Yes."

"What happened?"

"It's none of your business, Miss Fremont."

"It explains so much about you. You might feel better if you talk about it."

Bradshaw spun around and found she'd risen, clutching her book. Her eyes were full of pity. Something inside him exploded. He ripped the book from her hands and threw it across the room with such force it splayed against the wall with a crash before dropping to the floor. He stormed from the parlor, taking the stairs two at a time. Only his son sleeping in the next room prevented him from slamming his door until the house shook.

◇◇◇

When he came downstairs a half hour later, he found Missouri in the kitchen, washing out tea things at the sink, back erect, her pale bare neck vulnerable.

She turned toward him, and he thrust a yellowed news clipping out to her. She dried her hands and, without meeting his eyes, took the clipping from him. She brought it nearer to the gas lamp by the sink and began to read.

Her shoulders folded inward. He couldn't see her face, and he was glad of it, but he continued to watch her read, hearing each word as if the clipping were being read aloud.

YOUNG WIFE SWALLOWS CARBOLIC ACID

BOSTON, November 12 – A dinner party hosted by Mr. and Mrs. Bradshaw in their home ended tragically last night. According to Mrs. Bostwick, who attended the affair, Mrs. Rachel Bradshaw had grown distraught by the bitter silence of her husband. In the midst of the meal, she rose from the table, strode to the sideboard, and filled her wineglass with carbolic acid. She toasted her husband with the words, "If silence is what you want, I give you an eternity of it" then swallowed the acid before any of her astonished guests could stop her. Immediately, she cried for help, but within seconds she could no longer speak and though the doctor was quickly summoned, Mrs. Bradshaw could not be saved. She was twenty-six years old. She leaves her husband and an infant son of four months.

◇◇◇

Bradshaw sat alone in the dark parlor. Only the muted light from the kitchen and the dying embers softened the darkness. He heard Missouri enter and move toward the lamp.

"No," he said. "No light."

She stood gently silhouetted. Her voice was rough from her tears. "Uncle Henry never told me."

"I swore him to secrecy."

"You aren't to blame."

He didn't reply. He often felt he was to blame.

"Was she unkind to you?"

He laughed, and the sound was bitter and hollow. "Unkind? She hated me."

Missouri stepped softly on the carpet and knelt at Bradshaw's feet.

"Tell me."

After a moment's hesitation, he did. There in the darkness, as the little mantel clock ticked away the night, he began to speak of things he never spoke of. Slowly at first, hesitantly, but as the memories came flooding back so did the words. He told her everything. He told her about the hectic courtship to Rachel Sutherland in Boston. He told her of the wedding plans, the hopes and dreams they'd shared. He'd been young, unobservant, oblivious to what should have been obvious signs of Rachel's true nature. He'd not questioned why such a beautiful and wealthy young woman was willing to settle for a poor, newly graduated engineer and teacher. She could have chosen any man, he'd thought, and so he'd been flattered when she chose him.

Immediately after the wedding, she'd revealed her true self. She had refused to move to Seattle, although that had been their plan. Everything he wanted, everything they'd planned, she suddenly despised. When she discovered her pregnancy, she was furious. For nine months, Bradshaw had cowed to her every whim and mood, terrified that her violent temper would endanger the child she carried. When at last his son was born, he'd wept with relief and joy. Rachel had thrust the child away and refused to have anything to do with him. Bradshaw had taken over the care of his son, feeding him Mellin's Infant Food, bathing and changing him. His parents hired a nursemaid to help him, but Bradshaw only left Justin in her care when he had no other choice, when he had to work. His son became his entire life.

"At dinner, that night, she kept saying things, talking about the future, about the boy, as if she were a devout mother and we were such a happy family. I—I couldn't stand it. I was growing ill listening to her lies. She had lied to me from the very beginning. She only married me because she thought I would be easy to manipulate. Because other men were smart enough to see her for what she was. I finally could take no more. I told her to keep quiet. Before all our guests I told her to just keep quiet! And that's when she did it. She must have planned it. She must have egged me on until she knew I could stand no more." He pressed his temples. "She must have put that bottle there before the meal was served. My God, it didn't belong on the sideboard, but hidden away with the cleaning supplies in the kitchen! She must have planned—" He put his fists to his eyes and rubbed as if trying to rub away the vision of that night.

"It was horrible. I don't think she knew how horrible it would be. I don't think she knew it would really kill her. Her parents told me the next day of her past attempts. She had cut herself in front of them. She'd climbed on bridge railings. She'd even taken poison. Not out of depression or melancholy. It was selfishness. Always to get attention and sympathy and her own way. And they'd never told me. I was never warned."

After his wife's death, he'd gone a little mad. He'd moved with baby Justin into his old bedroom in his parents' home. He'd done nothing except care for the boy. He didn't read, he barely slept, he ate only enough to stay alive. He couldn't see from one minute to the next. He'd once had his whole life planned, and then suddenly he didn't know what he would be doing in five minutes.

And then he'd seen the calendar on his bedroom wall. Balancing Justin in his arm, he'd picked up a pencil, found the day's date and wrote "FEED JUSTIN." In the next day's space he wrote "TAKE JUSTIN TO PARK." And in the next "BUY JUSTIN NEW CLOTHES." His mind began to clear. The neat boxes of the calendar were so easy to see, so easy to understand. Life was no longer a huge blur but a series of neatly ordered boxes. He began to plan. He wrote in another space "APPLY UNIVERSITY WASH.," and then "SELL HOUSE." This last he stared at a moment before erasing and rewriting "VISIT ATTORNEY." Yes. That was the first step in selling a house, especially since his was still encumbered. Justin had begun to grow heavy in his arms, so he set him gently in his cradle then took the calendar from the wall, went to the writing desk and spent the next hour putting his life in little white boxes with his neat, engineer's printing.

He'd been keeping his life in order in that same way ever since.

Missouri, still kneeling at his feet, reached up and slipped her hand into his. Her skin was warm, her hand light. "I had noticed you put some rather obvious things on your calendar."

"Obvious?"

"Yes, like on Sundays, 'attend Mass' and 'read newspaper.' Would you forget to do those things if they weren't written down?"

"No, I wouldn't forget. I just feel better when I have it all down."

"You never leave any day blank?"

"No."

"Have you ever?"

"No."

"Not once in eight years?"

"No. Never a blank day."

"Tell me what you did next, after you began to fill in the calendar."

"There were no openings at the university. The engineering department hadn't yet been established. I moved out here anyway and worked for a year as a lineman for Seattle Electric."

"And eventually became a teacher."

"Yes. And, well, nothing much has happened since. I've kept busy raising my son and teaching." He looked into Missouri's dark, simmering eyes. "I'm sorry about your book."

A crooked smile touched her mouth. "It was very dry reading."

"Oh? I find the telephone fascinating."

He was relieved it was over. He'd told her, they need never speak of it again. His life with Rachel had become like a photograph too often inspected and he could see nothing anymore but the grains, the tiny pieces. He was unable to feel anything but concern for his son.

"Justin must never know. You do understand that, don't you?"

"Yes, of course. Of course. There are some things a child should never be told."

He searched her eyes. "Thank you," he whispered.

She moved closer, pressing her body against his legs to grasp both his hands. She was warm and soft, her soul visible in her eyes, open and tender. He hadn't been this close to anyone since the early days of his marriage. He hadn't been looked at with such warm affection by anyone other than his mother, ever.

She spoke softly. "I know I haven't known him long, but I do love your little boy. There's something very precious—"

He didn't recall lifting his hand, but he found he was stroking her face, his fingertips skimming her warm skin along her cheek. Her mouth was open slightly, but she was no longer speaking. Her eyes had widened and were looking at him in wonder. Her breath quickened, he was aware of it, and she was pressing yet closer, but he had no thoughts, only overwhelming desire that seemed on the verge of drowning him.

His fingertips continued on toward her lips, and he felt her breath, warm, moist—and alarm struck him like a physical blow. He pressed her away and sprang to his feet, nearly toppling her.

She stood facing him, a hand on her cheek where he'd touched her, her mouth still open, her eyes—confused? Alarmed?

"I'm sorry. I don't know what—it was all the talking, and you said—" *You said you loved my son, and I saw in your enchanting eyes that you meant it, and my God, I love you.* "I'm sorry." He turned, heart racing, and fled to his room.

Chapter Twenty-five

Golden sun slanted through the sheer curtains into Bradshaw's bedroom, mingling with the fresh spring air and birdsong wafting in through the open window. He lay in bed, hands behind his head on the pillow, watching the leaves of the birch tree shiver. He'd slept deeply most of the night, dreaming only as dawn approached of crackling sparks, waves of smoke, a mouth warm and drowning sweet, pulling him over the edge of a waterfall.

That's when he woke.

That's when he knew.

The truth had come to him, slipping under the edges of sleep, and he wondered if he had known all along.

A moment of self-examination told him no. All he'd lived and learned since Oglethorpe's death had brought him here to this knowledge. His chest felt heavy. He didn't relish what he must face today.

Not any of it.

He bathed and dressed and joined his household at the kitchen table for a breakfast of thick crisp bacon and brown-sugar-sweetened oatmeal. Missouri had cooked, and it was she who served him, placing the fragrant food before him then taking her own seat. He avoided catching her eye, but he watched her. He couldn't help himself.

A tinge of color on her cheeks might have been from standing over the hot stove. But why did the color linger? And what had she done to her hair? It was puffed a bit, the short ends curled. As he looked, she tucked a curl—self-consciously—around her ear. He tore his gaze away.

Mrs. Prouty placed the morning newspaper beside his plate. She'd folded it to highlight a headline that read: *Man Defies Falls!* A black-and-white photograph of Snoqualmie Falls, taken from the trail below, revealed the black outline of a figure in a crouched position at the brink holding a round object aloft. Bradshaw's eye swiftly caught details: *Unknown daredevil, wheels reported stolen at Fall City, Dittmar baffled.* He turned the article face down and picked up his fork. Mrs. Prouty expected the full story. But not now. Not in front of Justin.

The boy was trying to balance what Mrs. Prouty called a "rasher" on the tip of his nose.

"Bacon goes in the mouth, not on the nose."

"Yes, sir."

Missouri held her bacon as if about to join Justin's antics and she flashed Bradshaw a mischievous grin he was too slow to escape. His heart gave a little leap. Did he imagine he saw a flickering question in her eyes? Did she look away so quickly on purpose?

He lifted his own rasher, and balanced it easily on the tip of his nose.

Justin's delighted laughter was his reward. "Dad, you're a lot more fun than you used to be."

"Senility." He removed the bacon.

"Nonsense," Missouri countered. "It's spring fever. Gets us all eventually. Uncle Henry got it first."

Was she giving him an excuse for his behavior last night? Would he be forgiven as easy as that? He felt her watching him but couldn't bring himself to look.

Justin tapped his bacon on his plate. "Uncle Henry has *gold* fever."

"True," Missouri agreed, "but gold fever in the spring is the worst. I've got a bit of it myself. Or maybe I should call it school fever. I'm itching to explore the women's dorm up on the university campus."

Mrs. Prouty, standing at the sink, straightened up. Bradshaw froze.

Justin's young voice asked, "Why?"

"Because I'm going to live there when I go to the university."

They were all silent. Mrs. Prouty remained motionless at the sink.

Justin was the only one to voice his concern. "But you live here."

"I'll live on campus once school starts in the fall. If I pass my exams that is. I've got a lot of studying to do."

"Can't you live here like dad does and ride a bike to school?"

"I have my job at the hotel, remember. I can't be spending all my time going back and forth. No, I've given it some thought and I'd like to live on campus like a real co-ed. Don't you want to live on campus when you go to university?"

Bradshaw's appetite had fled. He'd done this. He'd frightened her from the safety of his home.

"I'm always going to live here with Dad and Mrs. Prouty," Justin said, with all the certainty of youth.

Missouri feigned surprise. "Always?"

"Uh-huh."

"What about when you get married?"

"My wife can live here too. She can help Mrs. Prouty."

Justin chewed happily, seeming content with his vision of life at his childhood home, his wife scrubbing pots with Mrs. Prouty. Bradshaw wondered if their domestic arrangement had given him too narrow a view of women.

"Dad, when will Uncle Henry get to Alaska?"

Bradshaw cleared his throat and stirred his congealing cereal. "Another few days yet."

"Can I send him a letter?"

"I'm sure Henry would be happy to hear from you. But remember what it was like when he went a few years ago? The mail can be very slow and is often lost."

"I could write him every day, and then if some get lost, he'll still get the others. Will you do other fun stuff I can tell him about?"

Missouri tousled Justin's hair, and the boy beamed. "How about we all write him letters, you, me, your father, and Mrs. Prouty. We'll bombard him with letters."

Mrs. Prouty grunted, and moved again for the first time since Missouri's announcement. "Me? I ain't got a blessed thing to say to Henry Pratt. What would I put in a letter?"

"You could write about things you do during the day," Justin innocently supplied. "You could tell him about making bread, and about the moving picture you saw on Saturday with your cousin. He'd like to hear about that."

Mrs. Prouty mumbled something about giving it some thought, then turned the faucet on full bore and became consumed in the washing up.

"Dad, you have to write Uncle Henry about the moving picture they made at your school. Remember he wanted to see if he was in it? Was he in it? Did you see it yet?"

"Someone made a moving picture at the university?"

Bradshaw kept his eyes on his breakfast. He could hear curiosity in Missouri's voice, he knew she was smiling. He did not need to look to know. "Henry was on campus the day the senior students had their camera set up. He danced a jig and made a general fool of himself. The students loved it, but they didn't include it in the picture they showed us."

Justin snorted. "Aww, that's no fair. What did they put in?"

"A lot of very boring stuff, like shots of stuffy old professors gesturing at blackboards, a tour of the campus and laboratories—" The hair on the back of Bradshaw's neck stood on end.

"Dad?"

"Huh?"

"You stopped talking." Justin giggled, and Bradshaw realized he had. He had also stood up.

"I've got to go." He kissed the top of Justin's head, nodded in Missouri's direction, and when he passed Mrs. Prouty on his way to the door, he said, "Pardon me," and tipped his hat to her as if she were a total stranger.

◇◇◇

The dreadful images flickered against the plaster wall of the walk-in utility closet. Bradshaw, sweating slightly from the effort of learning unaided how to feed the eighteen millimeter film around the series of internal spools in the wooden cabinet of the Kinetoscope, waited impatiently for his own hideous image to vanish. And yet—he recognized how much he had changed since the film was made. He knew his face no longer drooped in that resigned manner. His step, his movements, now had energy and life.

Professor Hill was next, curly-headed and youthful, looking cheerful as usual. And then there was Oglethorpe. Professor Oglethorpe, tall and arrogant, his pompous stance making the shallow curve of his bones appear all the more concave. On the plaster wall, Oglethorpe was strangely animated, returned to a ghostly sort of life. Bradshaw wished that image could speak. What would he have to say about the mystery of his death? If someone else had died, would Oglethorpe have solved it by now? With his brilliant mind for theories, where would he have looked for evidence?

"The trouble with you, Bradshaw," Oglethorpe had once said to him, "is that you can't see past the end of your nose."

There was truth to that, Bradshaw knew. He liked the visible, the concrete. He knew who had killed Oglethorpe, now he needed to know how. He needed proof.

He went over the clues again. The ink flakes in Oglethorpe's hair and clothes and on the back of McKinley's chair. The angled burn mark in Oglethorpe's left palm. The fragments of McKinley's bulb.

He knew where the lethal current had come from, but how had it been delivered in such a manner that Oglethorpe allowed himself to be in harm's way?

The Kinetoscope continued to play. The Electric Machine appeared now, flickering against the wall as it had been a few weeks ago, completely assembled. The "Welcome McKinley" sign was there. Bradshaw halted the film and stepped closer to the wall, squeezing past the brooms to get a better look.

He set the picture moving, stopping it when the image revealed the lab in full. He went close again, peering at the black-and-white image of the ceiling, trying to count the wires that ran beside the conduit. But each time he got close enough to see, his head was in the way of the projected image. One, two, three, four. Five? Was there a fifth in the image?

He switched off the Kinetoscope and opened the closet door, letting in the streaming sunshine. He fetched the ladder he'd used the other day, and, after placing it where the Electric Machine had been, climbed to the top step and stretched his fingertips to the ceiling to hold himself and the ladder steady. He was too focused to celebrate his lack of dizziness. One, two, three. Four. Just four insulated wires ran parallel the conduit. Four dark insulated wires that were easily accessible so that they could be moved to different experiments. He looked down the length of the ceiling, following the wires to where they disappeared in the far wall.

He came down off the ladder.

He pulled from his jacket pocket the white handkerchief he'd brought from home that contained the dried flake of India ink he'd pinched from Oglethorpe's hair. He opened the cloth carefully, and shook the flake gently onto the glass plate of the lab microscope. Under magnification, the sparkling black bit revealed its secrets. It was thin and curved, telling Bradshaw what he suspected—it had been painted lightly onto something with a rounded surface. Painted onto a bare copper wire.

Now he knew *how*.

A fifth wire had been temporarily strung up this wall and across the ceiling, just above the marked spot where McKinley was to sit holding up his souvenir bulb. The end of the wire had been stripped of its protective insulation. The exposed gleaming copper had been painted with black India ink. India ink was made of nearly pure carbon, a superior electrical conductor.

That fifth wire had been harmless until connected to a source of high voltage. It was this that had puzzled Bradshaw up until now. But he had seen with his own eyes a mysterious small black box transform low voltage to high. That demonstration had been, impossibly, of direct current from batteries, but he'd been told by its inventor that the device also worked with alternating current—with the current available at every electrical outlet in this lab.

How the components of that small black box worked still puzzled Bradshaw, but that didn't matter just now. It was enough that he knew that if the black box was connected to the building's current it could step up the voltage to dangerous levels. Like turning on a faucet full blast. And that black box had been connected to that fifth black wire that was tripped, as designed, and fell.

It unfolded as if before his eyes. The trap had been set for President McKinley. But McKinley's visit was canceled and so Oglethorpe had been convinced to play the part of the President, to sit in the chair before the Machine holding the bulb aloft. Then the trap had been sprung, the line energized and released, falling down toward Oglethorpe. He'd reflexively thrust up his hand as protection and dropped the bulb. His palm had touched the wire, and the high voltage had burned him and caused every muscle in his body to contract, to make him leap away.

The live wire hit the floor, and the high voltage spilling from the shattered inked end of the wire did what power line current always does—it went to ground. It sought the earth in order to complete the path back to its source. The concrete floors were unable to provide protection under such conditions. The voltage was greatest where the wire touched the floor, growing weaker in concentric circles, creating something lethal called step-potential. Like the ripples on a pond when a rock is dropped into its center, the electric ripples spread upon the floor, and Oglethorpe standing with his feet apart—well, those ripples would move through him, pushing current through his flesh, up one leg and down the other. A current strong enough to stop his heart, but not strong enough to scorch his shoes or leave any other trace of evidence.

Bradshaw took a deep breath.

There had been two parallel human circuits after all. A harmless one involving Henry Pratt and Artimus Lowe and oil stock. Marion Oglethorpe, by pointing out the newspaper article, and by her unusual relations with Dr. Swenson, had been a part of that harmless circuit, distracting Bradshaw from seeing the truth.

◇◇◇

Bradshaw climbed the stairs two at a time to his office, pulled his grade-book from his desk drawer, and ran an unsteady finger down the names.

Daulton, Oscar. Weekly Exam: A.

He closed his eyes and put himself back in his chair at home with Daulton's exam paper. He concentrated until he could see Daulton's spidery handwriting, the neat diagrams, and then the final answer to the final question circled in pencil. A circle the same shade of black as the rest of the exam. And below, the words inscribed by every student at the completion of the exam, swearing his honesty. This oath, however, was of a darker shade, for Oscar Daulton had been using Bradshaw's own pencil. This was the only writing Daulton had put on the paper after he snapped his pencil in two.

◇◇◇

He found Sara Trout studying in the attic library, Glen Reeves in an English class, mangling Shakespeare. He brought them both back to his office where they sat like frightened grammar school children on the edge of their chairs.

"Oscar Daulton intentionally stalled while taking his test last Thursday. He finished his exam on time, yet he pretended he had not. He was so nervous, he broke his pencil. He waited until the building lights fluctuated, until I was sure to become curious enough to go down to the lab. Why?"

"We've no idea," said Reeves unconvincingly. Miss Trout kept her head down. "Why are you asking us?"

"Why did Miss Trout faint on Monday, in Oglethorpe's office, when I mentioned the idea of an accomplice to his murder?"

Reeves looked helplessly at Miss Trout.

"Is there some medical condition which is making you prone to fainting, Miss Trout?"

She shook her head and turned that mottled red he'd witnessed the other day.

"Are you in the family way?"

She made a squeaking gasp.

Reeves jumped to his feet. "Really, sir. There's no call for you to be so rude."

Bradshaw waved him back into the chair. "I'm merely trying to determine the truth. You both led me to believe you'd had a rendezvous in the woods last Thursday, what else am I to think? And if you weren't having a dalliance in the woods, then where were you? Oscar Daulton had help framing me for Oglethorpe's death."

"No, Professor Bradshaw, we didn't mean to frame you, we thought we were saving you—"

"Sara!"

"Mr. Reeves, let her speak."

Miss Trout rushed on anxiously. "I never went to the hut with Glen, Professor. I've never been to any hut with any boy, you must believe me. It was the only thing we could think of that would stop you from asking more questions. It was Glen's idea and I never should have agreed, it wasn't his reputation at stake."

"Where were you then?"

"In the lab. We'd gone down to get supplies for our exhibit projects. When we saw Oglethorpe on the floor of the lab, such a short time after he'd gotten that note from you, we thought you'd killed him. We could understand why, of course, Oglethorpe was so evil, especially toward you. We didn't want you to go to jail! We still don't!"

"But I didn't kill him."

Miss Trout didn't look as if she believed him. She said, "Oscar was there, too, when we found Oglethorpe and so we came up with the plan of putting Oglethorpe in the cage and turning on the Machine so it would look like an accident, only we couldn't find a safety key to turn it on."

"Oscar was with you? Do you mean he arrived with you?"

"No, Glen and I arrived together, and then Oscar was there. I don't remember exactly how it all happened, we were too shocked at seeing Oglethorpe dead on the floor. We were so afraid you'd done it. We told Oscar to go on to your class and to not let you leave until he saw the lights flicker and he knew the Machine was on and then you'd have a witness to your whereabouts. It never occurred to us the police would be involved or that there'd be a coroner's inquest."

Reeves said, "It was my fault it took so long. I had to get into Oglethorpe's office when no one was looking, and then when I finally got in, I searched everywhere but couldn't find the key to the Machine."

Miss Trout said, "I thought I'd die, waiting down in the lab. And then Glen came back without the key and we realized where it must be. We had to go through Oglethorpe's pockets. It was so horrible. And then Artimus Lowe came in before we could get the Machine turned on, and we had to hide. We thought he might ruin everything by saying he saw Professor Oglethorpe dead before the Machine was on, but he wasn't even called to testify. Poor Glen was. I don't think I could've survived that witness chair. But I'd testify in a heartbeat, Professor Bradshaw, to save you from prison."

"I thank you for your loyalty, Miss Trout, but in every possible way your plan has only made things worse. Why did you suppose I was investigating the matter?"

She said earnestly, "So you would look innocent. And we, Glen and I, thought you must have been going crazy trying to figure out who moved the body, but we couldn't tell you."

He looked at their earnest faces, oddly flattered that they thought him capable of murder and warmed by their loyalty.

"You both must immediately go to the police."

He listened patiently as they argued, tripping over each other's pleadings for him to not be foolish, to not abandon them and their fellow students, to have a mind toward his future and their own.

"Mr. Reeves, Miss Trout, for the last time, I promise you, I did not kill Professor Oglethorpe. But I know who did, and I need you to go to the police and withhold nothing. I'm not sure what sort of crime you have committed, but your voluntary admission will surely help toward leniency." He took a sheet of paper from his desk and wrote quickly, then sealed the note in an envelope.

"Ask to see Detective O'Brien, and give him this note. I can trust you both to do as I ask?"

Miserable but defeated, they nodded, and Bradshaw let them go.

He sat for a quarter hour in his office in silence, until he could put it off no longer. It was time to face a young man brilliant enough to invent a revolutionary electrical device, and disturbed enough to use that device to kill.

◇◇◇

"Thank you." Bradshaw gave a polite but dismissive nod to the resident custodian, an elderly gentlemen, who'd let him into Oscar Daulton's dorm room.

The custodian shuffled in place. "Maybe you should wait downstairs, Professor."

"Here will be best, thank you."

"He's a good boy, that Oscar. Well-mannered. Doesn't cause a lot of nonsense like most of them do."

Bradshaw didn't comment.

"He served in the war, in the Philippines."

"Yes, I know."

"Made a man of him, in my opinion. His freshman year, before he went off to fight, he was sulky, kept to himself, angry with the world if you ask me. Well, life's been hard on him, often is on the weak. I don't think he gets much attention from his family. Never seen one of them here."

"No?"

"You'd think at least one of them would stop by, wouldn't you? Mom or Dad, one of the brothers. He's the middle of seven. But he doesn't seem to mind. Like I said, since he came back from the war, he's got a new pride about him. Like he's found his place in the world. And he's got his books and his motors. He's awful smart, that Oscar. Awful smart."

"The cleverest of his class."

"Is he now? I believe it. Well, I'll leave you to wait. It's not about a new job, is it?"

"I just need to speak with him."

The steward scratched an ear. "He was counting on that money he was earning to go to Buffalo this summer."

"Buffalo?"

"He was hoping to get to see the Pan-American Exhibition. He was disappointed when President McKinley canceled his plans to come here. Oscar hopes to see him in Buffalo. But after that fire at the tent factory last night, he's out of work until he can find something else. But he's a bright boy. He'll find something." The custodian left then, keeping the door open.

Bradshaw put his hands in his trouser pockets and stood in the center of the braided rug, in the center of the room. The narrow bed against the wall was neatly made. Above it was a Seattle Sundodgers' pennant and a framed military certificate. Beneath the window was a desk, textbooks piled to one side, a writing blotter in the center. Against the other wall was a dresser upon which stood a shaving set, mug, brush, and razor folded into its celluloid handle. The razor strop hung from a hook on the side of the dresser. Beside the shaving set was a model ship with three sails.

Bradshaw's stomach did a nauseating flip. How ordinary the room looked. It could belong to any boy going to college, any boy who had hopes and dreams. And fears. It could be, in a few year's time, Justin's room.

Bradshaw crossed the room to the door and quietly closed it. Then he began a slow, methodical search.

On the floor, lined against the wall, sat a disassembled electric fan, a working model Ferris wheel, and a few chem lab glass vessels. He looked into the dresser drawers, under the bed, inside the wardrobe. He found nothing out of the ordinary, nothing incriminating. Oscar's exhibition project, the baffling, revolutionary cigar box that, perhaps, stepped up D.C. voltage was missing. Where else would the boy store it?

By the window, a framed quotation caught his eye: *"The time will come when our silence will be more powerful than the voices you strangle today."* No source was given, but Bradshaw recognized those famous words. They were the last spoken by anarchist August Spies before his hanging.

No, never Justin's room.

He moved to the nightstand and picked up the small book resting there, Walt Whitman's *Leaves of Grass.* Not the sort of book one found easily. Bradshaw had seen only portions of it; passages of sensual poetry and provoking irony that were hand-copied and handed secretly around when he was in school. The leather was worn from use, and the book fell open to a marked page.

Respondez! Respondez!
(The war is completed—the price is paid—the title is settled
   beyond recall;)
Let every one answer! let those who sleep be waked! let none
   evade!
Must we still go on with our affectations and sneaking?
Let me bring this to a close—I pronounce openly for a new
   distribution of roles;
Let murderers, bigots, fools, unclean persons, offer new
   propositions!
Let the old propositions be postponed!
Let faces and theories be turn'd inside out! let meanings be
   freely criminal, as well as results!

Such bold, radical prose. What appeal did it have to a brilliant young man like Oscar Daulton? A boy weak in body and nerve, as the custodian said, yet so very strong of mind? A boy who had put on a uniform to fight for his country and seen death and brutality Bradshaw knew he could not, and would not let himself, imagine? Oscar had been changed by his war experience. The custodian had seen it. Bradshaw had seen the change but not truly noted it until after the boy's stunning Exhibition presentation. Whitman's appeal had been power. His writing inspired the notion that the weak need not accept being bullied by the strong. That physical strength did not equate to moral justice. It would be but a short step to the precepts of anarchism. Oscar had taken that step with religious zeal. Bullied all his life, traumatized by war, he'd found an ideology that at last gave him control.

He'd turned his genius against McKinley, then used his foiled trap to kill Oglethorpe. It took no stretch of the imagination to understand why Oscar had hated Oglethorpe. Next he'd used his lethal device on the Pinkerton guard who'd come to Seattle to protect those with money and power, and yesterday, he'd killed his own employer at the tent factory, who'd refused to let the workers organize for fair wages. All of them had been typical anarchist targets—and, except for McKinley, all personal enemies of Oscar.

But he had forgotten a victim. He'd forgotten himself. He was not Oscar's enemy. He'd considered himself rather a mentor. Oscar had always come to him for help. So why had Oscar tried to send him over the falls? Because the police had considered him a suspect. His death would have been considered a suicide, and thus an admission of guilt. And the investigation into Oglethorpe's death would have been closed.

Bradshaw had not died, but no more attempts had been made on his life. Why? Because the police, as far as the public was concerned, had another suspect. Artimus Lowe. This morning, Lowe had been set free on bail. It had been in the papers.

A wave of fear as cold as the Snoqualmie River flooded Bradshaw. He threw open the door and shouted for the custodian. The elderly gentlemen came at a slow trot down the hall.

"What time did Oscar go out today? Where did he go?"

"I don't know, rightly. I didn't see."

"Where's your telephone?"

"Down in the first floor hall."

Bradshaw was already running down the stairs; the palm of his hand burned and squealed on the newel post as he used it to fling himself around the corner. He grabbed the phone's receiver, fumbled it, then pressed it to his ear.

"What number please?"

"I don't know. The Lincoln Hotel. It's urgent. Please hurry."

"Yes, sir. Just a moment please. Yes, here you are."

It seemed an eternity before the line was picked up. "Lincoln Hotel Apartments, Mr. Randall speak—"

"I need to speak to Artimus Lowe. Is he in?"

"No, sir."

"Do you know where he is? Has another student been to see him? By the name of Oscar Daulton? Thin, nervous type, hair falling into his eyes?"

"I know nothing, sir. Even if I did know, I couldn't say. We have strict privacy policies at the Lincoln. You can sit outside the hotel with the other reporters and wait."

"I'm not a reporter! This is urgent, a matter of life or death."

"I'm sure it is." Mr. Randall sounded bored. "Do you wish to leave a message?"

Bradshaw slammed down the receiver. A waft of cool air came down the hall from the open front door. The custodian came through, pulling another man from the porch with him. This middle-aged man wore a soiled white cook's apron and was smoking a cigarette. He waved the cigarette at Bradshaw. "You looking for young Daulton?"

"Have you seen him? Where? When?"

"Oh, 'bout half an hour ago. He came to the kitchen over in the women's hall, borrowed a picnic basket and made a few sandwiches."

"Did he say where he was going?"

"West Seattle. Going on a picnic to cheer up a friend."

West Seattle. The ferry. *Another drowning.*

Bradshaw ran out the door, leaped off the porch without slowing to take the stairs, and sprinted across the expanse of lawn toward the Administration Building that glinted in the sunlight. He grabbed his bicycle from the rack and stood on the pedals to race toward 15th Avenue.

For the next four and a half miles, Bradshaw was aware of nothing but his goal and defeating the obstacles in his way. He plunged down the center of the roads, evading traffic in both directions. He snubbed the warning sign giving streetcars the right of way across the wooden trestle of the Latona Bridge and escaped collision by a mere three yards. His bones jolted over cobblestones, his muscles flamed up the hills, and his lungs exulted on stretches of fresh asphalt. He dodged horses and wagons, carriages and pedestrians. At intersections he said a prayer but didn't slow down, despite policemen blowing whistles or clanking streetcars screeching their warnings. On the blessedly steep hills of the city, he flew down toward the waterfront, both wheels airborne for seconds at time as he crested the avenues. As he descended, the traffic grew heavier, the intersections riskier. He scattered screaming pedestrians on Third Avenue, toppled another bicyclist on Second, was nearly flattened on First, and caused a minor wreck on Western that he didn't turn around to inspect. When he hit Railroad Avenue, the final major obstacle, he skidded to a halt, unable to penetrate the tangle of delivery wagons and freight trains. He abandoned his bicycle to finish the race on foot, ignoring the shouts and curses from those he pushed out of his way. The noise was deafening—the traffic, the construction—and the smell ripe with oil and creosote and the rank tide flats.

At last, he punched through to the waterfront at the foot of Marion Street. Before him, wedged between towering warehouses, was the dock. The ferry, *City of Seattle*, a single-decked steamer, was blasting her whistle as she prepared to depart. Bradshaw kept running. He leapt over the chain meant to restrict his entry, and as the thick rope was thrown from the deck to the dock and the boat began to pull away, he jumped aboard. His shoes, slick from puddles and oil and no-doubt horse droppings, slipped on the deck, and he landed hard on his behind at the feet of an amused crowd. An official-looking chap in a uniform and cap looked down at him with a scowl.

Chest heaving, Bradshaw dug into his jacket pocket and palmed the only coin there. Not a dollar, just two bits. He extended his hand to the scowling official, who obliged by pulling him to his feet and accepting the coin in the bargain. He looked at the measly quarter with disdain, showed it to the crowd, and bit it as if to prove it were real. The men guffawed and the women and children laughed. The official shrugged, pocketed the coin, and turned his back on the professor to a smattering of applause. The excursion crowd was in high spirits.

Bradshaw ducked through them into the dim interior that was filled with a shiny new buggy, a lumber-laden wagon, another of produce, and several dozen bicycles. He tried to touch his hat with a polite nod when passing a clutch of women in pale spring linen, only to find he hadn't the strength to lift his arm—and he'd lost his hat. He sprinted out into the sunshine at the opposite end of the ferry, fearing he was too late.

But he found them, Oscar and Artimus, perched side-by-side on the wide polished ledge of the white bulwark, a wicker picnic basket between them. They each wore crusher-style hats mashed tight on their heads to keep the wind from whipping them off. There was no railing behind them. Nothing but balance and cocky youth kept them from dropping backwards off the ferry into the deep cold.

The world began to spin.

Bradshaw propped himself against the bulkhead beside the boys, unable to talk, strangled as much by exhaustion as by the sudden and unexpected return of vertigo. He'd apparently pushed his luck too far.

They stared at him as he gasped and heaved. Sweat poured off his face, stung his eyes, but he didn't have the strength to lift his hand to his pocket for his handkerchief. He was glad for the buffeting, cooling breeze. His clothes were soaked through and clung to his skin, and his tie was choking him. After a full minute, he managed to lift a trembling hand to tug it loose.

All the while, they simply looked at him, Artimus Lowe with an amused eyebrow lifted. Oscar Daulton, with guarded wariness. Bradshaw kept his gaze on the picnic basket, willing the nausea to subside.

Artimus lifted his voice above the wind and the rhythmic thrum of the ferry. "To what do we owe the pleasure of your company, Professor?"

Bradshaw couldn't yet answer.

"Nearly miss the boat? Why the melodramatics and perspiration?"

Bradshaw lifted a finger.

"Yes, alright, we'll give you a minute to compose yourself. No fun getting old, I'll wager. And are you feeling guilty about abandoning me in jail? You should. It was a foul thing to do. Everyone seems to have abandoned me in my greatest hour of need, except for Oscar here. My father did wire the funds to spring me, but he also sent word I'd been disowned. So there you are. I hope it weighs heavy on your conscience. If it wasn't for Oscar, I might have resorted to flinging myself off the roof of the Lincoln. The management wouldn't have liked that. But Oscar came, clever chap, slipped past the damned reporters up to my room with a picnic basket and a plan to get me away for the day. You know," he said, turning to Oscar. "I didn't think you much liked me, after that ripping I gave you in Debate. I judged you wrong, Oscar. I'm sorry."

Oscar made a movement that was more like a twitch than a shrug. He glanced around at the other passengers huddled in clusters on the deck and propped on the opposite bulwark. No one was paying the professor and students any attention. The wind isolated the three of them.

Bradshaw still felt his heart thudding, but he had breath now to say to Oscar, in controlled gasps, "I believe—you've misunderstood—Whitman."

Oscar's eyes widened. They were a pale blue, young and anxious. Bradshaw realized he'd expected to see something more in his eyes, something dark and evil. But there was just this frightened boy. Just Oscar. And he understood. He understood Bradshaw had been in his room, looking through his things, looking for evidence. He licked his lips; his Adam's apple bobbed. "Walt Whitman died when I was a child, sir. I never met him, I know only the words he set down on the page. No one can know what those words meant to him. I know only what they mean to me."

"Tell me—about the Philippines."

"What do you want to know?"

"Why did you volunteer?"

Artimus Lowe sat forward, watching the interchange. Amusement had left his features.

Oscar squared his shoulders and pressed his palms on his thighs. "I believed in the uniform."

"I don't understand."

"Men wear military uniforms. Men who are strong and brave and respected."

"That's true."

"It's not true. It's a lie. It's all a lie." Oscar turned his face away, toward the choppy water of Elliott Bay and the wooded hillsides of West Seattle. "Do you have any idea what war is like, Professor?"

"No, not personally." He kept his gaze on Oscar's profile, keenly aware the boy's hand inched toward the picnic basket.

"You're lucky. It's awful. If you'd seen what I've seen, you'd know the truth. You'd know the uniform is just an excuse to murder innocent people."

"Sometimes war is necessary to preserve freedom."

Oscar huffed. "America claims to be a country that believes in freedom. Freedom and equality. But we send soldiers off to foreign parts with orders to subdue the natives for their own good. Do you know how to subdue a native, Professor? You give him a shovel and tell him to dig a hole. When it's deep enough, you shoot him, and he falls dead into the hole. Then you give the shovel to another native." Oscar's laugh was bitter.

Bradshaw didn't laugh. Artimus was going pale.

Oscar looked again at Bradshaw. His face held all the misery and anguish of the world. "I couldn't do it."

"Do what?"

"Shoot them." He ran his thumb along the fancy carvings of the wicker handle.

"Not everyone's meant to be a soldier."

"Once you put on the uniform, you don't have a choice. Unless you're clever."

"I don't know any student cleverer than you, Oscar."

"I've had to be. My whole life people have thought I wasn't good for anything. I figured things out on my own. I can get people to do what I want."

"The army sent you home sick."

"That was easy. Everyone had dysentery. It would have been harder not to get sick."

"How did you learn about anarchy?"

Artimus gasped. "Anar—" Bradshaw silenced him with a lifted hand, never taking his eyes from Oscar.

"You say it like it's something bad, Professor. They've got you fooled, too."

"Who has me fooled?"

"The people with power. The newspapers, the people with money, the military, the government. That's how they keep control. They get everyone believing what they're doing is right or noble, for the greater good. Manifest Destiny. A load of lies, Professor. What do we need with the Philippines? Or Cuba? Isn't America big enough? If those people want to run their own country, why don't we let them? We attack them and they're too weak and poor to fight back. Just like me. Just like a million other poor fools. They put a gun in my hand and told me to shoot because they wanted some godforsaken bug-infested hill on some bloody island. My commander said I was weak. A coward. Well, who's the coward now, Professor? I would have killed McKinley when he came. Me! I would have done it because I'm not a coward. McKinley's a coward. They're all cowards, taking from the weak and poor. Not me. I'm on the right side of history, you'll see."

Bradshaw let the chugging and swooshing of the ferry, and hiss of foaming seawater fill the silence. Oscar stared once again out toward the bay. Artimus, mouth agape, begged with his eyes for Bradshaw to explain. Bradshaw indicated silently, with the slightest shake of his head, that now was not the time.

Oscar spoke suddenly, his voice full of anger. "He tried to steal my invention."

"Who?"

"Professor Oglethorpe. He took it out of Denny Hall, the day before the exhibition. He took it down to the lab and broke it open."

"Oh, Oscar."

"I caught him at it when I went down to dismantle my trap. I'd read about McKinley's visit being canceled. Oglethorpe was in the lab when I got there, with my invention. He wanted to know how it worked and I refused to tell him. He said he was my teacher and that anything I made was school property and he had the right to know."

"That's not true."

"I told him I'd explain it to him after I performed a demonstration. It was really very easy. You should have seen his eyes. Fame and glory. That's what he thought he was going to steal from me. I sat safely on a lab stool, my feet off the floor, while he sat in McKinley's chair and held up that bulb like he was a king."

Artimus was, thankfully, too stunned to comment.

"Why did you kill the others, the Pinkerton man at the hotel and your manager at the factory?"

"They're my enemies, Professor, in my war against injustice. They kill workers every day, but it's a slow death of degradation and so no one notices. No one cares."

"Why did you try to kill me?"

"I didn't want to hurt you, Professor." Oscar's blue eyes shone bright and sincere. Bradshaw was struck again at the lack of dark insanity to match the murderous actions. "You were always so good to me. But my cause was greater than your life. You see? The police suspected you, and I thought that if you were gone, they'd close the investigation and I wouldn't be found out."

My God, Bradshaw thought. What had he seen in the Philippines that would push him this far? What sort of inner hell drove him to believe he should try to kill a man he considered a friend?

"Was it you who lodged the velocipede wheel at the top of the falls?"

"I couldn't be sure you'd be curious enough to go look. But you did."

"I did. Your wheel saved me."

"Did it? Well, it was a gamble. I needed it to look accidental. I tried to make them all look accidental so no one would know."

"Can I have the basket, Oscar?"

Artimus jolted, scooting away from the picnic basket as if from a snake.

Oscar shook his head and curled his fingers around the handle. His eyes were now distant. "You taught me about resistance, Professor. You taught me that unimpeded current has no limits. But resistance draws heat and light. Resistance draws attention. It eventually destroys the circuit path and the current ceases to flow. My fellow anarchists are foolish and vain to boast of their accomplishments. They leave their symbols blatantly as a signature of their work, but bragging only draws resistance. Feeds resistance. Silence is an anarchist's friend." Daulton's eyes glazed as his vision turned more deeply inward. He said reverently, "Silence is his unending line of power," then closed his eyes, and threw himself backwards.

Bradshaw sprang forward, but his abused muscles had cooled and tightened. They not only screamed with pain, they impeded his movement. He managed to grab a fistful of Oscar's jacket in one hand and halted the boy from tumbling overboard. He gave a mighty yank to pull him off the bulwark toward the ferry deck, and he succeeded, but Oscar had a firm grip on the heavy picnic basket and a plan of his own. He spun on his heel, the basket outthrust, and hurled it up and over. The lid flapped open, dumping a red-checked cloth, pale flashes of bread, and a large brown cigar box wired to three black cylinders strapped tightly together. They disappeared with a splash. Still gripping Oscar, Bradshaw looked over the bulwark at the receding water. The checked cloth, the bread, even the basket, floated on the churning wake. But the cigar box and cylinders—three dry cell telegraph batteries—had sunk out of sight.

A crowd had gathered, and the ferry was slowing. Oscar lay unhurt on the deck but unable to move because Bradshaw stood over him, pinning him down.

Artimus looked sick. "He was going to push me overboard, wasn't he? And make it look like suicide so I'd get the blame for Oglethorpe." He shook his head, unwilling to believe he'd been so close to death. "He would never have succeeded, you know. He'd never overpower me." He kept shaking his head, as if to say he could understand how a decrepit old man like Bradshaw had been easily pushed, but he was far too young and strong to become a victim of Oscar Daulton.

"He would have overpowered you easily once he'd shocked you with the device in that picnic basket."

Artimus' mouth dropped open. "Is that—my God, Professor. My—you saved my life."

Bradshaw felt his muscles weaken. He knelt down over his prisoner. "No plan is perfect, Mr. Lowe."

Chapter Twenty-six

Three hours later, Bradshaw gave a thoughtful lecture to the bright young faces in his electro-magnetism class. He said nothing of Oscar's arrest. How he could possibly explain to those inexperienced bright-eyed young men the tragedy forged from Oscar Daulton's beliefs?

On the way home, he pedaled his battered bicycle slowly, his muscles aching. He really did need to start using the university gymnasium. The front wheel gave him trouble because it was bent. It had been run over by a coal wagon when he abandoned it near the waterfront.

On Gallagher Street, he dismounted, and pushed the wounded bicycle along the tree-lined sidewalk. As he passed the Oglethorpe mansion, he glimpsed through the newly planted laurel hedge Dr. Swenson playing with Olive and Wesley. He heard Marion Oglethorpe's voice blended with those of the children. Perhaps, with time....

When Bradshaw reached 1204 Gallagher, he stood outside the white picket fence. Clumps of damp grass lay in long stripes across the small lawn, filling the air with a sweet earthiness. The rhythmic thrumming whir-whir of the push mower told him Justin was now cutting the back lawn. Colorful blossoms nodded a welcome from the beds beneath the parlor window. An image of Missouri—cheeks flushed, tucking a curl behind her ear—flashed in his mind. He forced the image away. But his fingertips tingled. How much longer would she be with them?

The whir of the mower silenced momentarily, and laughter, his son's and Missouri's, floated to him. She was there in the back garden, keeping his son company, delighting him.

Bradshaw's heart tightened, his eyes stung with tears. How fragile it all was, the haven of his home, the happiness of those he cared most about. Just a week ago, he'd taken it for granted, living like a half-dead man, plotting his life carefully by his calendar, trying his best to avoid living at all.

He didn't want to return to being that dour, plodding man. Yet what a relief it was to be home. His heart ached for Oscar, Oscar's family, his victims. Their tragedy made the sight of his home all the more precious. He didn't know whether he wanted to laugh or cry, but he did know he didn't want his household to witness either.

It was a warm afternoon. Mrs. Prouty had the windows open, letting in the smell of cut grass and spring blossoms. The curtains billowed inward, paused, then relaxed with a flutter, almost as if the house were breathing.

The screen door opened with a squeak and a smack, and Mrs. Prouty stepped onto the porch with her broom.

"Standing out there again are you, Professor?"

"I like the view."

"Well, when you're through gawking, there's a telegram in here from Henry you'll want to see. He wants to know what all the fuss is about."

"Did you wire him to explain?"

"Me? I hadn't a clue what he was talking about."

He beamed at Mrs. Prouty, nearly compelled to approach her stout figure with a hug.

Instead, he pulled his bicycle from the fence and in doing so glanced up the street. Loping toward him down the sidewalk was his least-favorite young man, well-dressed, hat at a jaunty angle. Quickly, Bradshaw opened the gate and pushed his bicycle into the yard.

"Is that your new broom?"

Mrs. Prouty's eyes were on the approaching figure. "Bristles sharp enough to sting."

Artimus Lowe put a hand on the gate and turned a lovesick face toward the house.

Bradshaw headed toward the backyard. "Use it at your discretion."

Mrs. Prouty beamed. "Yes, sir, Professor. I'd be most happy to."

Author's Note

While this story and characters are fictional, they are nestled and entwined with true historical events and detail. Researching is my favorite part of writing. I can easily spend three hours, or three days, rooting out a single detail. Seattleites might wonder about Professor Bradshaw living on Broadway Hill, but that was the hill's name until the fall of 1901, when it was renamed Capitol. Gallagher Street is not real, but the house at 1204 exists. It's where my grandmother lived when I was a child.

President William McKinley did plan to visit Seattle in May of 1901 and tour the Snoqualmie Falls Power Plant, but his trip was cancelled due to Mrs. McKinley's illness. The power company's president, Charles H. Baker, travelled to the east coast to present McKinley with the souvenir he was to have received on his visit. I can find no description or image of this souvenir, but it must have been impressive. According to an article in the *Seattle Daily Times*, McKinley said, "And does this represent that wonderful water power of which I have heard so much?" He then added, "And was this beautiful piece of work really done in Seattle?" Yes, it was. I wonder if it is now somewhere with presidential memorabilia. McKinley promised to visit Washington State the following July, but of course he was unable to keep that promise because on September 6 of 1901, while visiting the Pan-American Exposition in Buffalo, he unwittingly reached out to shake the hand of anarchist, who shot him twice.

The electrical engineering students at the University of Washington built and displayed a Tesla Coil (smaller and less elaborate than the fictional one in this book), an electric stove, and many other clever devices at their exhibition on May 18, 1901. The general public was invited to view the wonders of modern science, but the event was not scheduled to coincide with President McKinley's visit.

I had already written about the death of Bradshaw's late wife when I happened upon a 1901 *Seattle Post-Intelligencer* article and knew I'd found the particulars of that event. It's sadly surprising how many such deaths appeared daily in the news.

I modeled my Detective O'Brien after a photograph of a detective by the same name who worked for the Seattle Police Department in the 1920's. A handsome man with penetrating eyes and a Roosevelt hat—I'd confess to him in a heartbeat.

And the President of the University of Washington from August 1898 to June 1902 was, like my fictional president, named Dr. Frank Graves. He was the youngest university president at that time, and he did indeed have adorable ears.

To receive a free catalog of Poisoned Pen Press titles, please contact us in one of the following ways:

Phone: 1-800-421-3976
Facsimile: 1-480-949-1707
Email: info@poisonedpenpress.com
Website: www.poisonedpenpress.com

Poisoned Pen Press
6962 E. First Ave. Ste. 103
Scottsdale, AZ 85251